WAR & PEACE
and SONYA

Other books by the author

The Unsaid Anna Karenina

The Christesen Romance

The French Tutor

The Cook and the Maestro

The Maestro's Table

WAR & PEACE *and* SONYA

◇ THE STORY OF SONYA TOLSTOY ◇

JUDITH ARMSTRONG

Published by Unicorn Press Ltd

66 Charlotte Street
London W1T 4QE
www.unicornpress.org

ISBN 9 781910 06530 3

This edition published by Unicorn Press 2015
Published in Australia in 2011 by Pier 9,
an imprint of Murdoch Books Pty Limited

Design by Anna Hopwood/ahdesign

Printed in India by Imprint Digital Ltd.

To Piers and Lucien
in Paris

Characters

The Family of Count and Countess Tolstoy
at Yasnaya Polyana (Ash Glade), Their Country Estate

FULL NAME	KNOWN AS
Lev Nikolaevich Tolstoy, m.	Lyova, Lyovenka
Sofya Andreevna Behrs	Sonya, Sonechka
Sergei Lvovich Tolstoy	Seryozha
Tatiana Lvovna Tolstaya	Tanya, Tanechka
Ilya Lvovich Tolstoy	Ilyusha
Lev Lvovich Tolstoy	Lyolya
Marya Lvovna Tolstaya	Masha, Mashenka
Pyotr Lvovich Tolstoy	Petya
Nikolai Lvovich Tolstoy	–
Varvara Lvovna Tolstaya	Varya
Andrei Lvovich Tolstoy	Andryusha
Mikhail Lvovich Tolstoy	Misha
Alexei Lvovich Tolstoy	Alyosha
Alexandra Lvovna Tolstaya	Sasha
Ivan Lvovich Tolstoy	Vanya

Sonya's Family Background

FULL NAME	KNOWN AS
Liubov Alexandrovna Islavina,	–
m. Andrei Evstafevich Behrs	–
Elizaveta Andreevna Behrs	Liza
Sofya Andreevna Behrs	Sonya
Alexandr Andreevich Behrs	Sasha
Tatiana Andreevna Behrs	Tanya
Pyotr Andreevich Behrs	Petya
Vladimir Andreevich Behrs	Volodya
Stepan Andreevich Behrs	Styopa
Vyacheslav Andreevich Behrs	–

Lev's Family Background

FULL NAME	KNOWN AS
Count Nikolai Tolstoy m.	–
Princess Marya Volkonskaya	–
Nikolai Nikolaevich Tolstoy	–
Sergei Nikolaevich Tolstoy	Seryozha
Dmitri Nikolaevich Tolstoy	–
Lev Nikolaevich Tolstoy	Lyova, Lyovenka
Marya Nikolaevna Tolstaya	Masha, Mashenka

Prologue

My husband is now dead.

I am writing as always at Yasnaya Polyana, the home that I shared for forty-eight years with Count Lev Nikolaevich Tolstoy. We came to his ancestral estate south of Moscow in 1862, straight from our wedding in the Kremlin. Until that day I was Sofya Andreevna Behrs – Sonya to my family and friends. I had just turned eighteen. Lev Nikolaevich was thirty-four.

He is – was – is so famous his story will be told many times by many people. But will those accounts be true? Much will depend on what sources these clever people use. They will think that the facts are all there in his diaries, needing only to be transcribed. But diaries are not necessarily reposits of absolute truth.

I can say this because we both kept them nearly all our lives. When I began mine, it was to confide to those blank white pages my passionate love for Lev (whom I would also call Lyova, or Lyovenka, depending on how fond I felt); but whenever the relationship disappointed either one of us – and I must acknowledge that this occurred frequently – our diaries doubled as weapons. When either of us let our resentment boil over, a black notebook would be left around where it was sure to be discovered. The reader sometimes inserted responses. Or retorts.

This husband is now dead. But the person I adored and unfailingly served all my life – bearing his thirteen children, copying and editing his millions of words – that person ceased to care about me long before the breath left his dear body. And even before then, I often questioned the nature of the bond between us. Did the great writer understand what it was to love in real life?

As an infatuated girl, I took it for granted that he must, but eighteen years or so after our wedding, when he was so often angry and distant with me (though never in the bedroom), I became obsessed by two imperatives.

The first was to answer the question that sometimes made my veins run with poison rather than blood. Did his coldness mean that I had a *rival*?

The other was the realisation that although our life stories cannot be separated from one another, our inner lives were very different. And never, *ever* did he grasp what hidden knowledge I discovered about him as I pored over the pages produced by his brilliant imagination, ardently copying or editing them for publication.

And so now it is time to write my own story. Posterity *must* understand about my life with Lev Nikolaevich, and how I arrived at certain perceptions.

1

The Three Behrs
August 1862

The windows of my first-floor bedroom at Yasnaya Polyana look out over the park, the old and the young orchards, the stables, the greenhouses, the kitchen garden, and the avenue leading down to the ponds. Further on lies the village and the road to Tula, a good-sized town with a major railway station, about 12 versts away. The view from the other, north side of the house is mostly groves of trees, stands of darker green forest (splashed with gold in the autumn), cultivated fields and grazing pastures sloping down to the river Voronka, its dull satin ribboning in and out of view. Beyond is a vast plain where in summer a waving expanse of rye stretches.

The 'small Voronka', which flowed into a larger river of the same name visible from the upstairs window

The 'pretty fretted' porch at the back of the house, summer.

My first sight of this rambling, white-painted wooden house, with its pretty fretted porches, occurred when a vibrant summer was at its height, and when, incredibly, the owner of it all, Count Lev Nikolaevich Tolstoy, who often dropped in at our Moscow apartment, was little more than a long-standing friend of my parents. In fact, so frequent were his visits that my sisters and I, then aged fourteen, twelve and ten, had got quite used to him. But as time passed, I grew aware that my father, Dr Andrei Behrs, and my mother, Liubov, had high hopes that his presence was motivated by an interest in their oldest daughter, Liza. By rights, she should marry before either I or Tanya, who was the youngest of us three, could consider an attachment. The Count, from an old and noble family and already thirty-four, was showing himself to be a little cagey; yet he called so often that my parents were convinced that Liza's happiness must, in due course, be assured.

It was just as well – in more ways than one – that they did not have access to the Count's diaries, as was later to be my privilege, and my cross.

It was true enough that marriage was on his mind. I was to discover that three years earlier he had made a New Year resolution: 'I must get married this year – or not at all!' But that was only because he thought marriage would tame his deplorable promiscuity. Nothing came of it either that year or the two following. I'm sure he knew that Maman had her eye on him in regard to Liza, but unfortunately for her, this knowledge only caused him to note in the summer of 1862, 'Liza seems to be quietly taking possession of me. My God! How perfectly unhappy she would be if she were to be my wife.'

My poor mother could not guess that her aspirations, though running parallel to his, were most unlikely to converge. Mistakenly optimistic, she had no qualms about giving the Count a nudge. After all, she had known him since they were children living on neighbouring country estates. This happy connection now suggested a way of furthering her enterprise without alerting the gossips of Moscow.

'It is high time,' she announced to us girls, 'that I take you on a little

Sonya and Tanya in their teens.

trip to see your grandfather, and at the same time pay a visit to your grandmother's grave.'

She did not draw attention to the fact that her family's property at Ivitsy was only 50 versts past Count Tolstoy's country place. She innocently arranged for us to call in at Yasnaya Polyana on the way.

At Ivitsy, Maman and her five siblings used to play regularly with the five Tolstoy children. Family lore at both dinner tables talked up a famous incident when Lev Nikolaevich, aged about ten or eleven, pushed Liubov Isleneva (Maman) off a balcony, supposedly motivated by romantic jealousy. Both he and his brother Nikolai claimed to be in love with her. In those days the Tolstoy children, whose parents had both died, were looked after by guardian aunts, from whom they were always trying to escape. Life would surely have been much jollier in the happy Islenev household.

But all that was a long time ago. The Count's first encounter with Liubov Behrs was after he had returned to Moscow from a year in the Caucasus, where he'd accompanied his soldier brother Nikolai. Before that he'd been down in Sebastopol, serving in the Crimean war as a non-commissioned officer. Finally back in town after all these absences, he had renewed his acquaintance with Maman and a new generation of Islenev-Behrs. My mother was less than two years older than he, but a product of the social conventions of her time. She had been married to my father when she was sixteen, and had born her first daughter – Liza – a year later.

Lev Nikolaevich, who was then thirty, was by all accounts delighted to make our acquaintance – a trio of slight, but lively, dark-eyed girls. As we grew into late adolescence he seemed to find us even more charming. But although he was supposed to be keen on the idea of settling down, his intentions did not stretch to a *mariage de convenance* with Liza. I quickly realised that she was far too melancholy to be in the running. The one who really caught his fancy was our mischievous, high-spirited little Tanya, with her impish laugh and outrageous daring. Probably he also noticed her full mouth, which signalled a wayward sensuality that was later to lead her astray, and her sweet, slightly wistful gaze when she was meditative – which was not often. Her great virtue for the Count was that she was young enough to play and even flirt with, without being taken seriously by him or anyone else.

I, the middle one, was another story. I was never as playful as Tanya, but I know very well that he was stirred by my dark, intense gaze, in which there were depths he could not gauge and which therefore held a certain challenge. He told his diary (which, again, I only saw much later) that I was 'plain and vulgar', but admitted in the same breath that I 'interested him'. He meant, but of course could not say of a well-born girl, that of the three daughters I was the one who stirred him sexually. Nor could he know whether I was conscious of that. And, to be honest, at that age I wasn't. I had only the haziest, highly romanticised idea of what such a thing might mean. As a result, he felt helpless, and did nothing other than continue his visits to the family as a whole, while we were all thrown into varying states of confusion.

Our flat was wonderfully situated in the very heart of the city, within the Kremlin walls. 'A *kreml,'* Papa liked to explain to each child in turn, 'is simply the ancient word for the wooden palisade built around a village, or the fortified wall around a town or city. A *kremlin* is both the space inside the fence and the collection of buildings enclosed within it – churches, houses, businesses, sometimes a palace or a cathedral. Most of our towns and cities are built in and around a *kreml,* but none can compare to our Moscow Kremlin. How many cathedrals does it hold?'

'Three!' We all knew that answer.

'Right! And three palaces, plus a lot of buildings where people work or live.'

'Like us!'

'Indeed, like us. We are lucky, you know.'

It was considered very chic to live inside the Kremlin, and rather surprising that Papa was allocated one of the flats; admittedly he held an appointment as court physician, but he was not of the aristocracy, and collectively we hid an even darker family secret. Our darling Maman was technically illegitimate! Her mother, also a Sofya like me, had been forced when young to marry a Prince Kozlovsky, but she soon ran away from him in order to live with her true love, Alexander Islenev, with whom she produced six children, before her divorce from the Prince was finalised. She did in the end marry Alexander, but their children, having been born out of wedlock, were not allowed by law to bear the name of their father; in preference to Kozlovsky, grandfather had them all christened Islavin. Islavin was thus Maman's surname until she married, but she really belonged to the Islenev family.

Papa, Dr Behrs, was eighteen years older than she, but their marriage was another true love-match. Maman's great aim was to reproduce for her own six children the warm, lively family life she had revelled in at Ivitsy; but she also saw to it that we were all well schooled in languages, literature, music and dancing, and the girls taught to sew, cook and keep accounts. I even acquired a teacher's certificate, although I never used it professionally.

Count Tolstoy was so slow in getting to the point with Liza, yet such a regular visitor to our Kremlin flat, that I once overheard Papa quizzing Maman about the balcony story – as if he feared the Count could be still half in love with Maman! I knew that wasn't the case, because I'd seen him looking askance at her drawn cheeks and the thin hair that she had to comb carefully to avoid looking completely bald. No. It was more than obvious that we girls attracted him irresistibly whenever he was in town, but who precisely was the magnet had yet to be revealed.

And none of us, including me, had any idea at that stage how glad the Count always was to find himself leaving Moscow in order to roll up the long drive that led to this white-painted house at Yasnaya Polyana. There might be a dearth of society in the country, but he loved every blade of grass on his property, and was oblivious to the run-down state of the house.

This large estate, which is a place of great natural beauty, was left to him by his maternal grandfather, Prince Nikolai Volkonsky. The Volkonskys claim to be descended from Riurik, the Viking who came down with his men in the ninth century, and whose successor Oleg was the founder of Rus, the ancient kernel from which all the Russias grew. Apparently the Volkonskys considered themselves to be of extremely high birth – older even than the Romanovs! But the old Prince had fallen out with the court of Tsar Paul at the beginning of the century and retired to the country with his daughter, Princess Marya, as his sole companion. Marya's mother was already dead, but the father lasted until his daughter was thirty-one. He left her with a substantial personal fortune and just enough time to find a husband – if she hurried. Luckily, Prince Nikolai Tolstoy, five years her junior and completely impoverished, came forward, and the marriage was celebrated on July 9th 1822. Marya's dowry consisted of 800 male serfs plus Yasnaya Polyana.

It was exactly forty years afterwards that Maman decided to fulfil her filial duty by hiring a coach in which to visit Grandfather Islenev at Ivitsy, taking her three girls and our nine-year-old brother Volodya. (Our oldest brother, Sasha, was a cadet and had duties in Moscow. But in any case he would not have wanted to come.) And if she needed any further excuse to pay a call on her childhood friend, Lyova Tolstoy, en route, it transpired that his sister Masha, once Maman's best friend, was currently staying at Yasnaya Polyana after separating from her husband Valerian Tolstoy (he was also her cousin) and spending the winter in Algeria. It was all falling into place.

I wonder whether Lev Nikolaevich minded, or even noticed, how different was the house he now inhabited from the three-storey, fourteen-room mansion in which he and his four siblings were born. He had counted himself lucky to be the one who inherited Yasnaya Polyana, his favourite of the three estates belonging to the family; yet in 1854, from his army post in the Crimea, he had unaccountably sold the main house in order to raise money to publish a military magazine. He had already received the financial proceeds when he was told that permission for the project had been denied; he ended up gambling away the whole sum playing *shtoss*, his favourite card game, for two days and two nights.

When he got back, the main house had been dismantled and taken away, leaving only the two detached wings. Lev Nikolaevich used one of them to house the school he set up for the local serf children, and occupied the other along with his dear old Aunt Toinette, who had cared for the children after their mother died. (His mother's death occurred when Lev, the youngest, was not quite two. It was from Aunt that I heard most of this information.) There were also in the house Toinette's companion Natalya Petrovna, a maid, a manservant, and an old man who occasionally did some cooking when he was not too drunk. It could not have been very comfortable. The wooden floors were uncarpeted, and there were few upholstered chairs or couches. The Count did not even bother with bedlinen, preferring to lay his head on a hard red leather cushion and cover himself with an ancient plaid rug.

On that first visit, I did not dream that this house – now considerably extended but not much refurbished – would ever be my home, yet it developed a special resonance in my memory. Many years later, realising that, as the wife of a hugely famous man, some of my own recollections might be valuable to posterity (and, if I am honest, a little worried that other people's versions might project some wrong impressions), it was quite pleasurable to write a memoir about three young girls aged eighteen, seventeen and fifteen, all wildly excited by the new dresses their Maman had bought for them, and the prospect of a long excursion into the countryside.

Our longest stop was at Aunt Nadezhda's in Tula – a dull and dirty town, but nevertheless a welcome break because Aunt gave us a good dinner and told us stories about Ivitsy.

'So you're off to Yasnaya Polyana,' she said as we were leaving. 'Don't let the Count push any of you off the balcony!'

'We won't be stopping there for very long,' replied Maman rather crossly. 'The main reason for our journey is of course to visit Papa.'

We piled back into the coach and rumbled along through the late afternoon and early evening, the high sun beating down from a wide blue sky until the coach entered the shade of a magnificent forest. Called Zaseka, it is part of a huge strip of crown land running through the whole of Tula province and at one place bordering on the Tolstoy estate. We knew then we could not be far from Yasnaya Polyana.

The long drive up to the house was also green and cool, the branches of oaks and birches nearly meeting overhead; the horses pulled up outside the front porch of what was now a two-storey, white-painted country house, with a glimpse of stables and kitchen gardens to either side. Lev Nikolaevich, who of course we knew well, and his sister Marya Nikolaevna whom we did not, although her marital separation and independent travels intrigued us greatly, came forward to welcome us. Two elderly ladies, one of them Aunt Toinette, beamed in the background and chattered their greetings in French. The other, Natalya Petrovna, appeared to wink at Tanya, no doubt because my little sister was so merry.

The house seemed old-fashioned and sparsely furnished, our town shoes clattering on the bare floors. We were invited to make use of a large downstairs room that had three white wooden sofas set against the walls, with hard cushions covered in blue-and-white striped mattress ticking. There was also one matching chaise-longue, and a locally made birchwood table. The ceiling was high and vaulted, with hooks dangling from it.

'In the old days of the Prince,' said Aunt Toinette, 'it was used as a storeroom for hanging sides of meat.'

We dumped our bags on the wooden floor and rushed out to the garden to stretch our cramped limbs before the light faded. Hearing Natalya Petrovna's voice calling to us from somewhere behind the house, we had stopped dashing about in order to listen when she appeared from around the side.

'Would you like to help me pick the raspberries?' she asked.

It would have been impolite to refuse, so we nodded and followed

Natalya Petrovna to the beds of canes. The squishy red globes hanging amongst the slightly barbed silvery-green leaves were irresistible. When we surreptitiously popped every second or third one into our mouths instead of the basket, we were not scolded, even though the crop was almost at an end.

'Haven't you ever eaten raspberries straight from the vine?' the old lady asked.

Liza, representing us, shook her head. 'Even when we make raspberry jam at our dacha, they bring the fruit in baskets,' she replied.

'It's not the same,' replied Natalya Petrovna disapprovingly.

We left the darkening garden when swarms of whirring insects started to descend on us; inside, Maman sent me to help the maid, Dunyasha, make up beds on the sofas in the vaulted room. Dunyasha was wondering how to provide a fourth bed, when our host walked in unannounced and overheard the discussion.

'What about this?' he asked, pushing a square stool up against the end of the chaise-longue.

'I can sleep on that,' I offered.

'Good,' said Lev Nikolaevich with approval. 'I'll help you make it up.' He took a folded sheet from the pile and clumsily shook it out.

I felt slightly embarrassed to be standing on the other side of a bed from an older man while together we straightened and smoothed the linen on which I would sleep; nevertheless, I felt the odd situation to be rather nice. 'Intimate' was my word for it in the memoir.

'I had really come to call you to supper,' said Lev Nikolaevich, 'and to help you find the way to the dining room. It's upstairs. Come with me.'

Tall, stately Dunyasha followed us up to help serve the meal under the supervision of a squint-eyed butler.

I had never seen such a beautiful room as the one in which we were to eat. Large French windows gave onto a narrow balcony, and in the middle of one wall was a door which led to a little sitting room with an antique rosewood clavichord; from it too French windows led onto the balcony and its lovely view. It was so breathtaking I took a chair and sat alone outside, wanting to revel in a vista I felt I could love all my life.

No doubt it was the wide expanse of nature spread out in front of me, or perhaps the sense that my own life was about to open up to some kind of marvel – but whatever the cause, I felt overwhelmed by happiness, and what I described as 'an extraordinary sense of boundlessness'. When Lev Nikolaevich came out to tell me that supper was ready, I wouldn't move.

'I don't want anything,' I said dreamily but firmly. 'It's so lovely out here.'

Our host went back inside to join the others, and I could hear Tanya horsing around and showing off, but everyone was laughing and indulging her, as usual. Tanya was so merry and animated she got away with anything. My own style was quite different – more serious, but very passionate underneath.

Long before he could have finished his meal, Lev Nikolaevich left the table and came out to me again. I wish I could recall a bit more of the conversation other than just his opening words: 'How simple and serene you are.'

He could not have been more wrong, but I felt deeply flattered and did not correct him.

My happiness did not wane the whole evening, even carrying me through an uncomfortable night on the chaise-longue, whose hard arms enclosed me too narrowly. But it had been turned into a bed for me by the very source of my exultation.

Next morning at breakfast, Lev Nikolaevich, his small grey eyes snapping with pleasure under their bushy brows, announced that he had arranged a picnic. Within the hour a long wagonette they called a *katki* was brought around to the front porch, harnessed with quick-as-an-arrow Strelka, and a chestnut, Baraban. A pair of riding horses also stood by: a bay, Belogubka, sporting an old-fashioned lady's saddle, and a magnificent grey stallion who clearly belonged to the master of the house. As the preparations went on, another light carriage bearing a cheerful group of guests from Tula drew up; Masha greeted one of them, the wife of an architect, with particular pleasure. Curious to know more of Lev's only sister, I registered that the presence of two best friends, one from childhood, the other more recent, was making Masha positively playful; she'd said little the previous evening, but now her jokes and high spirits had us all laughing as we waited for the last hampers of food and drink to be loaded.

Under cover of the laughter, Lev drew me aside. 'Would you like to ride Belogubka, instead of going in the *katki*?'

'I – I'd love to! But I can't!' I answered, at once delighted and devastated.

'Why not?' he frowned. I almost hung my head with vexation, but answered, 'It's infuriating. I didn't think to pack my riding clothes!'

I did not add that today, thinking only of how to look my best, I'd put on my new yellow dress with the black velvet belt and buttons. Lev Nikolaevich gave a hearty laugh.

'If that's the only problem, don't worry!' he grinned. 'It's not an issue in this part of the country. There are no dachas here – nothing but the forest to see you.'

And with that he proved the point by holding out his hand to help me mount the bay mare.

Within minutes I was galloping down the road beside him, heading for Zaseka forest, where the party was to make the first stop. I was swept up in a wave of elation that I was never to experience again, however many times I took that road or picnicked in Zaseka.

The group congregated in a little clearing near a haystack, which, at Marya's invitation, we raced to climb, rolling down helter-skelter, pushing each other off and whooping crazily. The whole day was noisy, cheerful, and so hard to bring to an end there was virtually no evening left by the time we finally arrived back at Yasnaya Polyana. The Count's chaise-longue again received me in its hard, bare arms.

2

Ivitsy

August 1862

The following morning we were to take off on the expedition to Ivitsy, stopping en route in the village of Krasnoe where Maman was born; Krasnoe had been part of her father's estate until he gambled it away following the death of his wife. Maman was genuinely anxious to visit her mother's grave – for her, a solemn obligation.

'But you can't go so soon!' cried Masha. 'You've only just got here.'

'No, we must go to my father,' Maman replied firmly. 'You've already been more than kind.'

'But we insist – ' the Count began to interpose, looking sideways at me.

'At least come again on the way back,' said Masha, at the same time.

'Oh, yes, Maman,' cried Tanya. 'Let's go and come back quickly.'

'Very well,' smiled Maman, as though indulging her youngest daughter was her one thought.

'And to make sure,' added Masha, 'why don't you take our carriage and horses? Then you'll have to.'

Maman protested there was no need, but Masha would hear no objection. In the end we departed in the Tolstoys' carriage, drawn by the horses we had hired. Theirs might be needed.

In the village of Krasnoe we got out at the church and went through a little gate into the graveyard. We had no difficulty finding the tombstone of our grandmother – it was inscribed 'Princess Sofya Petrovna Kozlovskaya, born Countess Zavadskaya'. The implication was that her first marriage, however empty or unhappy, was the only one that counted in ecclesiastical eyes; but from everything that had been said, or whispered, I could see little in favour of either husband. Kozlovsky had been a drunkard to whom Sofya had been married against her will, while Alexander Islenev, who was not even a lawful spouse, had kept her endlessly pregnant and in the end gambled away most of his fortune, including the Krasnoe estate. Yet our mother remembered her childhood as very happy – Sofya seemed to have found real joy in her children, and they knew it. She must have loved Alexander too, despite his gambling. After all, it was a common enough sin, and far from the worst.

While we were gathered around the grave, a tall old priest came out to greet us, accompanied by his deacon, Fetis, a withered little man with sparse grey hair plaited into a skinny pigtail. When Maman told him the reason for our visit, both clerics spoke warmly of Sofya Petrovna. The priest confessed that he had committed the sin of performing her secret marriage with Alexander.

'She begged me to do it,' he said. 'She said she wanted to be the wife of Alexander Mikhailovich in the eyes of God, even if not in the eyes of men.'

'But that marriage was bigamous!' I nearly protested, quickly stopping myself when I realised the old priest had been fully aware of what he was doing. His human compassion must have overridden any concern for church or state law.

He was an unusual man on many counts, for he went on to tell us an even odder story: some time ago, he reminisced, Fetis had been pronounced dead, and a funeral mass had been said. But when the moment came for him to be buried, the corpse jumped out of the grave and ran off to his home!

We didn't know how to react. It was thoroughly unbelievable, but we couldn't cast doubt on the word of a priest.

'If that's really true,' I finally said, 'it's nearly as miraculous as Peter and Fevronia!'

'Ah! You know that story,' said the old priest, pleased.

'We've heard it a hundred times,' said Tanya impatiently.

We had. The church thrived on the improving stories it told. Peter and Fevronia were a fourteenth century married couple so united they managed to die simultaneously; although they were laid out in separate coffins, they turned up next morning in the same one, and became icons of marital devotion. Faithful wives were a frequent theme in our religious education, their fidelity supposed to symbolise the union between Holy Mother Russia and her husband, Little Father Tsar. The saintly Peter and Fevronia had surely inspired the legendary Decembrist wives of 1825, who voluntarily followed their condemned husbands to Siberia after the failure of the latters' attempted coup against the Tsar. Perhaps this ideal had even influenced Sofya Petrovna, whose devotion to the profligate father of her illegal children never wavered.

I was not even engaged to be married – no matter how promising the omens – but the whole situation was producing so many delightful conjectures I felt disinclined to bother my head about anything too precise. At that moment, my life and everything in it seemed fantastically full of beauty, magic and love.

As soon as the horses were rested and watered, and the clerics farewelled, we drove on in our borrowed carriage towards Ivitsy, the one estate our unreliable grandfather had managed to retain.

Alexander Mikhailovich, his large, aquiline nose prominent in a clean-shaven face, greeted us with the pleased formality befitting an infrequent family occasion. Then he quickly shepherded us inside, his powerful figure gliding across the floor in soft ankle-boots as he pinched the cheek of one girl, winked at another, and cracked a series of jokes, all the time screwing up his humorous little eyes. I could see immediately why Sofya Petrovna had been fatally attracted to him, and how, after she died, he had been able to capture a second wife. Even now he was still quite handsome as he enveloped us in warmth and kindness.

The second wife was also a Sofya, a woman no longer young, but clearly at one time a beauty, her black eyes still large and expressive. We had known her since we were children, and had always been fascinated by the long pipe that dragged on her sagging bottom lip as she smoked. Sofya Aleksandrovna had given her husband three more daughters, the middle one another beauty, cool and imperturbable, called Olga, who led us 'ladies' up to the room assigned to us. I was not pleased to find that I'd been allocated a cot behind a cupboard, with only a chair to put my things on. Unlike the chaise-longue, it embodied no special associations to dispel the lack of comfort.

The next day Olga took us to visit some neighbours with daughters of similar ages to ours, who had also invited other friends. The whole gaggle, though well mannered and pleasant enough to talk to, nevertheless felt alien to me. It was tantalising, because I couldn't define why they seemed so different. On the way home, with Maman and Olga rocked to a doze by the clip-clop of the horses' hooves, I asked Liza in a whisper whether she had had the same impression.

'Of course they're nothing like us, you goose. They've lived in the country all their lives!' she hissed.

For more than one reason, I tried for the first time in my life to imagine the holidays stretching into a permanent existence. We joyfully looked forward to staying at our dacha outside Moscow. It meant bright summer days and long, balmy evenings, haymaking and fruit-picking, picnics in leafy clearings, and bathing in a natural pool; if it rained there would be mushrooming in the forests and fields.

But the flat in the Kremlin was always there for us to go back to, and even at the dacha we spent a lot of time planning the muffs and fur hats we would buy for the winter, or the warm coats the tailor would make us. Winter was the season for balls and the Bolshoi theatre, for Christmas parties and New Year presents, for skating on Moscow's iced-over ponds. But the main thing was that all these activities took place in society, in the company of our own friends or our parents', amidst a constant bustle of gatherings and outings. Even the postman's knock would cause us to leap up and be the first to open the invitations that poured from his greasy leather bag. Surely city and country life were meant to complement each other in roughly equal measure, just as the sultry heat of summer set off the snowy sparkle of winter. Would I be capable of spending all my time on someone's rustic estate, confined to a ramshackle manor house, with the nearest neighbours only contactable when the weather permitted?

'How can they bear it, Liza, these people who live in the country and never come to Moscow?' I asked.

'What can they do? Some estates are too far away, or their owners don't have any money. They don't all have town houses like us,' sniffed Liza. 'And not everyone in Moscow has a dacha, you know, or relatives to stay with in the country.' She turned her head to the window, leaving me to my ruminations.

What she said was no doubt true for many Muscovites, but in our affluent circle everyone took such pleasures for granted. The crisp frosts of autumn following the gorgeous, lazy summer would gear us up for the winter round of socialising – and the move back to town. But several novels, particularly those by Mr Turgenev, insisted on the boredom of lives lived permanently in the Russian countryside. The one he'd published last year, *On the Eve* – the eve of the emancipation of the serfs – and his earlier success, *Rudin,* both showed the rigidity of life under our horrible Tsar Nicholas I, and the lack of improvement even after Alexander II came to the throne. Alexander put a large number of reforms in place – like that of the postal system and the railway network, which must have made an enormous difference to rural life. But we all knew that court protocol remained as formal and the government as dictatorial as they had always been.

My sisters and I, who thrived on romantic French novels, could not help but notice what a different story they told from ours. The Russian favourite, *Evgenii Onegin,* by our best-loved writer Alexander Pushkin was a good example. In it, the hero, obliged to make a duty visit to his uncle, finds life in the country so tedious he flirts outrageously with Olga, the fiancée of his friend Lensky. Enraged, Lensky challenges Onegin to a duel, but it is he who is killed, by Evgenii's bullet.

This tragedy is not however the end of the story. Olga has a younger sister, Tatiana, whose addiction to French novels leads her to fall in love with Onegin. He condescendingly turns her down, before being obliged to flee the country to avoid arrest over Lensky's death. Although still in love with him, Tatiana agrees to make a marriage of duty and *convenance* with a rich Prince; and when Onegin comes back after eight years abroad, realising that he loves Tatiana after all, *she*, the faithful wife, spurns *him*.

The story is told in a sparkling style that my sisters and I, and all our friends, adored, but no one could call it an advertisement for country life. Girls like the Ivitsy neighbours were living witnesses as to why. These landowning families were still as steeped in serfdom as if the emancipation had never occurred; their habits and outlook were virtually unaltered by progress of any kind. If they were not handy to one of the new railway lines, their interests were totally confined to their immediate neighbourhood. The men farmed and hunted, the women sewed and supervised the household or tinkled on out-of-tune pianos; the monotony was only broken by Easter and Christmas and name day celebrations.

'Those girls yesterday, with their tonged curls and quaint dresses – didn't you think they were like something out of a novel by Mr Turgenev?' I whispered to Liza. I liked mentioning this author, because he was a friend of Lev Nikolaevich, who had several times mentioned staying with Ivan Sergeevich in St Petersburg; unfortunately, he had little to say in his host's favour. Perhaps, both being writers, they suffered from a secret rivalry; but from what Lev Nikolaevich said, a greater problem was the difference in their personal styles. 'A European fop versus a Russian boor,' Maman once laughed.

Liza deigned to turn back to me. 'They certainly remind me of that novella of Mr Turgenev's called *The Correspondence*,' she was saying. 'Do you remember the part where the heroine writes a letter to her emotionally paralysed lover, describing herself as one of many girls living in the depths of the country, constantly dreaming about love and living for the day the right man will come along to save them?'

'Yes, I remember. She says that if a man only half good enough turns up,' I answered slowly, 'the girl immediately sees him as her hero, but in the end it all comes to nothing – they are always separated by "circumstances". Why is that? What circumstances? Is it just because it's a romantic novel?'

'No,' said Liza bitterly, 'it's because it's completely realistic! What does Marya say in the rest of that passage? That if only he were a hero, he'd be capable of anything. And then she goes on, "But there are no heroes in our time." She's right. There are no heroes. The fellows we see in town come from such aristocratic backgrounds they just loll around till they're so bored by cards and spoilt by pleasure-seeking they're unendurable. And down here in the country the men are all oafs who do nothing but stride around their estates.'

I did not reply. Although there was some truth in my sister's views, Liza expressed them with a vehemence that could only stem from hurt or anger. Of course I understood the cause, but what could I do about it? Liza was nearly twenty, and it was in all our heads, not only Maman's, that it was high time she married, and that Count Tolstoy was the obvious candidate. It was strange that Maman, whose own life had been so bold and controversial, was hidebound by etiquette when it came to her daughters. She was desperate to get her eldest married off, but everyone else could see that Liza held little sway over the Count. He was still happiest when Tanya, who was barely sixteen, was frolicking around. Only she remained impish and lively, whereas nowadays when the Count called, Liza and I were both on edge.

Our perceptive Aunt Olga, well aware of our parents' designs, took Tanya aside one day.

'Tatiana, why has Liza told me that Lev Nikolaevich means to marry her when my own eyes tell me otherwise?' she asked, but Tanya just shrugged and giggled, making her black curls bounce. Meanwhile, I wondered why no one had written a novel about a heroine who is not brought up in the country, but has to live there after she is married. In fact someone had – Count Tolstoy himself! But at fourteen I had been too young to read the magazine in which it was published.

3

The Name Day Engagement
September 1862

The fact of the matter was that Lev Nikolaevich himself was not at all clear in his own heart as to what he wanted. In the abstract it sounded simple enough: as I see it now, he needed to marry in order to satisfy between the sheets of a marriage-bed the voracious sexual appetite that led him so often into uncontrolled debauchery. He had long condemned as abhorrent his youthful lack of restraint – and particularly its inevitable aftermath, when he despised both himself and the woman. The woman especially. But whether such a step would truly cure him was another matter.

When circumstances first produced the charming little group that triplicated his playmate Liubov Isleneva, it was natural that he'd be collectively attracted to all three of us, and easy enough for him to go along vaguely with Maman's expectations. But he was not moved by the prescriptions regarding an eldest daughter, and in any case the cryptic scribbles in his diary confirmed that Liza never gave him a good feeling. (Of course I did not at that point have access to his diary, that was still to come.) After a 'pleasant' June day spent at our flat, something had provoked him to write, 'But I daren't marry Liza.' Why *daren't*? In September there was further reluctance: 'Liza Behrs tempts me, but nothing will come of it. Mere calculation isn't enough, and there's no feeling.'

Yet he continued to revel in our company. After we left Yasnaya Polyana to go to Ivitsy, he felt bored and restless (as he explained to me), curious to know what we were up to and jealous as to whether we were enjoying ourselves more there than at his house. Well, Ivitsy was only 50 versts away – surely, he thought, the cure was to ride over and find out! He set off on the grey stallion, and by the time he arrived and was met with a warm welcome from our grandfather, who'd been a good friend of his father, he seemed in splendid spirits, although momentarily taken aback to find that he was far from the only visitor. Olga had organised a dance for the evening, and guests kept arriving all through the day. There were some officers garrisoned nearby, and a few local landowners to equalise the large number of females. No band could be obtained at such short notice, but several ladies offered to play the piano.

I was smoothing down my mauve and white dress with lilac ribbons fluttering from the shoulders – it was in the style called '*suivez-moi*' – when to my astonishment Lev Nikolaevich materialised from behind the stove. He complimented me on my appearance and said he wished Aunt Toinette could see me.

'*Merci*,' I said, disguising my pleasure with a mock curtsey. 'But why aren't you dancing?'

'Too old,' he replied laconically. Yet his lively conversation kept everyone entertained well after the dancers and card players had left off. I was transported by the certainty that he had come to see me, and wanted to please me; the evening flowed around me like the loveliest of dreams. I always remembered it as the most significant night, the highlight, of our courtship, yet I could never recall him saying anything specific. I realised that our relationship had to be a wordless one, based on hints, looks and mutual understanding, but I was no less thrilled for that. In fact I felt supremely confident and elated by the time he left to gallop home in the moonlight.

We left Ivitsy the next day, calling at Yasnaya Polyana on the way back to return the carriage. But there we were greeted by a new issue. Marya Nikolaevna wanted to go to Moscow with us.

'It's rather urgent,' she said, taking Maman by the arm and leading her into the garden. 'There is someone pressing me to come …' Her voice faded as they moved away, but given my curiosity about Lev Nikolaevich's interesting sister, I followed them into the raspberry canes, where I could hear their conversation without being seen.

'He wants me to go to Sweden with him,' I heard her say. I knew she must be talking about a new lover, but only learnt later that he was called the Viscount de Kleen.

'What does the family say?' my mother asked.

'Aunt Toinette is the main problem.'

'Of course! She adores you, and she'll miss you badly if you go off again.'

'It's not only that. Remember, my horrible husband is her nephew. I can't imagine how darling sweet Toinette can be related to such a ghastly man, or how she can fail to see that he's impossible to live with. She was so thrilled when we got married, she simply refuses to believe that he makes me dreadfully unhappy. So will you take me with you?'

'Of course,' said my mother, sounding slightly worried. 'If it will make you any happier.'

I looked on with sympathy at the leave-taking. Poor Aunt Toinette was lugubrious. I could see that Count Tolstoy was enormously attached to her, and resolved to ask Maman as soon as possible about her role in their lives. Meanwhile I felt as though there were two side-plays going on amidst the bustle of our departure – one elegiac, involving Masha and Aunt Toinette, the other a glorious prologue to a future that no one could glimpse except myself and Lev Nikolaevich. Nevertheless, it was evident that some people suspected something was going on. My sisters in particular kept giving me dark looks.

Before we climbed into the coach, we sat with Aunt Toinette, Natalya Petrovna, and of course our host, for the customary quiet moment. But, apparently on the spur of the moment, certainly to everyone's surprise, Lev Nikolaevich announced that he wanted to go to Moscow too!

'How could I stay here?' he asked. 'All dull and miserable?'

But there were already going to be six people in the coach – the most it could hold. It was decided that Lev Nikolaevich would ride the whole way on one of the two outside seats, while Liza and I took it in turns to keep him company on the other. Whenever I, well wrapped up, sat outside, he told me stories about his time in the wild and romantic Caucasus mountains. I noticed that he sounded a little hoarse, as though moved by these memories. Or by something … I on the other hand kept falling asleep as we travelled through the night, waking at each jolt to hear that thrilling voice soothing and exciting me at the same time. When we were at the last staging post before Moscow, I was looking forward to taking my turn again on the outside seat when Liza leaned over to me with a different idea.

'Sonya, I find it terribly stuffy in the coach. Would you mind if I stayed outside?' she simpered.

I felt very resentful, but when we all came out of the post-station I climbed inside. She was the eldest.

'Sofya Andreevna!' cried Lev Nikolaevich, 'Isn't it your turn to sit at the back?'

'It is, but I'm cold,' I replied without conviction. The carriage door slammed shut on us, hiding the murderous look I flung at Liza. However, seeing that Masha was sleeping soundly, I asked Maman to explain about Aunt Toinette.

'Their mother died when Lev Nikolaevich – he was the youngest of the five – was only two,' she began in a low whisper. 'He was too young to remember her, and there wasn't even a likeness of her anywhere in the house.'

'So Toinette brought them up?'

'She did. She played a vital role in all their lives, but specially Lev Nikolaevich's because he was a little toddler. Mind you, there was also their grandmother, but she was bedridden. The Tolstoy children used to take us upstairs to visit her; we were fascinated by her white hair, white nightdress, white sheets and the high white pillows she was propped up on. But the Tolstoys loved her very much.'

'Yes, we used to climb in beside her in that high, white bed,' murmured

Masha, without opening her eyes. 'And the boys had such a kind, indulgent tutor, and several of the servants were extremely fond of us all; but it was definitely Aunt Toinette – Tatiana Ergolskaya – who meant the most.'

'Well, if you're awake, Masha, you can explain to Sonya who exactly she was. I know she was some relation …'

'She was actually a cousin of our father's. He was attracted to her in his youth, but our grandparents ruled her out of the running because she had no money. But Toinette loved Nikolai so much she accepted, even embraced his rich bride, and was grateful to live with them as a member of the family. And a wonderful asset to us all after our mother died.'

'How long did your father last after her death? Not very long, was it?'

'Eight years. And grandmother followed him the year after. That was when Aunt Alexandra, Countess Osten-Saken, became our official guardian.'

My mother giggled. 'I remember her! She was very religious and very smelly. You children tried to make us believe it was because she never took her clothes off even to wash!'

'Well, that's what we believed. But she died too, after about three years, and we were taken away from Yasnaya Polyana, where we'd been so free, and sent to live with Aunt Yushkova, in Kazan.'

'Miles away!'

'Four hundred. Halfway to Asia.'

'What was it like?'

'Awful. The boys went to the local *gimnasium* and Kazan's so-called university, but we all wanted to escape. Then finally the family inheritance got sorted out, and the three estates were allocated among the boys. Lyova got Yasnaya Polyana. He was thrilled because it was always his special favourite. He abandoned Kazan and the university – he was failing all his subjects anyway – and went back to Yasnaya.'

She gave a great yawn. 'That's enough ancient history. I'm going back to sleep.'

Maman's eyes were already shut.

The next day Marya Nikolaevna left Moscow to go abroad and our whole family went to stay at our dacha, Pokrovskoe, just outside the city. Lev Nikolaevich remained in town to work on an educational magazine for use in peasant schools; he had rented a small apartment in the house of a German shoemaker. However, he visited the dacha by train nearly every day, often travelling back to town with Papa, whose presence in Moscow was frequently required.

If Count Tolstoy realised how patently obvious it was that his inclination was veering towards me, he paid little heed. At Pokrovskoe we took long walks together, talking our heads off the whole time. He even joined in the childish games we still tended to play when we were there. Once I jumped into father's unharnessed cabriolet and shouted, 'When I'm Tsarina I'm going to drive about in a carriage just like this one!' Lev Nikolaevich stepped between the shafts, seized one in each hand, and started pulling the cabriolet along at a loping trot. 'I'm already taking *my* Tsarina for a drive,' he grinned over his shoulder.

The large first-floor drawing room was always the focal point of our dacha. After evening tea – the usual hours were coffee at 9 am, lunch at one o'clock, dinner at 6 pm, and tea at nine – the whole family liked to linger on the balcony in the cool night air. Often we sat up so late Lev Nikolaevich had to stay over. The evenings were long and the moon so brilliant that when he and I walked down to the little glade, we would be bathed in light as we gazed at the silvery pathway on the pond. I was proud that everyone found the Count's company interesting and jolly, but aware that my own feelings went well beyond the general appreciation. But if the still undefined situation made me prey to waves of agitation, who knew what it must have been doing to Liza?

One afternoon I was so overwrought I took refuge in my bedroom, with its French windows looking towards the pond and, beyond it, the church and all the places I'd loved since I was a child. I did not want my carefree girlhood to end, and yet the next step seemed so inevitable it made my heart pound. I knew I could not bear not to seize the unknown, no matter how terrifying it might be.

While I was standing there, Tanya ran in. 'What's the matter, Sonya?' she asked, looking at me with concern.

'*Je crains d'aimer le comte*,' I whispered. 'I'm afraid I've fallen in love with the Count.'

Tanya reacted with a cry of astonishment and alarm.

On one walk Lev Nikolaevich asked me if I kept a diary.

'Ever since I was eleven,' I replied proudly. 'And last summer I wrote a long story as well.'

'Let me read your diaries,' he said quickly.

'Oh, no! I couldn't let you do that!' I gasped.

'Well, the story then?'

I agreed to let him have that, and next morning asked anxiously for the verdict.

'I've had a look, but I only had time to skim it,' replied Lev Nikolaevich rather casually. I was hurt, but the truth, which I only discovered much later, would have been embarrassing for him and possibly distressing to me. He told me that he had in fact stayed up all night reading the story, agonising about the implications. He hardly registered my literary style, but in the main character, a Prince Dublitsky, he was sure he recognised himself. And I had written, 'The Prince was extraordinarily unattractive in appearance, and was always changing his opinions.'

Poor darling! Anxiety probably added to his hypersensitivity, yet, if truth be told, no photograph has ever been able to turn L.N. Tolstoy into a handsome hussar. His grey eyes are not large, are very deep-set and a little too close together; they appear even smaller because they are overhung by bushy brows and a huge forehead. Cameras usually bring out a lowering, truculent gaze; but they of course do not see with the eyes of a girl in love.

In any case the real problem lay as much with me as with him. It was not simply that I wasn't the eldest, but rather that at seventeen – admittedly

I was about to turn eighteen in the middle of the month – I must have seemed to him inordinately young: 'A child!' he wrote in his diary. He wanted to reach a clear and honourable position, but doubted his own motivation. 'What if this is the desire for love, and not love? I try to look only at her weak sides, but nevertheless. A child! But it could be!' (I must reiterate that I did not at the time know about anything in his diary.)

The next day he was trying to 'think less about Sonya', but when his thoughts turned, inevitably, to me, it was 'good'. And two days later, in the entry in which he tried to persuade himself that I was 'plain and vulgar', there was also that give-away confession – I 'interested' him.

Lev Nikolaevich passed two more indecisive days in Moscow, an agony for both of us. On the third, he was impelled to write the most momentous and strange letter of his personal life to date – so momentous in fact that he had to pretend that giving every word in it only its first letter was just a game, a game of acronyms: 'Worked a bit; wasted my time writing to Sonya in initial letters,' he recorded. (It may seem strange that I am describing L.N.'s state of mind more than my own. But I know only too well how I felt; this account is in part an endeavour to understand the mind and heart of Lev Nikolaevich Tolstoy, as well as to leave a record for posterity.)

He then went to our flat in the Kremlin and by good luck found Papa about to set off for Pokrovskoe. Lev had already decided to accompany him, being desperate to know the fate of his cryptic epistle. But although, or because, I had been unable to decipher his code, showing it to my father was the last thing I was likely to do. So, 'nothing, nothing, silence …' recorded the diary. The evening at the dacha was, on the surface, as pleasant as usual – he even experienced 'a good, sweet feeling' – but I could hardly wait to catch him alone and ask him to decipher the missive for me. The moment came – or rather, was snatched when the others decided to have a song at the piano – but he was unaccountably embarrassed, and wouldn't go through it with me! We were both horribly on edge, and I very frustrated by his refusal to explain. Instead of the declaration I had dared to hope for, there was a scene. I went to bed in tears.

For the next week Lev Nikolaevich ricocheted between Moscow and Pokrovskoe, while I remained on tenterhooks. I could not of course know then what I have since read – that he was convinced that he was too ugly to have any hope, yet felt ever more keenly attracted to marriage as he saw it – 'so simple, so timely, with neither passion, nor fear, nor a moment's regret'. This time he was not writing in code, yet, with hindsight, I cannot help wondering whether 'ugly' stood for wicked, and 'passion' for lust.

He too was hyper-tense for several days, telling his diary that he was as much in love as ever, but beginning to despair of a successful outcome. Deciding that Liza was the obstacle, he stopped feeling sorry for her and began to detest her. He could not sleep for anxiety, and even felt too nervous to come to the dacha. Every day he dithered and agonised. On September 9th he apparently wrote a letter setting out what he had meant by the initials in the earlier note – but failed to send it!

Five days later he tried again, insisting that I get out the first letter, which I had kept in my handkerchief drawer, well away from prying eyes. We sat down together to solve the puzzle. 'Y.y. & n.f.h ...' it began. How could I possibly have made anything of that?

'"Y.y. & n.f.h ..." These letters stand for "Your youth and need for happiness",' he explained to me, stabbing at the page with his stubby fingers. '"T.v.r. ... too vividly remind me of my age and incapacity for happiness."'

Once he had given me a few of the words, he seemed to think I should be able to guess some of the next sentence, but I was still completely at sea. 'Your family has the wrong idea about me and your sister Liza. You and your sister – ' he read, stopping at the capital T.

'Tanechka?' I murmured.

'Of course! "You and your sister Tanechka must protect me."'

We did not tell Maman about the letter, but she must have seen from my shining eyes that I'd received some kind of declaration. It was not of course what she intended. Poor Liza was equally aware that something was afoot, masking her humiliation with a furious display of temper. Papa did not bother to hide his irritation at what he still saw as Count Tolstoy's recalcitrance in making an offer for his eldest daughter.

Lev retreated to his room in Moscow, but could not keep away from Pokrovskoe for long. He came, and even stayed the night again. At least to himself he rejoiced that his future life 'with a wife' was presenting itself 'clearly, joyfully and calmly'. But he still had not formally asked me, or even made his intentions clear to my parents; our mutual happiness was referred to by no one and disapproved by everyone. Even Tanya looked unusually serious and severe.

As for me, it was as well that I did not then have access to his journal. To escape the tension in the house, he went down to the village with my brother Sasha. The shameful record tells that 'a wench, a peasant coquette' aroused his attention.

'Alas', he wrote of what ensued. As if one word could wipe the slate clean!

Within a few days we all went back to Moscow, and on September 16th, when the Kremlin flat happened to be noisy with a crowd of Sasha's cadet friends, Lev called me into an empty room – my mother's! – and thrust a letter into my hands, saying he would wait there for my answer. I rushed downstairs to the bedroom I shared with my sisters and tore it open. It was quite long and shot through with anxiety: basically, he could not leave but dared not stay … However, towards the end, he urged me, with my hand on my heart, in all honesty, to tell him whether I did or didn't WANT TO BE HIS WIFE …

At these words I ignored the rest, intent on racing upstairs to tell him what he wanted to hear. But there was Liza barring the doorway, frantic to know what was happening.

'Le comte m'a fait la proposition,' I babbled, as Maman also appeared. She took me by the shoulders and propelled me towards the stairs. 'Then go and give him your answer,' she ordered.

The next day was my name day and Maman's also, being the combined celebration of the virtues of Faith (*Vera*), Hope (*Nadezhda*), Charity (*Liubov*) and Wisdom (*Sofya*). A constant succession of well-wishers came through the door and, to their amazement, were presented to Count Tolstoy as my official *fiancé*; we were toasted innumerable times in Papa's supply of name day champagne. Our French teacher was the only one with a thought for Liza, remarking, without much French logic, '*C'est dommage que cela ne fût Mlle Lise; elle a si bien étudié.*' (It's a pity it was not Miss Liza; she's worked so hard at her studies.) But our poor Liza had learnt something: looking pitiable and depressed, she forced herself to kiss and congratulate the man who would only ever be her brother-in-law.

Incredibly to everyone except Lev Nikolaevich, whose impatience knew no bounds, the bridegroom insisted that there be only one week between the engagement and the wedding. He simply could not see the point of a long engagement, and I suspect that my parents were too afraid he would back out to put up much of an objection.

For me these eight days passed like a bad dream, while Maman, still too stunned to have an opinion of her own, resorted to shopping. She expected me to accompany her on the innumerable expeditions required to accumulate a proper wardrobe of dresses, jackets and underwear, leaving Lev and me virtually no time by ourselves. We only managed to exchange one kiss, standing by the piano. I could not imagine why Lev was not more eager to see me alone, but now I understand that he was on the whole relieved by my enforced busyness. There was a burning issue he had yet to sort out.

He had convinced himself that if I really knew him, not as he was now, but as he had been in the past, I would immediately cease to love him. In fact, he was persuaded that I was deceiving myself altogether about him. Terribly agitated, he decided he could not let me marry him while I remained in this state of virginal ignorance. He had to come clean; 'she' had to *know*.

Thus, on one of those whirlwind days between the name day party and the wedding, something occurred that I can never, ever forget. Lev Nikolaevich gave me all his past diaries to read. Through confession he would attain absolution, while I, presumably, would see that he had at least aspired to virtue. The crux was his shameful sexuality and resulting self-disgust, of which it was absolutely imperative that he purge himself – never mind the effect those revelations might have on me.

'At home Klara – she filled me with disgust,' I saw for the 24th of September 1857. The 15th–16th of June 1858: 'Had Aksinya ... but I'm repelled by her.' There were many, many such entries. Sickened, I shut that yearbook, only to seize another and again, utterly repelled, let it fall from my cold fingers. I have read and reread them all frequently since then, in my efforts to understand the man I married, but not even time can erase the impact of that initial shock.

He had recorded in particular his success, or lack of it, in adhering to his self-formulated Rules of Life, frequently admonishing himself for the countless failures to keep them. As well as an inordinate sexual appetite, he also accused himself of vanity, boasting, conceit, sloth, apathy, affectedness, deceitfulness, instability, indecisiveness, waiting for miracles, a tendency to copy others, cowardice, contrariness, excessive self-confidence, inclination to voluptuousness, and a passion for gambling – all in one month (March 1851)! The only sin missing from this list was drunkenness, although it cropped up often enough elsewhere.

Naturally I was devastated. I tried to tell myself that Lev Nikolaevich was acting out of an excess of honesty; perhaps I even perceived, however confusedly, that what was most strange about the confessions was less the behaviour itself than the loathing and disgust with which he castigated his own weakness. It was almost as though he suffered from an *excess* of moral sensibility. But that made it all the more wrong of him to seek salvation at the expense of *my* trust and innocence. Shattered and weeping, unable to get the revelations out of my mind, and suddenly terrified of how the beast within him would behave towards *me* when the time came, I was far from having recovered myself by the time the wedding was upon us.

'On the wedding-day, fear, distrust and the desire to run away.'

I might well have written those words on the 23rd of September 1862, but they were in fact my husband's, the day after the ceremony, and almost the only thing he wrote at all concerning the momentous event. 'She was in tears,' he added in staccato phrases. 'In the carriage.' But then he had consoled himself. 'She knows everything and it's simple.'

But it wasn't.

4

At Birulevo
September 1862

'At Birulevo.' The jotting in Lev Nikolaevich's diary the day after the
wedding night was followed by, 'Her timidity. Something morbid.'

I myself put nothing on paper at the time. Given my realisation even
then that I might need to record *my* view of our marriage rather than have
posterity misled by somebody else's, I tried to fix in my mind as much as I
could of that portentous night. But – write it down? That is both difficult
and embarrassing; yet I must force myself not only to clarify my own
feelings, but to try to probe *his* likely experience of our wedding, and of
the night we spent together in that unfamiliar place that I have never, ever
wanted to revisit.

The ceremony had been set for eight o'clock in the evening of Sunday,
September 23rd, which meant that a whole day had to be endured with
nothing to do but get the bride ready before I would set out for the last time
as a daughter of the house.

Until it was time to start dressing, I tried to occupy myself in the box-
room, where our trunks stood ready to be stowed on top of the coach. I
was prising open the smallest suitcase to squeeze in a pair of gloves – even
in the country they might be needed, if only for warmth – when a servant
tapped on the door.

'The Count is here to see you, Sofya Andreevna.'

Lev Nikolaevich! He shouldn't be dropping in uninvited on the very day of the wedding! What could he be thinking? I had only two seconds to contemplate what I should do before he was shouldering his way into the room, red-faced and agitated.

'I don't see how you can really love me!' he blurted out. 'You know, there is still time to call it off.'

I was deeply shocked that he could even suggest anything so far from my wishes. It must mean that it was really he who didn't want to go through with it! So terrified of losing him that I was unable to speak, I began to weep. Then my mother, no doubt apprised by the servant of his presence, marched in and in one glance assessed not only the situation, but the necessity of saving it.

'You've chosen a fine day to make her cry,' Maman reproached Count Tolstoy. 'A girl's wedding day is hard enough on her without the husband sneaking in and upsetting her. Look at her crying her eyes out! You've both got a long journey ahead of you, so be off and don't come back here! We'll see you in church.'

Abashed, Lev Nikolaevich went off sheepishly to dine with his sponsors, who were charged with the responsibility of getting him to the church before the bride arrived. His aunt would drive with me, his brother Sergei having gone on ahead to Yasnaya Polyana to make sure everything was in order for our arrival.

Shortly before seven o'clock my sisters and girlfriends started to dress me. After they had dropped the tulle frock – thin, light and open at the neck and shoulders – over my satin petticoat, I again raised my bony, childish arms, this time in order to fix my hair. I had vetoed a hairdresser, who would contrive something stiff and artificial that Lev would hate, but I let the girls pin some fresh flowers under the swathed white tulle of the veil. And clip a single string of pearls around my neck. And draw on a pair of white muslin gloves ...

At last I stepped into the waiting shoes and stood ready to leave. But before that could happen the best man had to come and let us know that the bridegroom was in the church. So far there'd been no sign of him.

Unwilling to crush our dresses by sitting down, we stood about stiffly, tapping our feet impatiently.

An hour or more passed and still no messenger appeared. Strung out emotionally and exhausted by the prolonged standing, I convinced myself that Lev Nikolaevich had run away. All I wanted to do now was faint.

At last there was a knock at the door and in a great flurry a small, squint-eyed little fellow rushed in. But he was not the best man. He was Lev Nikolaevich's valet, Alexei, who had been despatched to open one of the suitcases and get out a clean shirt for the groom, who had packed *all* his clean clothes! He had sent someone out to buy a new shirt but forgotten that it was Sunday, when the shops were shut.

It took an age for a suitable shirt to be selected and taken round to the groom, and for him to be escorted to the church, and for the best man to finally arrive at the Kremlin flat with the announcement that the ladies could now depart. But not until that happened did I feel I could bid farewell to the servants and the well-wishers who were not invited to the ceremony but had come to the house. The servants in particular wept and sobbed, but even my family and friends were tearful that I was going off to live in the country.

'However will we manage without our little countess?' snuffled my old nurse.

'I'll die of grief,' proclaimed Tanya tragically, for once bereft of her usual merriment.

My little brother Petya fixed his big black eyes despairingly on me, while my mother pretended to be busy with the supper preparations. My father, who was not well, had declined to attend the church, so I went to say goodbye to him in his study. They checked that the traditional bread and salt were ready for our return, and Maman took down the icon of St Sofya the Martyr so that and she and Uncle Mikhail Islenev could bless me with it. My uncle's lips twitched, but he forbore to make the joke that the saint's unfortunate name clearly suggested to him.

At last we set off for the Palace Church of the Virgin Birth, which was within the Kremlin walls and only a five-minute carriage ride from the flat. I sobbed all the way.

The carriage stopped at the palace garden where Lev Nikolaevich was waiting for me. He took my hand and walked me to the door of the church, where the priest stood in his white and gold robes and bulbous hat. He took both our hands and led us past the three hundred guests, known and unknown, and down the aisle towards the iconostasis. The glow of dozens of candles lit up the darkness and the choir sang 'Come, O Dove'; at the foot of the altar my brother Sasha and his friend Mitrofan, my best men, were patiently waiting. Golden crowns were held over our heads as the choir chanted and the candles were snuffed and relit.

The long ceremony passed in a daze until suddenly I was alone in a carriage with Lev Nikolaevich, driving back to the flat that was no longer my home. Only close friends and relatives had been invited to the reception; they drank champagne and ate fruit and sweets.

It seemed no time before I had to change into my going away clothes and say a final goodbye to everyone except the old chambermaid Varvara, who was to go with us. Lev Nikolaevich had purchased a brand new coach of the kind called a *dormeuse*, which was supposed to be roomy enough to allow travellers to sleep comfortably in a sitting position. Drawn by six horses, it also had plenty of space for luggage on the roof, but it took a while for our heavy leather trunks to be hoisted up and strapped securely. Lev Nikolaevich fidgeted with impatience, while I wished that the preparations for departure would never come to an end. My throat ached with the effort of trying to hold back my sobs, as it dawned on me ever more forcefully that I was leaving the only home I had ever known, and every member of my dear, darling family, *forever*. My sisters were unashamedly in floods of tears, and little Petya had to be taken off to bed, unwell on account of the amount of champagne he'd drunk in order to overcome his sadness. The baby, two-year-old Vyacheslav, was already sound asleep, but I went into his room and made the sign of the cross over him, tearfully embracing my old nurse and even Stepanida Trifonovna, an elderly lady our parents had harboured for thirty-five years without her ever taking the least interest in us girls.

I saved the last long embrace for my mother, both of us sobbing uncontrollably. Then I climbed into the carriage and arranged my skirt. Lev Nikolaevich slammed the door shut, and we felt the coach shake as his valet and my maid got up onto the outside seat at the back. Although I couldn't bear to look at the little group forlornly waving from the steps, the piercing cry Maman gave rent the air above the rumble of the wheels and the clop of the horses' hooves.

By now it was raining, and the puddles in the road reflected the advancing carriage lamps and the apparent streaking of the streetlights. I shrank into my corner, wretched, miserable and hiccupping.

My husband seemed puzzled and somewhat offended. Finally he said gruffly, 'If it upsets you so much to leave your family, you can't love me very much.'

I had no answer; at that moment I was not sure whom I most loved, but Lev Nikolaevich Tolstoy was not at the top of the list.

The autumn night had drawn in quickly, and the further we left the lights of civilisation behind us, the blacker grew the darkness engulfing the carriage. I completely forgot how exciting I had found it a few months earlier to travel through the countryside perched up on the outside of a coach next to Lev Nikolaevich; instead I succumbed to waves of terror and exhaustion. I cowered in silence for a couple of hours, soothed only by the swaying motion of the coach.

'We'll be making a stop for the night soon,' announced Lev. 'At Birulevo.'

My mind leapt immediately to what that would mean. So, I could tell, did Lev's, for he coughed and ahemmed and finally broached the question of what instruction I might have had.

'Sonya,' he began, softening his naturally gruff voice, 'Did Liubov Isleneva – did your mother – ?' It was obviously hard for him to raise the issue; and as it is equally hard, but absolutely necessary, for me to try to imagine what was going through his mind on that night, I am going to write down my speculations, most of which have been suggested by the horrors inscribed in those scarifying diaries. He did not go into intimate detail on the page, but I have deliberately *fleshed* out my terrified suppositions (the word is apt) with knowledge of what I discovered from experience only later.

He had never been bothered to ask that question before, because it had never been necessary. It was not that he had never had a virgin. He wouldn't have been able to count the number of hymens he must have broken in young peasant girls thirteen or fourteen years old. Perhaps they had screamed, because they were frightened or because it hurt, but he would not have seen that as his fault. Someone had to do it.

In any case, it would seem that he preferred married women, like Aksinya ... Aksinya! Her! Did he feel as angry with Aksinya for popping into his head at that inappropriate moment as I always did for her shadowy presence in our marriage? He had vowed in the diary never to go with her again, he seemed definite about that, even though she did live on the estate (!). But could I believe that, when every mention of her made her sound unconditionally receptive, enjoying their love-making to the hilt? Evidently she'd got a taste for it with her husband, and had then felt starved and full of longing after he lost interest, deserting her for the bottle. Of course the two of them had stayed married – what else were peasants to do? But then Lev, her master, had come across her in a deserted corner of the orchard, picking apples. After a quick glance around to see no one was looking, he'd slipped his hand down her blouse; her breast leapt in response, the nipple stiffening. He'd swung her round slightly so that he could put the other hand between her legs. Even through her skirt he could feel her convulse, but she wasn't objecting – all she wanted was to open her thighs so that the muscles could close more firmly around his hand and give her the pleasure she craved. Her own fingers went around his neck, pulling his face towards her, as their open mouths pressed together, their tongues avid;

her other hand reached down – teasing and playful at first, then familiar and urgent. They fell into the soft, long grass; slipping quickly and easily into her, he'd felt welcomed, like a delightful, craved-for treat.

Thereafter he had found it impossible to keep away from Aksinya … especially *after* she'd fallen pregnant. Even I understood from my reading of novels the huge difference between Russian and Western attitudes to babies. Russians believed ardently in the mystic fertility of motherhood, while Westerners seemed caught up with romantic dreams about virgin innocence. European novels seemed to revolve around falling in love, with many of them hurtling on from the quest for a marriage partner to the torments of adultery.

But the whole concept of romantic love was alien to Russian tradition. Russia hadn't even had any novels of her own until they started crossing the borders from Western Europe towards the end of the last century. There were the ancient chronicles, of course, but they were always about valiant heroes married to faithful wives – hence the Decembrists.

We had merged the bountiful Mother Earth of pagan times with Mary the Mother of God, who was never depicted on an icon without a babe in her arms; we never prized virginity. Our women were genuinely proud to become mothers. It was better for a girl, married or not, to show she was capable of bearing a child than to remain barren. There was no shame – or there hadn't been until the European notions started creeping in. Pushkin had got it absolutely right. If Tatiana hadn't filled her head with French novels she would never have fallen in love with Onegin and offered herself so brazenly to him. But in the end her Russian upbringing had triumphed, and she'd remained faithful to the husband her parents had arranged for her.

So there was nothing to wonder at if my husband found Aksinya even more desirable *after* she'd given birth to Timofei. Making her a mother did away with any scruples he might have felt vis-à-vis her drunken husband.

Suddenly I felt Lev's puzzled, wary eyes on me. For how long had this train of thought preoccupied me, preventing me from replying to his question? And how could I make reference to any of it?

He took my hand and held it in his large, rough paw. He smiled at me encouragingly; I let a wan quiver curve my cold lips. The coach slowed down and we heard the driver telling the horses to whoa and pull up. I peeped out of the coach to glimpse a building with lights in some of the windows, and a few log huts scattered around. We had come to a village. It must be Birulevo.

Lev Nikolaevich leapt to the ground and came around to hand me out. Huddled in my warm cloak and walking stiffly after the long drive, I followed him in the direction of the yellow glow spilling from a doorway. Alexei and Varvara had also climbed down and were heading for the inn, each carrying a handsome tapestry bag by its tortoiseshell handle; inside were the night things of their master and mistress.

The innkeeper, quickly realising that he was dealing with quality, ushered us into the 'Tsar's Suite', which consisted of three large, bare rooms, the sparse furniture covered in red damask. His wife bobbed a curtsey and enquired if we were hungry.

'No, no,' I answered, sure that the sight and smell of food would have a disastrous effect on my stomach. 'But if tea were possible ...'

The woman assured us it would arrive instantly and I sat down on the sofa; soon a samovar was brought in with glasses and sugar lumps. The woman placed everything on a round, cloth-covered table, poured hot water into the little teapot and put it back on top of the samovar. Again she left the room. I didn't move.

'Come now,' said Lev Nikolaevich in a jovial tone. 'You must be mistress and pour out.' For the first time he used the intimate form of address. I couldn't bring myself to reciprocate, either then or for some time to come, but I did manage to fill the glasses and hand him the sugar.

But tea drinking could not defer the inevitable forever. We were both desperate to put this 'first time' behind us, though no doubt for different reasons. Lev appeared discomforted by my timidity; I could only recall the day Maman had initiated that awkward conversation in the confines of a rather dark cab, her face wearing an expression I had never seen before – a strange mixture of embarrassment and a kind of knowing archness. We were on our way back from ordering half a dozen winter nightdresses and some bedroom slippers.

'Sonechka,' she'd whispered, laying her hand on my knee. 'I know you are familiar with the facts of – of procreation.'

I had swallowed and nodded. Of course I was. You couldn't be second oldest in a large family without hearing the sound of babies being born in another room, or spend every summer in the countryside without seeing animals mount each other. But the closer we'd got to the wedding day, the more I'd come to realise that this was little better than looking at pictures of Michelangelo's David. I had never seen the male member naked, but I had overheard jokes among the peasant girls about size and shape, and had a hazy notion that it could grow and dwindle according to the circumstances. I had also admitted to myself that during those moonlit walks with Lev I had experienced an urge in my own private parts that might in a novel be called desire; certainly that long kiss by the piano had set up an ardent longing to press closer and closer to him, to feel the full length of our bodies hard against each other, especially my small, taut breasts against his strong chest; but also, especially, *down there*. But by now all those exciting flutters of anticipation had died away, no doubt extinguished by the exhaustion of the day and fear of the unknown.

'Good,' Maman had continued in the cab, smiling happily. 'You know, the things that husbands and wives do between themselves are not just so that they can have children, although that of course is the main reason, as the Church tells us. It's also very – very *nice*. It's, um, *pleasurable*. For both of them.'

I could not doubt the confidence of my mother's tone.

'It doesn't hurt?' I made myself ask, since the vague picture I did have was like some kind of brutal invasion of the most mysterious and private orifice in my body.

'It will the first time,' Maman replied, a slight frown wrinkling her brow, although her eyes gleamed merrily, as though focused on something I could not see. 'But after that, it's wonderful.' Then, as if recovering herself, she added primly, 'God ordained it, you know.'

Thus, for me, and probably even more for Lev, the sex was something we both trusted would come good – very good, why not? – once we had got over tonight; but I still had to cope with the challenge of undressing in front of a man I hardly knew, of lying down next to him in a strange bed, and of enduring brief but unimaginable pain. If only I wasn't so exhausted, and didn't have to do it in these bare, alien rooms, so far from home!

I tipped the teapot once more, but it was already drained. Lev Nikolaevich, who had silently observed my attempts at procrastination, remarked huskily that it was getting late.

'I've had a look in the bedroom,' he said. 'There's a small dressing room off it, so I will go in there while you put on your nightdress and climb into bed.' He spoke almost as though I were a child, thinking perhaps that this strategy would be the most likely to put me at my ease. No doubt he personally believed night attire to be redundant under the circumstances.

And so it was that I at last took off my dressing gown and lay rigid under the cold sheets, waiting for Lev Nikolaevich Tolstoy to come to bed.

Our immediate union turned out to be above all a confusing experience. As Lev threw off his robe to reveal his naked body, I had a quick glimpse of a long, hard organ rearing up under the thatch of pubic hair; but in a minute he was under the sheet beside me, then lying half over me, his hands grabbing at my breasts to rub and squeeze them, his mouth planting kisses all over my face. There was an animal scent coming from him that I found foreign, intoxicating and a little frightening; but his limbs and torso warmed my cold skin and for that I was genuinely grateful. The organ was pushing against my own pubis, and just as I felt a flutter of response beating deep inside me, his large hand was using two thick fingers to force apart the sensitive folds of flesh. I gasped, and the fingers stopped probing for a second. I had a flash of concern – that intake of breath had been the wrong thing to do – and sought to make amends.

'It's – all right,' I panted. Not I exactly, but my body, *that* part of it, could not have borne it if he did not go on. But he did, pulling me apart, pushing in with his finger, clamping his mouth over mine, ducking his head to suck my breast, until with a great groan he heaved himself directly on top of me and the organ forced itself in. I let out a yelp of agony as I felt something tear inside me; yet, although it hurt so badly I felt sure a bruise would show through on my skin, there was also a sensation that could only be called thrilling. And satisfying. Though not completely; something more was urgently, very urgently, required; there was no time to sort out exactly what. There was a rhythm now to the organ's movement, like a kind of pumping that got faster and more – more – could it be *desperate?* – until I was flooded by a heavenly, warm liquid which gushed into that secret cavity where the sex was happening. Lev Nikolaevich groaned again, more loudly, and rolled off me. He lay on his back panting for a moment, then flung his arm over my breast, palm up; in two minutes he seemed, incredibly, to have fallen asleep.

I thrilled alone to the fabulous, involuntary convulsions that too soon died away.

5

Family Happiness
1863

It shocks me now to realise how little I knew the man I had married. When he was still courting who knew which daughter, I took it for granted that Lev's great virtue was his lineage and all that went with being a member of the nobility – like this great and beautiful estate spread beneath me every time I look out of my window.

So when did I become aware that the Count was also a writer? I would have been about eight when his budding literary efforts began to gain him some reputation, but at that time I had never even heard his name. Later, after he had begun to visit us, I overheard one of my father's patients mention that she never felt bored sitting in the waiting room, because there was always a pile of thick journals on the low table in the middle of the room. *The Contemporary,* though published in St Petersburg, was apparently well represented, which she was glad of because it contained the stories of her favourite writer, 'L.N.'.

When I asked Papa about the magazines, he replied, 'I don't mind recommending young Tolstoy's efforts. Some people are rather impressed that we know him.'

So then I asked Maman how long they had been following Lev Nikolaevich's writing career.

'Much longer than you, dear,' she laughed. 'I can remember Papa and me sitting over breakfast one morning, it must be nearly ten years ago now. He was reading the paper and I had a periodical. Suddenly I cried out,

"Andrei! There's a whole story here by Lyova Tolstoy, about his childhood when we all played together, though he changes names and things." It seemed to be written as a memoir but it read like fiction. He was definitely in it, under a different name, but I think I was too.'

'Were you really? What did Papa say?' I asked, intrigued.

'He was a little alarmed, but I told him there was nothing to worry about, everyone was disguised, and anyway it was when we were all children. Soon I was able to assure him that the public response was excellent. Lyova's little stories were earning him quite a name even then.'

There was no doubt that *Childhood* by 'L.N.' was as successful as she claimed; he'd followed it up with *Boyhood* and then *Youth,* both of which made less of an impact but still pleased many readers. Papa became noticeably more friendly towards Count Tolstoy.

The first time Maman invited him to our dacha was in 1855, the summer after he returned from the Crimean war – which had been something of a disaster for Russia, dragging on for over two years and ending with a humiliating defeat. (We didn't have a Florence Nightingale on our side.) Maman thought our noisy family life might help him forget the carnage he'd seen in Sebastopol, which everyone knew about because our guest had recorded his impressions in three stories called *Sebastopol Sketches.* Published in consecutive episodes in *The Contemporary,* they were called *December*, *May* and *August.* He intended them to cause a stir, and they did. The first instalment was suitably patriotic; but *May* developed a rather caustic tone, and in *August* he roundly condemned the whole war. But some good came of it, because it turned Lev Nikolaevich Tolstoy right off soldiering and right on to his real calling.

'My career is literature – to write and write!' he'd carolled. You can find the words in his diary.

The instalments in *The Contemporary* were so popular they were soon bound and marketed as a book. Maman told me that people had begun referring to Lev Nikolaevich as Russia's first war correspondent. His success encouraged him to get on with finishing another story, one he'd had lying around for nearly ten years, since the time he was twenty-four – and I ten! (Of course I knew nothing of this then.)

At that time Lev Nikolaevich had accumulated gambling debts amounting to sixteen thousand roubles, and his one idea was to get out of Moscow for a while. This was not too difficult to arrange: his soldier brother Nikolai let Lyova accompany him when he returned to his peace-keeping post on the border with Chechnya.

The job of the Russian troops was to keep the local tribes – Chechens, Abreks, Circassians – in order. Mostly they fought amongst themselves, but the Chechens in particular had a history of rebellion against the Russian presence. A few years earlier, a Russian army of eighteen thousand men was required to force them all the way back to Grozny. And there was another large group, the Cossacks, who also had to be kept under control. They were not Muslims, but Orthodox Christians who took pride in serving the Tsar, yet remained a law unto themselves.

My future husband's romantic dream at this time was to remove himself from civilisation, live like a native in this beautiful, rugged mountain region, and find in the simple life something he conceived of as 'authenticity'. This quest informed the story he wrote there. His autobiographical hero, Olenin, who is billeted in the house of an old Cossack (as wily as he is wise), dreams of 'purifying' himself through the fresh, untrammelled love of a wholesome mountain girl. In the story he calls her Marianka.

When Lev Nikolaevich returned to Moscow nearly a year later, he brought with him the jottings of *The Cossacks*, and a learnt moral: Olenin has been unceremoniously jilted by Marianka in favour of her local boyfriend, and his good intentions have been disastrously misunderstood by the natives. In other words, it is impossible for a civilised man to turn himself into a noble savage.

If only Lyova had taken to heart this object lesson on the absurdity of trying to escape from reality ...

He revised this tale sporadically over several years, the final version only coming out at the beginning of 1862, in a periodical. But not *The Contemporary*. As soon as Mikhail Katkov, the editor of Moscow's *Russian Herald*, heard that the novella was finished, he waged a campaign to bring Lev Nikolaevich into his own stable. Trumping *The Contemporary* by offering Lyova a higher fee, he collared the man who would one day write *War and Peace*.

Business to do with the publication of *The Cossacks*, set for early in 1863, gave Lyova and me the opportunity to make our first excursion away from home. Shortly before Christmas we went to Moscow to collect the very useful advance.

Lev had once again gambled himself into debt, and I was pregnant.

Later that year his reputation was deemed high enough for all the stories and articles he had written so far to be handsomely bound and sold in an edition of *Collected Works*. The first three volumes included *Childhood, Boyhood, Youth*, the *Sebastopol Sketches*, and the fourth and final version of *The Cossacks*. But there were also several pieces I had never seen, many showing much more imagination than his war reports and memoirs. *After the Ball* was a charming, if bittersweet, short story; and *Kholstomer* (*Strider*) got right into the mind of a horse! However, another relatively new novella, *Family Happiness*, had more to say to me than I, an infatuated young bride, wanted to hear. (I had not at that stage learnt to read between the lines.) It had first been published in 1859, when the frequency of the Count's visits to our flat was becoming increasingly obvious. Perhaps if Maman had paid more attention to Lyova's fiction, she might have been less avid for a daughter of hers to become Countess Tolstoy.

Family Happiness was a moral tale told in the first person by Masha, an inexperienced, motherless girl brought up in the depths of the country by an older and wiser, but rather stodgy, guardian called Sergei, with whom she falls in love. (The circumstances were of course different, but didn't my parents notice the ages of these two characters? Masha was eighteen, Sergei in his mid-thirties …) Sergei marries the girl against his better judgment, his caution quickly vindicated when she grows bored with the quiet country life he loves. As a sop, he takes her to town and allows her to stay on after he returns home; Masha accompanies some friends to a German watering place. There she succumbs rather willingly to the attentions of a lascivious Italian marquis. Her honour is only just saved, mostly by good luck, but the message was to my mind terribly heavy-handed, and the happy-ever-after ending rang hollow: the reunited couple are shown bending tenderly over their first baby, as Masha determinedly intones:

> [A] new kind of love for my children and the father of my children
> laid the foundation of a new life and quite different happiness,
> which I am still enjoying at the present moment …

I swore I could hear the girl gritting her teeth, but it never occurred to me then to draw any parallels.

As far as Lyova was concerned, getting the *Collected Works* out of the way was like clearing the ground for the much longer work that he was contemplating – something historical yet relevant, he muttered. But when it came to pinning down a scenario, the recent past of our embattled country offered an *embarras de richesses*. Where should he look to start? With the pivotal Decembrist uprising of 1825, the first time liberal aristocrats had tried to challenge the Tsar? Or would it be better to go further back, to the influx of foreign ideas that flooded in after the French retreat in 1812? He couldn't discuss the former without bringing in the latter, but then to talk about the retreat without reference to the invasion itself was nonsensical … The only thing he was sure of was that he was no longer interested solely in battles. It would be equally important to show civilian life – its organisation and activities, of course, but also its more intimate aspects – both in the city and in the country, involving both men and women, and different generations and classes.

And the extremely important question of how children should be brought up would have to be included.

So many tantalising thoughts seemed to hover in front of him like butterflies that he often looked quite panicked. He decided aloud that probably the only solution was to make an arbitrary beginning and then simply get on with it, however many chapters might need to be rejected and rewritten. Anxious to be involved in the project, and keen to help him get started, I offered him my best handwriting, should he want anything copied. He turned to look at me with dawning appreciation. It was probably the first time he realised that as a wife I might actually be useful to his writing.

I should admit here that the initial three months of marriage had been something of a challenge. Not easy, probably, for either of us, if I am honest. There was no doubt in our minds that we were passionately in love, but underlying my joy was the inability to rid my mind of those diaries. Time and time again I went over and over their revelations, which had lost not one whit of their power to shock and dismay.

I realised I had to ask myself why their impact was so deep-seated, so ineradicable.

I had not been so naïve as to believe that young men led the same cloistered lives as girls did; but Liza and I, being older than Sasha, had had little opportunity to see past the formal behaviour adopted by the young aristocrats who turned up at balls and parties. Most of them held sinecures in the Civil Service or commissions in fancy regiments, but we only saw them in public – politely partnering us in the mazurka or brazenly appraising the talent from their boxes at the ballet. I assumed, calmly if vaguely, that unlike their brides they would come to the marriage-bed already initiated; I had not been overly distressed to discover that Lyova lost his virginity in a Kazan brothel, conducted there by his brother Sergei. But I was certainly taken aback to read at what age this had happened. He had been fourteen – three years younger than Sasha was now! The explanation – that Sergei was doing his brother a favour because Lev had been too inexperienced to take advantage of their aunt's appetising little maid – did nothing to dispel my disgust.

From then on, the confessions had got worse by the page.

No doubt peasants and gypsy girls were fair game, even though they were the obvious cause of the outbreaks of venereal disease for which Lev Nikolaevich had frequently to seek a cure; nor did I criticise the upper-class girls who attempted to draw him into the practice of discreet flirtation. I did not even have a problem with his various attempts to fall in love, because I understood that his ultimate motive was Christian marriage. One of his early mistakes was Valeria Arseneva, a girl from a neighbouring estate whose dying father had short-sightedly appointed Lyova, at the age of twenty-eight, to act as her guardian! Lyova had dutifully courted Valeria, trying sincerely to fall in love with her, but, thank goodness, his intention was never likely to be fulfilled. (*Family Happiness* was, I am convinced, a projection of what might have happened if he had married Valeria.) But having arrived at the sad conclusion that she was nothing but a wet noodle (his words), he wrote her a rather condescending letter freeing her of all 'obligation', though kindly admonishing her to take a walk every day and 'wear a corset'!

The relationship with Aksinya Bazykina was much harder to swallow.

The affair with her, the twenty-three-year-old wife of one of his peasants, had apparently begun in the summer of 1858, with the physical aspect on blatant record: 'I am in love as never before in my life. Today in the big wood … I'm a fool. A beast.'

As time passed, the attachment refused to die down.

'Continue to see Aksinya exclusively,' he wrote the following year; and the one after, 'It's no longer the feelings of a stag, but of a husband for a wife.' (My heart had lurched sickeningly at that line.) Timofei, Aksinya's son by Lev Nikolaevich, was born in the summer of 1859 and later accepted as a pupil in Lev's own school; Aksinya and Timofei remained fixtures on the estate until Timofei became coachman to one of our sons. Neither Lev

Sonya after three months of marriage.

nor I could fail to encounter one or the other of them most days; and I have to say I was murderously jealous of that fat, white slug of a woman. With whom my husband had broken off all sexual relations at least two months before the wedding, as I knew for a fact. So why should I feel so threatened by a *past* liaison? Was it not insane to torment myself with excruciating mental pictures of those vile couplings, when I had to admit they had taken place before Lev even had a fiancée, let alone a wife?

Such imaginings were clearly absurd, yet I found it impossible to refrain from self-torture. For forty-eight years I have never ceased to relive the hurt and humiliation Aksinya caused me. My own diaries bear witness to the surges of emotion that have constantly assailed me. As early as the fraught first fortnight of married life, when I was overwhelmed by confused feelings, I discovered how valuable it was to write down my desperate efforts to get some grip on the peaks and troughs of my reactions. For example, while Lyova's diary revelations were nothing but repugnant, I was unimaginably transported by the ecstasies to which he brought me in the bedroom. Embarrassingly, their effects were visible to all. Visitors who stayed with us, from my younger brother Sasha (!) to Lev's writer friend Afanasy Fet (a nice man but never a discreet one), could not refrain from commenting on the glow that apparently lit up my face. It seems that a smug and gorgeous satiety emanated from my walk, my laugh, my voice. Lev too had a new lightness to his step, and often joked like a twenty-year-old. He even noted, 'My happiness seems to absorb me completely.'

Yet he must have been aware that I was troubled by unspoken resentment; and while we discussed none of it, he must equally have suspected that it was caused by his past activities, by those things he'd felt obliged to reveal to me in order that our marriage could be based on mutual frankness and honesty. I understand that he thought it imperative for me to know what sort of person he had been; but would not ignorance have been a less destructive option?

Not in his view. He felt that I simply failed to accept his confessions in the spirit they were offered, and that therefore it was I who was the problem, not him. To unload his burdens was to eliminate them, according to him, even though I could not see it that way. Accordingly, he told me after two brief months of our living together that he had no confidence in my love for him.

I was shattered. Admittedly, there was a germ of truth in his accusation, but I was unable to articulate to him my complicated, pent-up defence. My magnetically sensual husband made *me* the guilty party without clarifying what exactly I was guilty of. I on the other hand knew exactly where our relationship had gone wrong. I had already written:

> Always and for ages I used to dream of the man I would love as a
> completely whole, new, pure person ... Now, having got married,
> I have had to recognise how foolish these former dreams were, yet
> I cannot renounce them. The whole of his (my husband's) past is so
> horrible that I don't think I shall ever be reconciled to it.

Nor was I, ever; but the writing helped. It came to me that it was not the lechery and depravity *as such* that were the real torment, but the fact that his formation was so utterly different from mine it had created an abyss between us, forcing me to recognise a hard truth: even two beings joined by God and man in one flesh are irremediably divided from each other by the independent lives they have led previously. I continued:

> He cannot understand that his past, with its thousand different
> feelings, good and bad, can never belong to me, just as his youth,
> squandered on God knows what or whom, can never be mine either
> ...

I know my words were overcharged, going on for two whole pages, swinging wildly between anguish at the gulf separating me from a frighteningly unknowable husband, and my desperate desire for our love to flow freely and bravely between us.

But, I wrote:

> Whatever I do, I can't forgive God for arranging it that people must
> sow their wild oats before they can become decent people ... I cannot
> bear the way he is slowly wearing me down, down. And yet he is a
> wonderful and dear person ...

Another issue was that everything in *his* life conspired to take him away
from me. He would leave me alone for hours and hours, with only the two
old ladies for company, when I had been brought up in a houseful of sisters
and brothers, and used to the constant visits of many friends. Couldn't my
brilliant husband see why I resented every single moment he gave to the
estate or the peasants or his pupils, instead of spending it with me?

Overwrought I no doubt was, but my state of mind was not helped by
Lev's insistence on having a bed of his own; every time he retreated to it I
felt rejected and hurt. I would have felt even worse if I'd known then that
he regarded sex during pregnancy as 'swinish and unnatural'.

A few days before our first Christmas together I wrote:

> Love is hard – when you love it takes your breath away, you would lay
> down your life and soul for it, to keep it as long as you live. It would
> be narrow and mean, the little world I inhabit, if he were not in it. Yet
> for us to join together our two little worlds is impossible.

Impossible, in the end, as I now know, for any husband and wife – at
least to the point of seamless unity that I once longed for, fondly imagining
it to be the norm.

6

Pickling Cucumbers
1863–64

There weren't many interesting things to do at Yasnaya Polyana, and certainly no kindred spirits to talk to. Lev would not let me have a carriage to go about in, and seemed these days to prefer riding by himself. To get anything out of the available activities I would have had to enjoy such occupations as breeding hens, tinkling on the piano, reading a lot of fourth-rate books (dusty old things from the library shelves) or pickling cucumbers. Anyway, that's how I saw it.

Nor did it help that, in contrast, Lyova could hardly keep up with the countless interests vying for his attention. He loved to range far and wide on horseback, yet returned eagerly to an estate he found endlessly absorbing, both mentally and physically. He ran horses, cattle, sheep, pigs and bees, and oversaw orchards, kitchen gardens, a greenhouse, a forge, a carpentry and a granary; and he still taught the peasant children in his school. Paradoxically, his interest in the peasants also kept him in touch with the most important issue of the day in national politics – the chaos still thrown up by the controversial edict of emancipation of two years ago.

Theoretically the serfs had been given their freedom, but in practice they'd had to buy the land they had for centuries farmed though not owned. The purchase price was almost impossible for them to meet, and they certainly did not believe that freedom left them better off materially. But the Tsar ignored their protests, having already moved on to other reforms. The mobility offered by the railway system was wonderful for people of our class, but it did little to appease the peasants. A movement called Land and Liberty even promoted socialism, with the unforeseen result that the already severe censorship became particularly punitive. Lyova was soon to feel its effects, and react with a mixture of contempt and irritation; but otherwise he rather enjoyed getting caught up in political passions. I therefore tried to take some interest in the 'woman question', which aimed to give females our own internal passports and allow us to be admitted to the universities, but it was all a little remote for a new bride unable to see beyond the problems of married love. At the time I wrote, 'He is fortunate because he is talented and clever, but I am too stupid to do anything but sit and think about him.' I don't believe that I was stupid in general, but it is perfectly true that my thoughts revolved incessantly around my husband. My emotional dependence was alarming even to me.

> I cannot love him any more than I do, for I love him utterly, with all
> my heart and soul, I need only him ... Lord, what if he loses interest
> in me altogether?

These hysterical fears were partially caused by my pregnancy. I dreaded the time when I would have to deal with divided loyalties, convinced that I would be torn by guilt whatever I did. If I truly loved the baby, I would be over-playing what I called 'the womb's vulgar love for its offspring' (such language!); if I didn't, it would be because of my 'somewhat unnatural love' for my husband. That was closer to the truth, but neither option made much sense. Thank God for the comforting presence of my mother, who came to see her second daughter through her first confinement. I had yet to turn nineteen.

The baby, a boy we christened Sergei but called by the pet name of Seryozha, was born on the 28th of June 1863. The long labour took place on the old leather couch that normally stood in Lev's study. He, his brothers and his sister had all been born on that couch, which he insisted on dragging into my bedroom for the birth. He, surprisingly, attended it. As soon as I was capable, I wrote:

> I suffered for a whole day. It was terrible. Lyovochka was with me the whole time, and I could see that he felt very sorry for me; he was so loving, his eyes shone with tears, and he kept wiping my forehead with a handkerchief soaked in eau-de-cologne ...

I was all the more shocked therefore, later on, when I discovered his attempt to elaborate what should have been a life-changing experience for both of us. His diary entry of August 5th tailed off, unfinished. He did comment on how beautiful 'the darling' looked, despite the untidiness of her black hair and the red blotches on her face (!); fortunately her dark eyes were 'big and burning' and he was deeply moved by her expression of 'seriousness, honesty, strength and emotion'. But then he moved on, somewhat incoherently, to less complimentary comments:

> Her character gets worse every day ... her grumbling and spiteful taunts ... her unfairness and quiet egoism frighten and torment me ... I've looked through her diary – suppressed anger with me glows beneath words of tenderness ... To give up everything ... the poetry of love and ideas and work for the people – and to exchange it all for the poetry of the family hearth, and egoism in what concerns everything except one's own family; and in place of everything to get all the worries of a tavern, worry about baby powder and preserves, as well as grumbling, and without anything that brightens up family life, without love and without a peaceful and proud family happiness, only outbursts of tenderness, kisses etc! I'm terribly depressed ...

So was I – and more so after reading that. My fears of loving the baby too much or not enough had evaporated – clearly there is room for different kinds of love in the female heart. But now I was assailed by a new worry: I was sure I would not be able to do my duty by my growing family because I was insufficiently educated. It was not just the children who daunted me: my lack of self-esteem also made me timid with Lyova, to whom I felt I was becoming a burden. I taunted myself with the thought that even if I did love this child, it was only because he was Lyovenka's.

That makes me smile now. My perceptions were as usual far from accurate. The baby quickly became an unalloyed source of joy, while the most immediate of the difficulties with Lyova could be put down to a practical problem – the physical agony I suffered every time little Seryozha suckled at my inflamed nipples. The intense pain led me to beg for a wet nurse, but this aroused Lyova's scathing anger. To him, the request was not only outrageous, but unnatural.

> It is abnormal not to feed one's baby, but what can I do about a
> physical weakness? ... He wants to wipe me from the face of the
> earth because I am suffering and not fulfilling my duty ...

Thankfully, my delight in Seryozha, especially when he began to recognise me, gave me daily a glowing happiness that compensated for everything.

That autumn I observed that Lyova was brooding over a new project, which he did not discuss with me – further proof, I wept, that he had come to regard me as unworthy of his confidence. He used to share many thoughts with me, and we'd had some blissful, happy times together. But now they were all gone. At least when he disappeared these days I knew where to find him. He would be in his study, writing his *History of 1812*. At that early stage he had no idea that this new work would change its title and focus at least twice, and occupy him for the next six years. Nor did he once acknowledge that it might not have been finished at all, without my secretarial contribution.

I began staying up nearly every night, *joyfully* transcribing an avalanche of pages covered in his almost illegible hand. Nearly every morning Lyova would arrive at his desk to find my beautifully clear transcripts waiting for him in a tidy pile; and every day he would be dissatisfied with his work, crossing most of it out and cramming his second and third thoughts into the spaces above and below the lines, or up and down the margins. I would copy them over and over until he was satisfied with what he had written. I loved it. Our second son and third child, Ilya, who was born a year after his sister Tanya and about halfway through the writing of the magnum opus, commented in later years that my transcriptions must have added up to seven fair copies of the two-thousand-page novel. He saw my labours as excessive, and I had to remind him that I used to wait with genuine eagerness for my pages after Lev Nikolaevich had finished his day's work; that I would copy on and on in a state of feverish excitement, always discovering new beauty in his writing.

My husband was truly a genius, the way he brought people and places to life – of that there was no question; but I admit that part of the pleasure for me was that this labour of love was mine alone; no one else came into it. There was, exceptionally, a rather unhappy period in late 1864, soon after Tanya was born, but by then my distress only showed how much copying Lyova's work meant to me.

A few days before the birth, which was on the 4th of October, Lev Nikolaevich was chasing a hare, when he was thrown from his horse. He landed badly and broke his arm; we had to drive him into Tula straight away to get it set. The local doctor made such a hash of it, however, that I decided we must go to Moscow to get it properly attended to by Papa.

It was by far the best thing to do, Lyova agreed, but, callously, he chose to leave me behind at Yasnaya Polyana, looking after Seryozha and the very new baby, little Tanya, while he stayed with *my* family in *my* old home in the centre of Moscow. That in itself was bad enough, but to add insult to

At Yasnaya Polyana with Seryozha and Tanya.

injury (literally!), he stayed on for weeks and weeks, until long after the arm was healed. How *could* he be so insensitive as to leave me mouldering in the countryside with two babies to take care of, while he enjoyed the company of the people *I* missed so much – my darling mother, my busy father, my lively sisters and brothers – and the society of our many friends? But what was even more hurtful during that interminable time he lingered in town was that he asked my sisters to take dictation for his new book. Not only was I deprived of my favourite task – I was the last to hear of my husband's authorial about-face, when he radically changed his project for the second time.

Even before he left Yasnaya he'd stopped writing about 1812 in order to focus on the famous but unsuccessful revolution of December 1825, when most of the men involved had ended up in chains, trudging their way through the snow to a dismal Siberian prison. In Moscow's liberal circles the Decembrists were held up as national heroes, but like all Russian girls, my sisters and I were more thrilled by the story of their legendary wives. These splendid women voluntarily followed their men to Siberia, and ended up being hailed in both the history books and popular opinion as secular saints. Lyova of course had not been going to write about *them* ... In any case, it now seemed that he had decided to switch again and begin his story twenty years earlier, when the Russian nobility were following from afar the conquests of the French general Napoleon Bonaparte, and mocking his imperialist ambitions. The title of Lyova's book was now *1805*.

More importantly to me, however, he hatched this idea while he was in Moscow, and it was to my younger sister Tanya, not his loving wife, that he gave the thrill of copying out the earliest accounts of the delightful Rostov family, including the girlish games and romantic dreams of mischievous, impetuous Natasha, the youngest child and only daughter of the Count and Countess. Tanya could hardly have failed to notice the similarities between herself and Natasha – two little enchantresses – or to be flattered by Lyova's reliance on her, and his consequent gratitude.

Confined to Yasnaya, babies and old ladies, I felt ill-used and resentful, especially when my thoughts turned back even further to the time when Lev constantly visited the Kremlin flat, but kept his intentions undeclared. Liza and I had hated each other then, both riven by jealousy, but neither of us had been worried by our little sister, whom Count Tolstoy sought out for a good romp. But what if Tanya had been older? Could she have swept our suitor off his feet, and left me as well as Liza to endure the humiliation of rejection? Was it simply timing that led Lev Nikolaevich to choose me? That appeared quite likely now, given Tanya's favoured treatment as his Moscow copier and Natasha's model. But oh, how hateful it was to wish my own little sister out of the way, and my fickle husband removed from temptation! Of course I did not think for a moment that there was anything untoward between them – yet how mean of Tanya, how cruel of Lyova, to ignore that mystical link between a writer and his true amanuensis! Copying let me into his mind and made him dependent on me; it was the saving grace that almost made up for his premarital activities.

Fortunately it turned out that even while I was looking after Seryozha and little Tanya, and brooding over Lev's absence, I wasn't so far out of range as to be completely useless. Lyova posted me a few passages of the new novel to copy, but only those concerned with a rather minor character who also had to spend her life in the country. Poor Princess Marya, obliged to dance attendance on her irascible widowed father and forgo any life of her own! The old Prince depended on his daughter too much to countenance her ever leaving him, even though it meant she would never get married.

I felt sorry for the Princess, but I hardly needed a chapter from a novel to tell me what it was like to be confined to a country estate!

Nevertheless, I despatched the fair copy back to Moscow, accompanied by a note saying how much I admired Princess Marya – 'such a splendid, sympathetic character'. But my compliments did not elicit any further pages. I reverted to feeling utterly wretched and increasingly angry with my gallivanting, neglectful husband. The sense of being personally out of touch, as well as redundant to his work, left me with only one friend: my faithful diary. On its patient pages I poured out all the hurt and jealousy that welled up every time I anguished at the thought of the lively goings-on in the Kremlin flat.

I always stowed my past diaries in a safe place, but usually kept the current journal in or near my desk. It would not be my fault if Lyova happened to come across it one day and be smitten with guilt at the misery he'd put me through. Though even that strategy, which I'd already resorted to more than once, had been known to backfire. When for example I was enduring that terrible bout of mastitis and unable to breastfeed Seryozha, Lyova had reacted more harshly than I'd ever thought possible – ranting on and on about how shamefully I was failing in my maternal duty, et cetera. I certainly hurled that moment of despair at my diary. 'How can one love an insect that never stops stinging?' I wrote, jabbing the paper so viciously it made a hole through several pages. But then, apparently, it had started raining, and in alarm I've added, 'I'm afraid he'll catch cold. I'm not angry any more. I love him, God bless him.'

Well, when he came back Lyova did read that page – the diary happened to have been left open – and in a lengthy insertion begged me to forgive him:

> I have always recognised that I have many failings and very little generosity of spirit. And now I have acted so cruelly, so crudely, and to whom? To the person who has given me the best happiness of my whole life and who alone loves me. I know this can never be forgotten or forgiven, Sonya, but I know you better now and realise how badly I treat you. Sonya darling, I know I have been vile – somewhere inside me there is a fine person, but sometimes he seems to be asleep. Love him Sonya, and do not reproach him too much.

How wonderful it would have been to read those beautiful words exactly as they were written. But he had quickly lost his temper again and crossed them out before I had a chance to see them unspoilt.

7

The Mangy Dog
1865–71

The following year caused great excitement for Lev Nikolaevich and further chagrin for me. I should have guessed that he would be among the first to volunteer for the new local government committees, the *zemstva* that had been proclaimed the year before. He was bound to want to put his finger in these country pies that were to take responsibility for everything the central authorities routinely neglected, from rates and roads to hospitals and education. They were an important first for Russia, although idealistic landowners like Lyova had long been canvassing for them, and I approved in principle – but I also knew that *zemstva* meetings would provide further reason for him to be away from home.

However, there was another, quite different matter that now seized my attention; and I must acknowledge it provided living proof that my jealousy of Tanya had been utterly baseless. The eighteen-year-old who came to spend New Year with us was no longer the fun-loving child whose merriment had once captivated Count Tolstoy. Tanya was now a young woman about to plunge into a love interest of her own, one which not only failed to include my husband, but worse, earned his stern disapproval. I was naturally more inclined to be sympathetic to the situation, but I was also utterly fascinated by the affair. It was the first time I'd been close to an emotional drama against which I could measure the surges of my own mercurial and overwhelming passions.

*

Tanya was a frequent and favourite visitor at Yasnaya Polyana. She usually came for the whole summer, and again more briefly at New Year. During past visits she had often encountered Sergei, Lev's older brother by two years, who for a long time had been living not far from us on his estate, Pirogova, with his gypsy mistress Masha Shishkina and their six children. His domestic situation barred Sergei from going into society, but he seemed content enough with his farming, horse breeding and family life. He often came to Yasnaya Polyana, but always alone, knowing better than to try bringing his companion with him.

However, to our astonishment, Sergei suddenly fell in love with Tanya, and she with him. I was delighted, both for them and for me. It was like a gift from God, the unlooked-for possibility of my much-loved sister becoming a near neighbour. But Lev was less enthusiastic, and Tanya's happiness was not unclouded.

With Sergei always appearing by himself, she had only an imperfect idea of his personal arrangements, and kept longing for their mutual attraction to be brought into the open. But nothing happened over the New Year.

In the spring Tanya made another visit, innocently reviving my reprehensible jealousy by accompanying Lev on many hunting, riding and walking excursions, while I stayed at home with the children. 'The two of them have gone off to the woods alone to shoot wood snipe and I am imagining God knows what ...' I wrote. Unfortunately, my diary reveals the worst of me.

Finally, on June 7th, Sergei proposed to Tanya. Thrilled, she accepted him, and the wedding was set for June 29th, at Nikolskoe, Lyova's other estate, before the heat of summer could wilt the magnificent roses that thrive there. I again expressed my great delight, but Lev continued to display his disapproval without disclosing his reasons.

Darling Tanya, meanwhile, had no idea of the conflict poor Sergei was having to put himself through in order to be able to act like a free man. The marriage would require him to send Masha back to the gypsies, along with all their lovely children.

Within a few days, Sergei had stopped visiting Yasnaya Polyana. Tanya was bewildered and desperately upset.

Soon afterwards two letters were delivered, one to Lev, the other to her. In the explanation he gave his brother, Sergei described the following scenario.

Coming back to Pirogova early one morning, he found Masha praying before the icon in the red corner, where an oil lamp burned permanently. As he gazed, conscience-stricken, at the back of her bowed head, he realised that on several counts it was simply out of the question for him to send her and the children away.

'Throughout these ten miserable days I have been lying, believing that I was telling the truth, but when I saw that I must finally break with Masha I realised this was completely impossible,' he confessed to his brother.

In his letter to Tanya, Sergei tried to enlist her understanding and forgiveness by placing more emphasis on Masha's feelings than on his own. But when Tanya learned of the collapse of all her hopes, she ignored the plea for sympathy. To us she stormed, 'He led me on, he deliberately kept from me the real nature of his relationship with that woman. I despise him! I want nothing more to do with him, ever! Please ban him from your house when I am here.'

To our parents she wrote, 'Do not be surprised or grieved; I could not have done otherwise and would always have had it on my conscience. All may now be for the best.'

But this was to comfort them. The underlying shock became evident to all of us when she tried to poison herself. Although the attempt was too half-hearted to be successful, it made her seriously ill; she remained in a catatonic daze for several months. Thankfully, our near and dear neighbours, the Dyakovs, stepped in, inviting Tanya to stay with them for a while and offering to take her to Italy for a holiday.

Lev Nikolaevich thought Tanya's letter wonderful, and her behaviour noble and splendid, but he was furious with his brother and told him so in writing. I was at first too upset to record any of the saga, but finally, on July 12th, I took my diary with me on a drive to Nikolskoe, which needed some attention from Lyova even though there was to be no wedding there. I laid no blame at Masha's door – in fact, I describe her as a good woman for whom I felt very sorry. But I too gave vent to savage anger and disgust with Sergei.

> He has behaved like a scoundrel … He's repugnant. Wait, wait, he kept saying, and all the time he was just leading her by the nose and playing with her feelings for him … What a villain …

This was not entirely just, however, for soon afterwards Sergei married Masha, legitimising the children and giving their gypsy mother legal proof of his genuine affection.

Tanya also married, but too hastily and not for the best. Her husband, Alexander Kuzminsky, could not provide her with the marital happiness I was able – sometimes – to exult in. The continuation of my entry proclaimed:

> My own family life at home is so lovely, calm and happy. Why has such happiness come to me? The children have been well, as has Lyova, he and I are such good friends, and outside the weather is wonderfully warm and summery, and everyone and everything is superb.

I had gained enough self-knowledge, however, to conclude with a question: 'I am happy – but for how long?'

Our daily diaries were by now a major issue for both of us, especially after we'd learnt to exploit them. At first they had been simply a useful strategy by which either of us could acquaint the other with sensitivities too difficult to voice – and God knows there were plenty of those. But

Lyova soon came right out with it, snarling at me, 'When you're cross you take to your diary!' For a while his accusation upset me so much I left the current volume to gather dust, only reopening it while he was in Moscow cradling his broken arm and failing to involve me in the new novel. But I wasn't motivated solely by jealousy and resentment. My emotional trajectory was always a jagged graph of highs and lows.

On March 20th 1865 I wrote: 'Lyovochka makes me feel like a mangy dog.'

But on August 10th of the following year: 'There are days when you feel so happy and light-hearted that you long to do something to make people love and marvel at you.'

And that was a whole month prior to one of the most cherished events in my life, a point of reference for a long time afterwards, a rare celebration all the more memorable for being totally unexpected.

September 17th, my name day, had come around again. Many members of both our families and a number of other visitors called to offer their congratulations, as was normal. But when evening fell, it turned out that Lyova had organised a magnificent surprise for me. Managing to keep his plans secret until the last minute, he had booked the military band from the garrison at Yasenki to come and play during dinner, and ordered lanterns and candles to be placed around the veranda! In a mood of startling exuberance, he rushed about ensuring that everyone enjoyed themselves, and made not a single objection when I danced the night away with one partner after another. Though a mother of three, I was still only twenty-two years old.

I was thrilled at the combination of affection and freedom that he accorded me that evening, and although I was exhausted by the time I fell into bed, I let my love for him overflow joyfully and spontaneously, instead of him making the first move.

I treasure my memories of the pleasures that wonderful party gave me; however the following year, 1867, brought nothing but gloom. ('Yes, it *is* ruined,' I declared. 'There's such coldness, such a glaring emptiness and sense of loss …') As if symbolically, at ten o'clock on a bleak night in March a fire broke out in the hothouses, and all the little plants that Lyova had tenderly cultivated were burnt to ashes. 'Nothing can bring them back now,' I wrote, feeling his disappointment as if it were my own, 'and time alone will ease the pain.'

Even my love for the children concealed a down side:

> I love my children so passionately it is painful. Their least little hurt leads me to despair, and every little smile or glance brings tears to my eyes … It would be easier if I did not love my children so much.

As if that were possible! No wonder the sole entry for the whole of 1868 began:

> It makes me laugh to read my diary … What contradictions – as though I were the unhappiest of women! But who could be happier? Is there a happier or more harmonious marriage than ours! … I always write my diary when we quarrel. There are still days when we quarrel, but for delicate, emotional reasons, and we wouldn't quarrel if we didn't love each other … He often says that this isn't really love, but that we have grown so used to each other now we cannot live without each other. But I still love him with the same restless, passionate, jealous and poetic love, while his calmness occasionally irritates me …

I remember wondering about that word, 'calmness', which still reads as though I lacked the courage to explore what it really stood for.

During these years my diaries show more gaps than entries, but the reason is obvious. I was busy copying Lyova's *oeuvre*. The ecstatic sense of oneness with him that I derived from this activity was my most precious consolation, and also the reason I never complained about the exhausting nightly labour. Nor did I ever comment to him about the content of his works. However, I did allow myself to intervene when it came to their commercial handling.

When he began the book that would ultimately become *War and Peace*, Lyova had signed up with Mikhail Katkov at the *Russian Herald* for the usual serial publication; he was supposed to produce one episode per month, preferably with a cliff-hanger at the end to keep the readers tantalised. But his epic mix of history and romance, military and civilian life, and national and international affairs interwoven with those of the heart, did not lend itself to arbitrary cut-offs; and in any case, being an inveterate reviser, he found deadlines irksome. During 1865, for example, he had decided to rewrite all the battle scenes, unconcerned by the resulting delay in delivery. The gap in the serialisation lasted from April right through to November.

At this stage we could afford for him to be offhand with his editor because money was of less concern than it had once been. It was some time in fact since we'd been financially reliant on his writing. He had not only given up gambling, but after the usual legal delays following the deaths in 1856 and 1860 of two of his brothers, Dmitri, the middle sibling, and Nikolai, the eldest, he had been left heir to the lion's share of the family estates.

Katkov however was not at all pleased with Lyova's cavalier silence, and no doubt he would have been even more irritated had he known that I had a hand in it. With a different view of our financial situation, I was firm in my own ideas regarding our income. We were comfortable enough for the moment, but I needed to be sure we could provide for our children's futures. Lev might crow about the number of roubles per page that he managed to winkle out of the magazine, but once the fee had been paid, that was it – whereas I knew that books would go on generating royalties indefinitely. Serialisation was the normal way of doing things and a good source of publicity, but a more permanent format was equally desirable.

'Let me help you persuade Katkov to get out a hard-cover edition,' I urged Lyova. 'Why pander to him? All he's interested in is the sales of his paper.'

This was true. And fortunately for Mr Editor, there was another writer who needed the *Herald*'s money more than we did. At that stage almost all we knew of Fyodor Dostoevsky was that he was a hopeless gambling addict (Lyova had never been more than a binge player), then living in Wiesbaden – Germany was well known for its permissive attitude to casinos and card tables. From there he had sent Katkov a proposal about a work he intended to write which was apparently to be called *Crime and Punishment*. Katkov was more than glad to let instalments of this novel fill the gaps caused by Lyova's vagaries; subscribers to the *Russian Herald* throughout 1865 thus received the first twelve chapters of Dostoevsky's novel in January, substantial hunks of *1805*, as *War and Peace* was still called, in February, March and April, and after that, more *Crime and Punishment*. Meanwhile, never dreaming that Lyova would insist on further revisions, I saw to it that the first section of the work was published between hard covers in June.

It sold so well that the next year he ran with the idea himself, deciding to self-publish in book format a revised version of the continuation of *1805*. But here lay another pitfall.

'Self-publishing will cost *us* money,' I pointed out.

'But we get all the proceeds, instead of a stingy royalty,' he answered merrily.

'We'll have to borrow the capital to start with,' I frowned.

'Doesn't matter. We'll double it, triple it, in no time.'

There was no gainsaying Lyova when he was set on something. He went off to Tula and came back not only with the required funds, but a new fur hat and boots.

'The bank gave me more than I asked for,' he explained, only slightly abashed. 'They pressed it on me! If they're not worried, why should we be? Look, there's still more than enough for the printer. I can even choose my own illustrator! Who would you say is the top man in the field?'

'Mikhail Bashilov, of course. He's a distant relative of our family, as it happens.'

'All the better! I'll be able to tell him what *I* want!'

Not only did he do that, constantly arguing with Mikhail about the minutest details of the characters' hats and hairstyles, he also drastically cut the already serialised sections of *1805*. At the same time as he excised, though, he could not stop adding to it. He had envisaged and promised his readers a total of four volumes, but the public, he congratulated himself, couldn't get enough of it, and he wasn't yet ready to put his pen to rest. He produced a whole fifth volume, and finally a sixth and definitely last one, which came out in time for Christmas in December 1869. Even so, he only arrived at the absolutely final full stop after adding two lengthy epilogues. The first was a provocative illustration of his philosophy of marriage, seen through a kind of 'what happened after' viewfinder that was not part of the main story; the second, a verbose account of his philosophy of history.

Naturally I copied them both, as well as organising a little Christmas concert with the children, making New Year gifts, and getting in supplies for the inevitable guests. For the first time, as I transcribed the epilogues, my usual pleasure in Lyova's work sometimes escaped me. Moreover, the reason for this felt ominous.

Much praise had been heaped on *1805*. With each instalment in the *Russian Herald* Lev Tolstoy's fame had crescendoed, and now, as successive bound volumes appeared, the applause grew thunderous. But for me, when it came to the epilogues, doubts arose. I even felt my own self to be compromised. As well as being the original (but unthanked) advocate of the book format, I had heartily endorsed the simple, straightforward title, *War and Peace,* that Lev had finally come up with; but this minor advisory role did not make me a literary critic. So what right did I have to object to the lengthy add-ons I was now copying?

It was the first epilogue that really revolted and alienated me. By the time the once enchanting Natasha was married to Pierre Bezukhov, she had been drastically rewritten in reaction, obviously enough, to her author's personal marital experience. Natasha married was so made over,

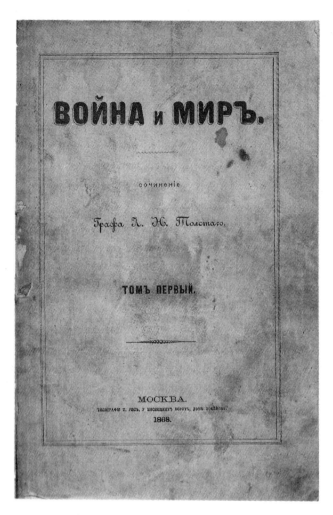

Cover of the first edition of War and Peace.

so very much a 'model' wife, that she could only be seen as a deliberate affront to any real one.

'Natasha,' wrote Lev Nikolaevich at the beginning of Part 10 of the Epilogue, 'had married early in the spring of 1813, and by 1820 had three daughters, and the son she had longed for *and was now nursing herself.*'

This was clearly an allusion to the problems I regularly experienced with breastfeeding. Even if no one else took the point, *I* knew they were a swipe at my desperate longing for a wet nurse. Who would have guessed that Lyova's anger could seethe and simmer so long?

It was equally impossible to ignore his comments about Natasha's figure. A wider girth and some slackness in the stomach muscles – a normal by-product of childbirth – had apparently affected Natasha rather more than myself. I was no longer the slip of a girl who slid childlike arms into her wedding gown, but, thank goodness, I had so far kept my figure. Stoutness, never an attractive quality, was quite out of character for anyone as passionate and emotional as I.

But in Natasha, stoutness was praised! Lev extolled her thickened waist as if it were a virtue! I looked again at the passage I had just copied.

> [Natasha had] filled out and grown broader, so that it was difficult
> to recognise in the buxom young woman the former slim, vivacious
> Natasha. Her features were more defined and she wore a sedate
> expression of quiet serenity. Her face had lost that constantly flashing,
> eager light which once constituted its charm. Now one often saw only
> her face and physical presence, without anything of the animating spirit.
> The impression one had was of fine, vigorous maternity.

Broad, sedate, and lacking in spirit! Would anyone other than Lev Nikolaevich Tolstoy laud such a depressing example of 'fine, vigorous maternity'? It was perverse, and wilfully provocative.

Nor was Natasha's increased girth her only 'improvement'. Lyova also expatiated on her willingness to renounce society and all outside activities on the grounds that she was too busy – not with her children, but with 'every moment of her husband's life'! She had even given up singing, although her sweet voice had once charmed all who heard it.

The author admitted that 'most people' would be amazed by the changes in his heroine. Only 'the old Countess' – Natasha's mother and his moral paragon – understood that her daughter's earlier 'waywardness' had proceeded solely from her need of children and a husband.

I was seething. The word 'waywardness' was deliberately misleading.

It covered everything from Natasha's innocent high spirits to her dangerous infatuation with the seducer Anatole Kuragin – the false love of her impetuous youth. Only later had she settled for the bumbling Pierre Bezukhov, who cut a less dashing figure but held views shared by Lev Tolstoy. Pierre was, in fact, Lev in disguise.

In the next paragraph he was asserting that, unlike many *clever* folk, such as the *French*, Natasha was *happy* to let herself go, *glad* to neglect her appearance and former accomplishments. She now *scorned* any attempt at 'witchery' (!), because feminine wiles were beneath a wife bonded to her husband 'as indefinably but as firmly as her own body to its soul.'

What a sanctimonious metaphor.

> Single-mindedly and enthusiastically absorbed in her husband and children, the only company she sought was that of close relatives to whom she could triumphantly show a nappie stained yellow instead of green.

As if an improvement in the colour of a baby's *kaka* represented the height of female aspiration!

Grinding my teeth but automatically picking up my pen and positioning the new sheet of paper, I went on with my 'fair' copy (Fair! It was blatantly *un*fair …), hearing his voice as if he were in the room when he elevated Natasha's peculiarities to the highest moral plane. 'Some people' (still not specified but clearly unreliable) were wont (fatuously of course) to argue and debate the rights and freedoms of women and the appropriate relations between husband and wife; but his Natasha was not only not interested in these subversive issues, she had absolutely 'no comprehension' of them. Such discussions, according to my pontificating husband, 'were like the question of how to get the utmost possible gratification out of one's dinner'!

Wham! I threw the pen down and with both hands grabbed a heavy iron paperweight in the shape of a Peter the Great sailing ship, and with all my strength slammed it down on the manuscript. The top page tore somewhat and several beneath bore a slight indent, but no great damage was done. Panting slightly and feeling a little better, I went on reading.

The tone now changed from sarcastic to arch. Natasha's besetting sin was jealousy – which Lev again seemed bent on turning into a virtue. Jealousy! It was and always had been my most intractable weakness. I'd been jealous of both my sisters; I still actively loathed Aksinya, although I knew Lyova had had nothing to do with the slut since our marriage; and I bitterly resented the individuals and activities that took him away from me – his gathering fame only making things worse. I'd tried to fight this vice for most of my life – yet here was Lev lauding it to the skies, explaining with fond indulgence that Natasha was jealous of her cousin Sonya, jealous of the governess, and jealous of every woman in the world that her husband looked sideways at, with the result that he could speak 'smilingly' to no female, did not spend money on a whim, and would not absent himself from home for any length of time except on business. What was he? A lapdog?

No, because in return for this role he was allowed to rule the domestic roost, his every wish anticipated by Natasha and implemented by the household. This kind of jealousy served them both very well. My pen was supposed to record in neat, obedient handwriting the notion of two different jealousies – a good one for Natasha and a bad one for everyone else.

Only Lev could get away with such idiosyncrasy.

And that would do with copying for tonight.

I undressed and went to bed, but was too angry to sleep. Lev's Natasha – an adoring wife willingly enslaved to her husband – had also been stripped of any sexual allure. The slender figure, the lively animation, the lovely singing voice had all been eliminated. But why? Because they stood for sensual temptation inappropriate to a wife?

It was repellent, smug and outrageous. *Outré*, the French would say. And, George Sand would surely add, pernicious to women's freedom. Of course, a lot of readers would simply shake their heads dismissively over such a message, unwilling to let it efface the enchantment of the main story. Nevertheless, Lev had written it and Katkov had published it. And who could guess what the public really thought?

But I for one determined that I would never, ever turn into a Natasha Bezukhova, whom I loathed and despised. Yet through her, I saw, I had begun to understand what Lev required of his own wife. The great gap between Natasha and Sonya explained better than anything else the growing gulf between me and Lyova.

8

The Fop and the Boor

1868–78

War and Peace was a thundering success with both the critics and the public, reaping us gratifying financial rewards as well as great fame for Lyova. But there was no denying it had taken its toll. At the end of the '60s both of us were exhausted and in poor health.

Lev Nikolaevich's daily occupation since finishing the great opus appeared to be sitting in his chair reading, or lying in bed recovering from the flu. But his hand hovered over the pile of folktales, fables and dramatic works that I had to seek and find in our library – Molière, Shakespeare, Goethe, Pushkin (whose *Boris Godunov* he dismissed as weak!) – while he toyed with ideas for writing a comedy.

Relieved of copying duties, I redeemed my maternal role by plunging into family matters. In the autumn of 1868 we all went to Moscow, to say goodbye to Papa, who was dying; but the following year sorrow was replaced by joy when our vigorous third boy, Lev, or Lyolya as we called him, arrived. In 1870 I fell pregnant again, but this time the baby, Masha, was born prematurely and I contracted puerperal fever. We both survived, but for a long time I remained extremely weak.

Lev felt so drained by all this that he was sure he was developing consumption. He decided when the summer came to set off on a trip to Samara, in the southern steppes of Russia, with my young brother Stepan. There the two of them lived in a Bashkiri tent made of felt, and Lev went on a regime of *kumis* – fermented mare's milk, which was widely believed, though not by me, to be full of restorative properties. Lev was so carried away by the romance of the open steppe he decided to buy an extensive parcel of land in the region.

Our tenth year of married life was chalked up in September 1872, but the whole year blessed us with an unusually auspicious lead-up. After a snowy January, the weather turned mild as early as mid-March, playfully ruffling our bare heads with the lightest of zephyrs. Lyova and I were unexpectedly so happy, healthy and harmonious that he ignored his diary completely, while mine extolled the joys of nature in short ecstatic entries. Throughout April and May, the spring sunshine thawed the snow, warmed our bones, and drew Lev out of doors to shoot the wood snipe nesting in the fields. One cloudless night was so brilliantly clear, and yet not cold, that he stayed up until dawn, mesmerised by the stars hanging so close overhead. By day he picked huge bunches of sweetbriar and blossom, their colour and perfume brightening the house and gladdening my heart. When spring showers fell, they produced vast crops of mushrooms; the children and I donned boots, hung baskets on our arms and in high spirits went out to gather the golden *ryzhiki* and buttery *maslyaki*. By June the air had grown so hot and dry we took our towels and filed all the way to the river, where the children splashed and shrieked with delight. I swam with more decorum but just as much enjoyment.

The heat and brilliance gently softened into a golden, hazy autumn. The 23rd came and went without either of us feeling the need to acknowledge our milestone simply for the sake of it. Amazingly, we seemed to have reached a plateau of contentment that needed no commentary. By the time the sweetbriar began to drop its blossom, the diaries, like much else, had dried up completely; perhaps we sensed that our happiness was too precious to risk any reminder of less idyllic times. I even wondered whether I had entirely misread the First Epilogue.

Since his return from Samara, Lyova had been busy supervising the publication of the third edition of his *Complete Works*, which, when it finally appeared in 1873, had grown to eight volumes.

But he repeatedly told me that he longed to be writing again, and with a gleam in his eye launched into an anecdote about a proud man of great brilliance travelling around Russia and making himself useful by educating people – at least that was what he said then. But that idea faded and instead he set out to learn Greek, starting with a few lessons from a theological student, but soon teaching himself. He was wonderfully quick at it, and never happier than when memorising new vocabulary or mastering a grammatical technicality. He would ask me to listen as he read out his own impromptu translation of some page or other, while I checked his version against the published one. He never made more than two or three mistakes, being as clever at languages as at everything else.

The shock was thus all the greater for both of us, though worse for him, when a new literary effort proved a total failure. After the Greek lost its charm, he had thrown himself into composing four little books for children of different ages, beginning with an ABC, for which we had both sat up until four o'clock in the morning getting the proofs corrected and sent off. But it was all for nothing. The government questioned his pedagogical qualifications – as if he hadn't run his own school for years – 'And look at the price the bookshops have put on it!' he exploded. 'No wonder no one can afford to buy it.' Lyova was terribly upset by the unforeseen slap in the face, and insisted to everyone who would listen that an ABC was of far more use to mankind than *War and Peace*.

'If my novel had been such a failure,' he said to me, 'I would have readily believed them and simply accepted that it was no good. But I feel quite convinced that my ABC is unusually good and they simply didn't understand it.'

Grumpy and unsettled, he picked up a history of Peter the Great and let his eyes run over a few lines. His mood cleared immediately as he fell under the spell of the extraordinarily energetic, Westernising, shipbuilding

Tsar, who, as a boy, had been seen as only an indirect heir to the throne. As a result he'd been brought up outside the walls of the Kremlin, and allowed by his mother to run wild.

'Just imagine,' Lyova called out to me. 'This man grew to a height of six feet six inches but was petrified by spiders! He tyrannised the court, but was terrified of bad dreams! We know that because he used to write them down.'

'But he also built St Petersburg,' I remarked. 'Such a beautiful city.'

'Italian, not Russian,' harrumphed Lyova. 'And a heartless monument to his own ego. Thousands of serfs died in the building of it. Peter may have made it the capital, but Moscow will always be the heart of the Russian nation.'

Nevertheless, the impulse to make Peter the subject of his next book grew stronger by the minute. The idea had apparently come to him several times over the past three years, but he'd always been held back by reservations. Now Peter seemed to have taken up residence in his head. He couldn't stop thinking and talking about him, even including me in excited conversations. He ferreted out all the historical information he could lay his hands on and made notes of the dress, customs and way of life of a century and a half ago. On a separate page he jotted down ideas for plot and characterisation. A vexed question as to whether high collars were worn on the short kaftans fashionable in Peter's time, or only with long coats, even brought him back early from a fox hunt. Every day we'd seen a wily red animal running over the bridge near our chickens, and Lyova had been determined to shoot it. But, even more set on tracking down the correct height of the collars, he came indoors to hunt this quarry instead.

He had already written ten versions of the first chapter.

For some time his health had not been perfect, and the summer brought little improvement. He was persistently troubled by a bad knee and a dry, rasping cough that would not go away.

'It might have to be Samara again,' he ventured, looking at me sideways from under his thick brows. He knew how much I'd hated his previous long trip away, and I did not try very hard to hide my resentment at the suggestion of another jaunt. After all, it was only one week since I'd given birth to our sixth child, little Petya – named obviously enough for Lyova's current hero.

'Why don't you come too?' he suggested, as if suddenly inspired. 'You've never seen the land I bought down there – not even I have, not all of it. I really should inspect my last parcel. We own sixty-seven thousand acres now, all very wild and wonderfully remote.'

I thought it was a mad idea. 'What about the baby?' I asked.

'He'll be fine. You'll be feeding him.'

Well, yes, but there were five other children to be nourished, as well as the retinue of servants we would need to help us. I was full of misgivings, but rather than be left at home by myself for weeks on end, I agreed to go to Samara, so long as the children came too. I couldn't leave them behind.

It was a terribly long journey – three hundred miles by train to Nizhnii Novgorod, another five hundred to Samara, and then another one hundred and twenty miles by carriage. Even so, the travelling was not as bad as the arriving. Our destination turned out to be a large peasant hut with a leaking roof and an open fireplace, whose acrid smoke did nothing to deter the swarming flies. The local crops had failed owing to drought, and there was an alarming shortage of even the most basic foodstuffs. It was all so primitive that Lev did not try to write; he and Stepan were camped out in their felt tent, while the little boys – Seryozha, Ilya and Lyolya – lived in a shed with the tutor. I shared the relative privacy of the smoky hut with Tanya and the baby, but I cannot pretend that I enjoyed the comfortless life. In fact, it was almost intolerable.

Lev on the other hand revelled in it, and by the time we were due to leave, claimed to be restored to perfect health, both mentally and physically. The baby, thank God, also seemed to thrive, though I don't know how. And once we were on the road back to Yasnaya, I was glad I'd made the effort. Shared discomfort was probably better than solitary moping.

At home in the autumn, Lyova was dying to get on with his work, but all I could pick up was that Peter the Great had apparently been abandoned back in Samara. The theme of a novel kept running through his head – something about a married woman who compromised herself morally – but the details remained obscure. Who she was and how she got herself into the situation he did not know, yet he found himself itching to begin while constantly wondering where and how to do so.

As if on cue, an event that had occurred twenty months earlier hove into his mind. It had taken place in our very own neighbourhood, although it did not involve anyone's wife. The ruined woman was Anna Stepanovna Pirogova, the unmarried mistress of one of our neighbours.

Once I recognised her possible significance in regard to the new novel, I felt yet again that I should set down certain facts for posterity. This time I bought a special notebook which I labelled 'Various Notes for Future Reference' (for there might well be other matters) and started to record the first item.

> We have a neighbour here, A.N. Bibikov, a man of about 50, not
> rich and not educated. He had living with him a distant cousin of
> his late wife, an unmarried woman of about 35 who looked after
> the house and was his mistress. Bibikov hired a governess for his
> son and niece, a beautiful German woman, with whom he fell
> in love and before long proposed to. His former mistress, whose
> name was Anna Stepanovna, left the house to visit Tula, saying she
> was going to see her mother, but she returned from there with a
> bundle of clothes under her arm (containing nothing but a change
> of clothes and some underwear), to Yasenki, the nearest railway
> station, and there she threw herself onto the tracks under a goods
> train. There was a post mortem. Lev Nikolaevich saw her with
> her skull smashed in, her body crushed, at the Yasenki barracks, it
> made the most terrible impression on him. Anna Stepanovna was
> a tall, plump woman with a typically Russian face and character.

She had dark hair and grey eyes, not beautiful but very pleasant looking.

I had witnessed the shock effect of this incident on my husband, but was less aware that it exemplified certain thoughts that had been in his mind for some time. They appeared to have been caused by a voracious reading bout on the theme of marriage. The feminist novels of the French writer George Sand had been influential in Russia for some time, but Lyova had devoured them only to rail against them. He especially liked to use them as ammunition when he was a guest at the dinner table of his sometime friend but more often thorn in the side, Ivan Sergeevich Turgenev.

Turgenev comes into my story at this moment because he was inclined to boast far too loudly about his mutual friendship with the celebrated Frenchwoman, but his on-and-off friendship with Lyova fascinated me more. He was really the only one of our great writers that we had much to do with; Lyova had little in common with Fyodor Dostoevsky even after that inveterate gambler changed his habits, and we only started inviting Anton Chekhov after he bought a country house in our region, some time later; in any case, Chekhov was twelve years younger than Lyova, and a very different kind of person. Admittedly, so was Mr Turgenev. What a contrast marriage to either of those two gentle souls would be!

As for George Sand, Ivan Sergeevich knew her in the context of her own country and its distinctive mores, whereas Lyova's only acquaintance with her was through her novels. He did read them in French, however, although they were available in Russian and very popular with young women. Before I married, I had fallen to some extent under the influence of 'Georgesandism', as we called it, but I became cautious when I realised that in Moscow she sparked a more revolutionary flame than she ever had in Paris. This was because her ideas received a significant twist on their arrival in our country. The reason I liked the novels was that they strongly advocated a woman's right to choose her own husband, I suppose in rebellion against the French custom of arranged marriages. Sand was convinced that being able to marry freely and for love would ensure that women lived happily and remained monogamous forever after. Although her personal life included many lovers, from Alfred de Musset to Frédéric Chopin, she did not preach promiscuity or illegal unions.

In our country the situation for girls has always been worse than in France, but less because of our moral customs, which in many ways are freer, than on account of our autocratic government. Passports, as I've mentioned, are required even for internal travel, but women are unable to hold them in their own name. As a result, many advanced Russian women use Sand's novels to campaign for political freedoms she was not concerned with. But my husband always regarded her influence as a threat to stable marriage, and had long ago written some scathing ripostes. *Family Happiness* was one of them, a clear warning against the dangers of unchecked romantic love; and it was followed by a play called *A Contaminated Family*, which savaged women's emancipation across the board. In these matters Lev Nikolaevich was unquestionably ranged with the archconservatives, and the more sparks he drew from his liberal opponents, the more he enjoyed demolishing their views.

Most of his friends sided with him. Nikolai Strakhov, for example, a literary critic, philosopher and dear man whom I liked very much – despite his ideas – had a few years ago published an article arguing that 'woman' was entitled by her physical and moral beauty to be considered the queen of creation – as long as this did not detract from her 'prime mission of giving birth'. It did cross my mind that I, who had borne six children, might be in a somewhat better position than he to pronounce on the virtues and trials of motherhood as a woman's sole vocation.

Mr Turgenev, in contrast, had long since espoused dangerously European views, which he reflected in both his novels and his private life. He lived in a *ménage à trois* with Pauline Viardot, a Spanish singer he adored, and her husband Henri, who seemed to make no objection to the arrangement. (I have heard it said that the relationship between Pauline and Ivan Sergeevich was a chaste one, but how that can be asserted I do not know.) Certainly Ivan Sergeevich's personal situation and political liberalism were always a greater cause of the disagreements between my husband and him than any rivalry over literary success. Both of them tried sincerely to maintain a friendship, but for nearly twenty years they succeeded only in offending each other.

It all started back in 1852, when Ivan Sergeevich, who was some ten years older than Lyova, composed a laudatory obituary for his friend and fellow writer Nikolai Gogol, who was mainly known for his novel *Dead Souls*. But Gogol tended to satirise the regime and thus died in extreme disfavour with the authorities; and as a result of the obituary, Turgenev was sentenced to a lengthy period of exile on his mother's estate. His confinement there earned the sympathy of most fellow writers, but Lev Nikolaevich refused to believe that Ivan Sergeevich's defence of Gogol was genuine. He told our mutual friend, Fet, that Turgenev was 'merely wagging his democratic haunches'. (I have already mentioned Fet's lack of discretion.)

Yet when Lyova returned from the Crimean War and had to report to army headquarters in St Petersburg, he accepted without hesitation Turgenev's offer of accommodation. Fet once told us about a visit he made to Turgenev's house at that time. Arriving around midday, he noticed a magnificent short sabre hanging on a stand in the hall. The servant informed him that it belonged to Count Tolstoy, who was residing with the master. The Count was at that moment sleeping. Fet and Turgenev then conversed in hushed tones for a couple of hours.

Finally Fet asked, 'Why are we whispering?'

'Lev Nikolaevich hates being woken,' answered Turgenev. 'It's what he does – carouses all night with cards or gypsy girls, then sleeps it off till two o'clock the next day. I've tried remonstrating, but it's no use.'

En revanche, Lyova loudly disapproved of the interest that Ivan Sergeevich briefly displayed in his sister Masha Tolstaya. Active in society, the suave 'older man' met her socially and started sending her the most flattering letters, which also praised her brother's talent. The literary accolades were, I believe, genuine enough, but in the company of others he referred to my Lyova as a *poseur* and a 'troglodyte' lacking refinement. I had yet to meet him, but I know that Lev Nikolaevich accused Turgenev of the identical vices.

Yet when *Childhood* was published in *The Contemporary*, Turgenev had praised it warmly. It was Fyodor Dostoevsky who remarked with more spite than prescience, 'I like Lev Tolstoy enormously, but in my view he won't write much of anything else ...'

When Turgenev returned from one of his regular trips to Europe in May 1861, he invited Lev Nikolaevich to his estate at Spasskoe, where he gave him a good dinner and handed him the newly completed manuscript of his novel *Fathers and Children*. Tactfully, he left the room so that his guest could read it undisturbed. But creeping back after a while, hoping to hear its praises sung, he found my future husband flat on his back on the sofa sound asleep, the manuscript dangling at his side. Tolstoy opened his eyes just in time to see its tactful author sidling out.

I admit that the squabbles of two grown men behaving like little boys entertained me at first, but later I became aware that their relationship was a cause for gossip in both St Petersburg and Moscow. Having already acknowledged my concern for Lyova's reputation in the eyes of future readers, I was upset by the idea of sniggering, sniping tales doing the rounds. The report that Anastasy Fet had devoted several pages of recollections to the saga made it abundantly clear that a more moderate version should be available. I therefore began a new section of 'Various Notes', in which I have to admit that I did to some extent water down my husband's truculence, and stress the ultimately gratifying reconciliation of the two of them.

My account begins with a description of a heated meeting between Lyova and Turgenev that took place at Fet's estate in Mtsensk fifteen years earlier. This was before I was married, but investigation has allowed me to reproduce what happened.

There was a conversation about charity work, in which Turgenev said that his [natural] daughter, who had been educated abroad, did a lot of good helping the poor.

[In Fet's more colourful language, she mended their 'tattered rags'.]

L.N. said real charity flows from the heart, doing good spontaneously, and giving with feeling.

[In Fet's account he was supposed to have said, 'I think that a well-dressed girl with filthy, stinking rags on her lap is acting in an insincere theatrical farce.']

Turgenev then said, 'Apparently you think I'm bringing my daughter up badly,' to which L.N. replied that he meant what he said, but had merely expressed what was on his mind and had not meant to be personal. Turgenev got angry, and suddenly said, 'If you go on talking like that I'll give it to you in your face.'

[Then, according to Fet, he ran out of the room, but returned a minute later to apologise to Fet's wife, a stunned witness to the outburst.]
    I continue:

Tolstoy got up and drove to Bogoslov, a station situated halfway between our estate at Nikolskoe, and Fet's at Stepanovka. From there he sent for his gun and some bullets, and sent a letter to Turgenev challenging him to a duel because of the insult. In this letter he told Turgenev he didn't want one of those vulgar duels in which two literary men with pistols meet a third, and the affair ends with champagne. He said he wanted a real duel, and asked Turgenev to meet him at the edge of Bogoslov forest and to bring his pistols.

Lev Nikolaevich waited up for him all night, sleepless. In the morning a letter came from Turgenev saying that he did not agree to fight the way Tolstoy suggested and that he wanted this duel to be conducted according to the rules. Lev Nikolaevich wrote back saying, 'You are afraid of me. I despise you and refuse to have anything more to do with you.'

After a while Tolstoy, in Moscow, had a characteristic change of heart, and in a wonderful mood of love and forgiveness he wrote to Turgenev regretting that they had fallen out and begging to be reconciled. Unfortunately Turgenev was by then in Paris, and did not receive the letter. He himself was still angry, writing to Tolstoy: 'You are telling everyone that I am a coward and would not fight you. For this I now demand satisfaction, and shall fight you on my return to Russia.'

Lev Nikolaevich replied that he found it utterly absurd that Turgenev should challenge him to a duel in 8 months time, that he treated this letter with as much contempt as the last one, and that if Turgenev really needed to justify himself in public, he would send him another letter, which he could show to anyone he liked. In this letter Lev Nikolaevich wrote: 'You said you would punch my face, but I refused to fight you.'

I wrote this sad tale down in 1877, but was relieved in the following year to be able to add to my account. Overcome with contrition, Lev Nikolaevich wrote to Turgenev in Paris, begging him to forget any enmity there had been between them. Turgenev replied affectionately, promising both to visit him next time he was in Russia and to shake his hand when they met.

He came to Yasnaya Polyana on August 8th 1878. Lev showed his goodwill by going to meet him at the Tula railway station, and I greeted warmly the tall, gentle man with grey hair who appeared at the door. I wrote:

> Turgenev's weakness of character has become very obvious, a naïve, childlike weakness. But he is obviously gentle and kind too. It seems to me that this weakness of his wholly explains his quarrel with Lev Nikolaevich. […]
>
> Turgenev spent two days with us. There was no mention of the past; they had a lot of abstract discussions and arguments, and I felt that L.N. was being slightly reserved but very friendly, not overstepping the mark. As Turgenev was leaving he said to me: 'Au revoir. I have had a very pleasant time here with you.'
>
> He kept to his 'au revoir', coming again at the beginning of September.

This time my husband did not hide his obsession with metaphysical questions – Why are we here? Is there a God? et cetera – about which Mr Turgenev had little to say. He tried to respond sympathetically at the time, but I know that he told others he feared Tolstoy was going mad, while Lev Nikolaevich found Turgenev's easy charm and relaxed attitude unendurable.

Shortly after returning again from Paris, Ivan Sergeevich made what turned out to be his last visit to Yasnaya Polyana. Before he left, he entertained our children by showing them the latest dance from Paris, which required him to hop up and down on one foot while he kicked the other high in the air.

They laughed and clapped and tried to imitate him, but Lyova wrote in his diary: 'Turgenev. Can-can. Pity.'

9

One Unhappy Family
1873

The psychological trigger of Anna Stepanovna's shocking suicide plus the more philosophical rejection of the West's infatuation with romantic love and tolerance of sexual freedom were inching Lyova towards his new novel. In 1873, between the births of our seventh and eighth children, Pyotr and Nikolai, he began writing *Anna Karenina;* but well before this, the startling moment when he'd mooted the idea of a married woman of noble birth who 'ruined herself' had been followed by a further refinement.

'The idea is to make her pitiful, not guilty,' he'd said, his grey eyes piercingly sincere and seeming to focus on something not in the room. 'It's suddenly become clear to me!'

Turning exultantly in my direction, but hardly seeing me, he went on, 'As soon as I imagined this woman, all the men and other characters came forward to take their place in the story!'

It seemed like a eureka moment, but for several months nothing further eventuated. Then, just as suddenly, in fact out of the blue on March 19th 1873, he announced, 'I have written a page and half and it seems good.'

He had begun at last! I wondered what had finally moved him to set pen to paper, but Seryozha, now ten, inadvertently provided at least part of the answer. Two days before, he had complained of finding 'nothing for Auntie'. Aunt Toinette was now aged and bedridden, and her eyes so weak she could no longer make out fine print, but the older children were usually willing to read to her.

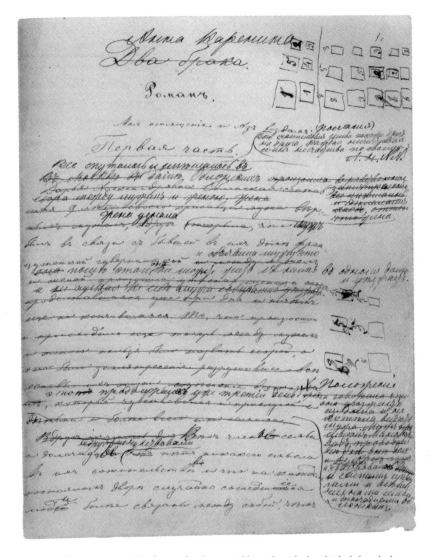

Page 1 of Anna Karenina. *The famous first line is visible on the right-hand side, below the boxes.*

Racking my brains and bookshelves for something that would interest both an old lady and a young boy, I came up with Pushkin's *Tales of Belkin*, a handful of short stories written in a lively style about the role of chance in matters of love and death.

'Take this,' I said, handing the volume to Seryozha. 'You could try reading her the one called "The Shot". It's about a duel.'

Seryozha went along to Aunt Toinette's room, but soon came back to report that the old lady had fallen asleep. I was busy stewing the new-season windfalls by then, and simply told him to leave the book on the windowsill in the dining room.

Next morning, while Lev Nikolaevich was drinking his coffee, his eye fell on *Belkin*; opening it up, he was instantly carried away. When I walked into the room he appeared ecstatic.

'I can always learn so much from Pushkin!' he exulted. 'He is my father and I should always be guided by him.'

That evening, March 18th, when a waning moon was riding low in a clear sky, he went away to write furiously in his study. Next morning, his face as radiant as the bright sunlight, he announced that he was very pleased. A week later, in a letter to Nikolai Strakhov, he mentioned that he had begun a new novel whose inspiration had come from reading Pushkin. Specifically, he said, he loved Puskhin's opening line, 'The guests were gathered at the dacha ...'

'That's how to begin!' he carolled, looking up from the letter, which he was reading to me before giving it to the post. 'In the middle of things!'

For some time, until a more memorable opening line came to him, his new novel began: 'The guests were assembling at Princess Vrasskaya's after the opera'; but the Princess was later shunted to the start of another chapter, and formality was replaced by familiarity: 'Princess Betsy went home before the end of the last act ...' – a much better line, in my opinion.

Within three weeks he was announcing that he had written a complete draft. I raised my eyebrows at this little exaggeration, well aware how constantly he would alter, excise and add. There would be plenty of copying for me to do for some time yet.

'All happy families resemble each other, but every unhappy family is unhappy in its own way.'

Lifting my head to gaze out the window, and wishing that the guttering candle would give as much light as the brilliant stars burning so close and bright, I wondered about this latest beginning to the no longer new novel. How many Chapter Ones had I copied out now? It was a long time since Princess Betsy had been demoted.

'It was all confusion in the Oblonsky household ...'

Confusion? 'Consternation' would have been my word for the emotions of a couple not on speaking terms, 'the wife' refusing to come out of her room ... But perhaps 'confusion' did more aptly suggest the disruption to their lives.

'How good it all was until now, how happy we were ...' This was of course Stiva, 'the husband', lamenting his plight. The couple's individual interpretations of what had happened were radically different. Stiva thought it ridiculous that a brief fling with the children's governess should permanently undo the marriage he had enjoyed for many years (although even now the rogue 'smiled fondly', as he recalled 'Mademoiselle's mischievous black eyes'); but Dolly, 'the wife', was so incensed when she learnt of the affair she had banished Stiva from her bed and told him to leave the house forever.

I had to admit that Lyova was disconcertingly good on the dynamics of discord. Yet I rather hoped that this version, to my mind the best so far, would end up as the definitive one; it was clever of Lyova to begin with Dolly and Stiva when they were not the central pair. I already knew that the heroine was Stiva's sister Anna, married to the bureaucrat Alexei Karenin, and that her family life in Petersburg was more decorous but no happier than her brother's in Moscow. I also knew that she would fall in love with the handsome Count Vronsky and run away with him, abandoning her husband and little son. But certainly, as the new opening implied, the flaws in the Karenin marriage were quite different from those in the Oblonskys'. Various details of the story would almost certainly change again and again, but not the crucial role of the beautiful Madame Karenina, the centrepiece of a passionate affair precipitating a great marital tragedy. But neither Anna's feckless brother, with his sparkling eyes and infectious bonhomie, nor her sweet, anxious sister-in-law, mother of five and faded at thirty-three, were likely to die as a result of Stiva's passing affair. There had already been too many others.

I put down the pen and rubbed the chill out of my clawed right hand. The heat of the stove had died, and I suddenly noticed how terribly cold the room was, how stiff my whole body. March had appeared to deliver an early spring, an unexpected thaw causing the thinner patches of snow to melt into puddles of black icewater; but the ground had remained hard and the air was sharp as knives. I again leaned towards the window as I stood up to stretch my cramped limbs, and saw amongst the glittering stars a gleaming half moon, the pearly light softer than the brilliant scattering of diamonds, but no warmer.

Without heat I really couldn't do any more, yet I was loath to leave Lyova's study, which in those days was part of the downstairs library. (The location of his study tended to shift around according to the need for children's bedrooms.) When I sat at the desk littered with sheets of paper covered in his beloved scrawl, every second sentence with a line through it and the corrections running up and down the margins, I felt closer to him than anywhere else, even in bed. But I knew I must stop. It was already past the time I should check on little Petya, whom at nine months I was still breastfeeding. My love for each of the babies was all-consuming, but I worried about Petya because he was inclined to be sickly. He and I shared a sweet, unproblematic devotion to each other – in glaring contrast to my relationship with Lyova. Not because Lyova was anything like his wayward character Stiva, or a dried prune with sticking-out ears like Alexei Karenin; it was simply because, as I had at last admitted to myself, the justly famous author of *War and Peace* could be a monster *in his own way*. The First Epilogue had shown that. A monster I loved and clung to, my whole happiness depending on him. Especially when we were united by his work – he writing, I copying.

Every evening, as night drew closer, I could hardly wait to finish my own chores and start my precious, almost sacred task; but getting to it these days was increasingly difficult. The blackened pages had to wait until the children and the servants were settled, the estate affairs in order, and the barns and livestock quiet. These responsibilities had been allocated to me a few years back, after Lyova lost his temper with a series of bailiffs and declared that he and I between us would manage the estate. He was supposed to be responsible for the fields, forests, vegetable gardens and beehives, but he usually got away with leaving most of their upkeep to the peasants.

I had fewer children then, and my own reasons for raising no objection to the new regime. The last bailiff had had an attractive, politically aware young wife, the obnoxious Marya Ivanovna, who declared herself to be a nihilist and was always going up to Lyova and engaging him in political conversations. I strongly resented her boldness, but was unable to bring up the matter with him on account of the then latest baby (our third child, Ilya). We were sleeping in separate rooms, and I was angry with him, enduring both mental and physical agony as the baby sucked on my painful breasts.

Fortunately, the Marya Ivanovna issue was defused in a way that only Lev Tolstoy could contrive. Our neighbour Dmitri Dyakov's wife was still alive then, and the family had come over on one of their many welcome visits. On such occasions, after dinner, we often played charades, but this time Lev had suggested a play-reading – there was a little comedy he had recently dashed off, called *The Nihilist*. The hero was a young male student staying in the house of a married couple. The husband (played by me) got the absurd notion that his coquettish wife (Tanya Behrs, who was staying with us at the time) was having an affair with the handsome student (Dyakov). The whole thing turned into a hilarious farce, such that we could hardly speak our lines for laughing. It forced me to see the Marya Ivanovna episode in a more sane perspective, but nothing could permanently tame the tiger of jealousy in me, forever poised to spring.

It was thus a great relief when Marya Ivanovna was no longer around, and I was glad of the opportunity to discuss issues involving the estate with Lyova, partly because they were not usually controversial. In too many common concerns our approaches could be at odds. For example, Lyova conducted the school he ran for the peasant children according to the precepts of the French philosopher Jean-Jacques Rousseau, who wanted children to educate themselves by making their own discoveries. This led Lyova to seriously question whether he should be teaching his pupils, or they him! Yet when I gave our own children French lessons, even writing a grammar book for them, it turned out that the habit adopted by most of our class of speaking French instead of Russian was another of those affectations that Lyova could not abide.

My nightly contribution to his writing thus remained *the* most binding of all our shared activities, profound proof that we *were* close. But it was also important for another reason. Before me, Lyova had simply burnt all his unsatisfactory pages, but, as well as retaining a clean copy of each version of his works, I carefully collected and put away every word he ever wrote or discarded. In the end I filled twelve large boxes with bits of paper covered in his handwriting.

Copying, and looking after the children, were not however my only occupations. At the price of earning a somewhat derisory reputation for volcanic outbursts of physical energy, I also sewed, gardened, bottled, pickled, preserved and took charge of the children's education. But if I fought off offers of help from any other quarter, I again had my reasons. One was of course my desire to please Lyova; but another was to keep at bay the black thoughts that overwhelmed me if I brooded too much. If I was not occupied, I soon felt stifled by isolation and boredom, and more inclined to give in to my dark obsession with Lyova's refusal to love me as I wanted to be loved. I never really adjusted to the profound sense of loneliness that had set in the very first day I arrived at Yasnaya Polyana, with no company other than the two old ladies.

I will concede that having my own children made me more appreciative of the role Aunt Toinette played in Lyova's early life. He still adored her, and as she was so essentially sweet-natured, I too slowly grew fond of her. Her cherished reminiscences filled in many gaps in my understanding of the family's early life, but one favourite story told me more about her than about anyone else. As a girl, Toinette had fallen in love with Lyova's father, Nikolai, but was ruled ineligible because she had no fortune. After Nikolai's wife died, he did ask Toinette to marry him, but she refused, writing something on a piece of paper which she enclosed in a pearl-embroidered purse. Many years later, after she was bedridden, she directed me to where it lay hidden in the bottom drawer of her wardrobe. I unfolded it, and read the following faded words: '16th August 1836. Today Nikolai made me a strange proposal: to marry him, be a mother to his children, and never leave him. I refused the first suggestion, and promised to fulfil the others as long as I live.'

Whenever I thought about Toinette's unselfish love, I would feel guilty that I was not more understanding of Lyova's motherless childhood. Perhaps it even explained his turbulent youth. But it could not excuse those aspects of it that still stuck in my gullet.

With feet like blocks of ice, I realised that I had been lost in my thoughts for a good quarter hour. I quickly picked up the candlestick and crept up the stairs to the nursery. Lyolya, Masha and Petya – the little cherubs – were all sleeping soundly, their breathing quiet and regular. I made the sign of the cross in the air above them; then, coming to rest in my own bedroom, I resolved to make Toinette my model in a firm effort to banish my propensity for jealousy. Far better to relive the moments of joy – such as the name day party – or relief, like the time when Lyova finally came back from Moscow, his broken arm healed, than to dwell on baseless and destructive fantasies. What joy it had been then to know that I was again his only helpmeet, privy every night to the vast, historic world his brilliance had brought to life in *War and Peace*. Apart from the cranky First Epilogue, I had revelled in every superb page, and even now hugged myself with secret delight at its power to bind the two of us in a common enterprise. As the new novel was also doing.

Once, I had tempted fate by putting this pleasure into writing: 'He and

I often talk about the novel,' I said in my diary, 'and for some reason he listens to and trusts my judgment (which makes me very proud) ... Could any wife want more?'

I have to admit that this one could. A few days later I'd added something less happy to that moment of self-congratulation.

> Lyovochka has been writing all winter, irritable, excited, and with tears in his eyes ... But he takes out his 'fatigues de travail' on his family and with me he is often impatient and bad tempered; recently I have begun to feel very lonely.

Always I was lonely, no matter how hard I fought against it.

But before long I was jolted out of that preoccupation into the greatest terror I had ever known. Little Petya developed a throat infection and from its complications fell seriously ill. He died of croup on November 9th 1873. His death was devastating.

> He was a healthy, bright, happy little boy. I loved my darling too much and now there is nothing ... He was very attached to me – does he grieve that I remain and he had to leave me?

The Lord giveth and the Lord taketh away. When Petya died I was already pregnant again. In April 1874 I gave birth to another boy, but poor little Nikolai only reached the age of ten months before he too succumbed to a ghastly death, this time due to meningitis.

Almost unhinged by the double tragedy, I threw myself into a frenzy of busyness. As well as copying Lyova's novel and caring for the remaining five children, I refurbished the main house, installing carpets and curtains to make it warmer, and, now that Lyova was writing full-time, transformed the old school wing into a guest suite. Once we were able to invite family and friends to stay in comfort it was easier to relieve my loneliness. Lev's sister Masha came often with her two little girls, and spontaneous, overnight visits from the Dyakovs could take place at a moment's notice. The warm friendship, begun many years ago when the two husbands were boys, had developed a special significance now that poor, sweet Dmitri Dyakov was widowed and in real need of society for himself and his children.

Only occasionally were we ourselves guests, journeying *en famille* to Moscow; more often Lev went by himself. When the children and I were allowed to accompany him, we were so numerous we had to sleep in a hotel, but Maman sent the carriage around every day to bring us all to the Kremlin flat. In those dear, familiar surroundings I revelled in visits from old friends and acquaintances, while they in turn would whisk me off to my favourite treat – musical recitals in the concert hall off the wide, gracious street called the Arbat. After *War and Peace* I often found people milling around me during the interval; I was a gratified beneficiary of the lionising that had started to snowball at any mention of the Tolstoy name. Lev claimed to loathe it, but I thought it was fun.

Trips to town were thus an increasing source of joy – in the anticipation, in the actuality and in recall – but unfortunately they were not frequent. Lev only went to Moscow when business called, and in any case preferred to make the trip alone.

When there were no visitors and no prospect of going anywhere, grief would claim me, forcing me to channel my manic energy into sewing and piano playing, supervising and contributing to the children's lessons even though there was a tutor and a governess in the house, and searching out appropriate staff, including some less aged help for the nursery. There was always someone leaving, or a new person to train.

Rather to my surprise, gardening became the most rewarding outlet of all. If only I could eradicate problems as easily and quickly as I tore out weeds! I could even smile when the children brought me in tiny bunches of violets, or armfuls of the tall yellow and purple irises I had planted in the autumn. *Their* favourite times were the summer holidays, when I made myself take them out for picnics, or in hot weather swim with them in the Middle Pond, where we had built a rough wooden bathhouse.

Visitors enjoy walking in the apple orchard, whose fruit Sonya bottled.

The long days of summer, which brought a stream of guests, also demanded that I tackle a whole swag of tasks that had to be performed out of sheer necessity – bottling the fruit from the orchard before it rotted or was eaten by birds; making clothes to replace those that the children constantly outgrew; reupholstering the shabby old chairs because getting someone to come from Tula was more trouble than it was worth. But although ticking off the items on my endless lists gave me a degree of satisfaction, collectively the tasks were banal. None of them had anything to do with Lyova's interests – literature, history, politics, religion – yet they reduced the time I had for him, or for the improving reading I knew I should be doing.

'I wish I were better educated,' I confessed to my diary, 'able to discuss clever ideas and read a lot of books.' But I knew that book-learning would only go part of the way towards overcoming the gulf between him and me.

Matching futility to wistfulness, I added: 'I also wish I were prettier.'

10

What the Chalk Really Wrote
1875

Several months further into *Anna Karenina*, Lyova explained to me the curious way he had come to understand an important fact about his unhappy heroine.

'I was sitting downstairs in my study gazing at the white silk embroidery on the sleeve of my dressing gown, which was very beautiful,' he said. 'And I wondered how it occurred to people to invent all these designs and decorations and embroideries, and I realised there was a whole world of women's work – fashions and ideas – through which women live. All this must be very delightful, I thought – I can understand why women enjoy it and occupy themselves this way. So of course all this led my thoughts (thoughts about the novel, that is) to Anna ... And suddenly this piece of embroidery suggested a whole chapter to me. Anna is deprived of all the joys of this aspect of a woman's life, because she is alone, other women spurn her, and she has no one to talk to about all the ordinary, everyday things that interest women.'

I hardly knew whether to laugh or to take to my diary. (I in fact did both, which is why I can accurately reproduce his words.) I did not find my harried domestic activities either jolly or fascinating, and Lyova appeared unaware that a woman did not have to commit adultery in order to feel alone. Although he was profoundly struck by his discovery that it was Anna's social isolation that deprived her of everyday consolations and was thus the cause of her unhappiness, he was quite unable to see that his own wife was equally, if differently, subject to loneliness. As I saw it, he chose to shut his eyes to any acknowledgment of the one thing that would make me completely happy: constant, ongoing emotional and spiritual union with *him*.

Yearning to be inside his mind every minute of every day, I suppose I underestimated how many thoughts he did communicate to me. Precious moments of communion cropped up, which I cherished both for their rarity and for the knowledge that they were shared with no one else. I particularly treasured an occasion when, upon finding the passage he was working on 'tedious', he treated me to a small but unparalleled insight into the demands of literary authenticity.

'You see,' he began, 'I've said that Vronsky and Anna were staying in the same hotel room, but that's not possible. In St Petersburg at least, [being unmarried] they'd have to take rooms on different floors. So as you see, this means that all the scenes and conversations and encounters with various people will be wrong. It will all have to be altered.'

Another reflection on his own work that was subsequently to become famous and widely quoted was confided to me when he was standing one blustery morning in March 1877 at his table. Deep in thought, he pointed to his notebook, and came out with something so portentous I rushed away to record it in 'Various Notes': 'My ideas are quite clear now,' he announced. 'If a work is to be really good there must be one important, fundamental idea in it which one loves. So in *Anna Karenina* I love the idea of the *family*; in *War and Peace* I loved the idea of the *nation*, following the war of 1812.'

Yet, copying these novels out so many times, I became convinced that these simple ideas were far from the whole story. I am sure that while one great framework preoccupied the forefront of his mind, his *brain*, he was not aware of the many subtexts that ran like underground streams beneath the surface. I believe now that I was trying to express the idea that they welled up from what Mr Freud in Vienna has since defined as the subconscious, though obviously at that time the science of psychology had not been invented.

In January 1875 the first fourteen chapters of *Anna Karenina* were published in the *Russian Herald*. The response was wildly enthusiastic, but sadly it hardly touched us. During the whole of that year we suffered one blow after another. Still grieving over the deaths of Petya and little Nikolai, we were painfully aware that even in our common loss we suffered separately, unable to comfort each other.

Then in November I gave birth to a baby girl, Varvara, whom we scarcely had time to get to know before she too died. The death of darling Toinette the year before had been a great sadness rather than a tragedy, and Aunt Pelageya had moved in with us to take her place. But she breathed her last in December, one month after poor little Varvara, and Natalya Petrovna, who had become so deranged we had had to put her in an old peoples' home, failed to survive a bad fall. It was a time of protracted and overwhelming sorrow, which gouged both of us with claws of iron. We had lost all three old ladies, and despite so many pregnancies, our little brood still consisted of only five living children – Seryozha, who was a dear boy, musical and wonderfully loving to me; Tanya, a darling; Ilya, always a little confused; Lyolya, irresponsible but so affectionate; and Masha, who was sweet but not strong – plus three small graves that broke my heart each time I put flowers on them.

Struggling with so many losses, but particularly those of the babies, I felt I urgently needed to protect myself from further griefs of that nature. The obvious solution was simply to avoid conception, but I had no idea how to go about it, and could not contemplate bringing the matter up with Lyova. He would be outraged, and shout that I ought to be ashamed of myself.

Yet I knew there were measures that could be taken. Guiltily I let my mind go back nearly three years to the time not long before Anna Stepanovna Pirogova threw herself under the train. She had not been a happy woman even before the German governess arrived, and although she and I were not close friends, we occasionally talked together. Goodness knows, unless Tanya or Masha happened to be staying at Yasnaya, I had no one to unburden myself to; I felt that I of all people could afford to extend a little sympathy to Anna Stepanovna, who was even more isolated.

I had come upon her one hot day near Zaseka wood, where we were both seeking consolation in its cool, rustling tranquillity. Anna Stepanovna was a pleasant-looking woman, tall and plumpish, with dark hair and grey eyes, but after exchanging greetings, I expressed some concern about her feverish colour.

'It's all right,' she replied. 'I'm just a bit worried. Well, very worried, actually.'

'May I ask what it is that's concerning you?' My words sounded formal, but I did not wish to pry.

'It's my period,' Anna Stepanovna burst out.

I was shocked. Constant pregnancies and prolonged breastfeeding meant I hardly ever had a period, but in any case I would certainly not bring up such a matter in conversation with a mere acquaintance.

'It's late,' pursued Anna Stepanovna curtly. She was twisting a handkerchief in her fingers.

'Do you think you might be pregnant?'

'Yes – no! I can't be! But what if I am?'

I saw that I had better begin at the beginning. 'You do – have – relations with Alexander Nikolaevich?'

Anna Stepanovna flashed me a look of contempt. 'What do you think?'

'Is that also your wish?'

'Wish? I don't have any say in it. But I love him, so I'm glad when he comes to me.'

'But is that – sometimes – too often?'

Anna Stepanovna laughed. 'Can't be too often for either of us. As long as I've taken precautions. But they don't always work, that's the trouble.' She bit her lip.

Thanks to Lyova's views, I was unable to discuss 'precautions'. But here was an unforeseen opportunity to go into them with this woman ... though how demeaning it would be! And also how very, very wrong.

'What is your method?' I asked impulsively, slightly emphasising the 'your'.

'Well, if I can get him to pull out in time, that's the safest way, but usually it doesn't suit him.'

I felt my cheeks reddening. I could neither ignore the avid desire to ask what I was desperate to know, nor make myself frame the words. I realised that Anna Stepanovna was looking at me curiously, and remained silent.

'Do you douche?' Anna Stepanovna finally asked. Receiving no answer, she gave another laugh. 'I get the picture,' she said. 'Try washing yourself straight away, but not just with water. That won't help. Add a bit of lemon juice. Alum works too, if you've got any.'

'Thank you,' I managed to whisper, looking everywhere but at her. My whole face was burning.

'I can't promise it'll work, but it's worth a try,' she said. 'Have you definitely made up your mind you don't want any more kids?'

'Well, not – not for the present,' I heard myself say. I soon discovered that I must have been already pregnant with Petya; but at the time I switched the focus back to Anna Stepanovna.

'I have five children,' I said, 'Whereas you have none of your own.'

'Nor want any. I'm not married, you know.'

'But perhaps, if you were to have a child, Alexander Nikolaevich might marry you.'

'And he might show me the door too, kid and all, and then where'd I be? Nah, I've thought about it often enough, 'cos I'd quite like one of my own, but it's not worth the risk.'

I thought of the intense love I felt for all of my children, and the great joy – almost my only one – that they gave me, and suddenly felt deep compassion for Anna Stepanovna.

'Children can be a great comfort, you know,' I volunteered.

'Not to everyone. Even if he were to marry me tomorrow, I still wouldn't have any. I mightn't be at his beck and call then, and he'd be jealous.'

I'd seen then that Anna Stepanovna was utterly dependent on the goodwill of a master whom she also loved, which made her situation both better and worse.

Now, nearly three years later, I still felt unnerved by the jealous despair that had driven her to kill herself when the German woman took her place. Meanwhile, I stowed away the wicked knowledge that Anna Stepanovna had passed on to me, while recognising that I would never be capable of putting it into practice. It wasn't simply Lyova's disapproval. I would rather have had Petya, Nikolai and Varvara for the brief time they'd been with us than not have known them at all.

In any case, if I did use contraception and Lyova found out, he might not 'show me the door', but he would surely never speak to me ever again.

Though Lev Nikolaevich was also cast down by the deaths of the children and the old ladies, he still wrote whenever he felt able, and was now deep into the next section of his novel. But he was often too depressed to get involved in it, and would seek distraction by being out and about. In the evenings he missed having Aunt Pelageya to unwind with; they used to play endless games of patience, while I copied away in the study. These days I had quite a lot of nights off, while the chunks of writing that were left for me were increasingly confusing, often out of sequence with those of the previous stint. Not only did Lev move sections of prose around, as with Princess Betsy's post-opera party, but new perceptions seemed to strike him all the time, and he would work on them immediately, leaving the previous paragraph up in the air. The higgledy-piggledy order made me lose track of the plot lines, as did his concentration on one character for chapters at a time while ignoring the rest. I often had great difficulty keeping the whole picture in mind.

Yet familiarity with the context was crucial when it came to deciphering his corrections. After breaking my head over several time-consuming puzzles, I started writing a timeline for each of the three central couples – Dolly and Stiva, the problematical pair who nevertheless stayed together; Kitty and Levin, whose marital path was not as smooth as it should have been; and Anna and Vronsky, the enthralled, doomed lovers. I noticed that the family trees I also constructed highlighted the secondary relationships – Dolly and Kitty being sisters, Stiva and Anna siblings, Levin and Stiva old friends – and forced me to think about the novel in terms of structure and significance. Which, as with the First Epilogue, was not necessarily a good thing. When I simply deciphered and copied words, I scarcely focused on their implications; but whenever I laid down my pen to address larger issues, I often felt critical. Or angry. Or threatened. The lead-up to the wedding of Kitty and Levin, for example.

Konstantin Levin, a landowner, falls in love with pretty Kitty Shcherbatsky and cannot be dissuaded from proposing to her, even though he has been told she might not be receptive to his declaration. Stiva has warned him that he has a serious rival in Alexei Vronsky, aide-de-camp to the Tsar, rich, handsome, well connected, and favoured by Kitty's mother. Advised to act quickly, Levin impulsively collars Kitty towards the end of a dinner party at her parents' house, and is dismayed to be rejected, however gently. He returns straight away to his house in the country, where he lies low and licks his wounded pride.

Stiva, coming to shoot game at Levin's estate (called Pokrovskoe, like my parents' dacha!) tells him that Vronsky lost interest in Kitty the moment he set eyes on Madame Karenina, who'd come to Moscow to try to patch up Stiva and Dolly's marital problems. In this she was wonderfully successful, but she was less clever at hiding her attraction to Vronsky, whom she met getting off the train, and again at a ball attended by *le tout Moscou*. Kitty, sitting out because she had saved the mazurka for Vronsky, who instead asked Anna, is alerted to their mutual passion by the telltale glow in their faces. Mortified, she falls ill and is taken abroad. Anna, back in St Petersburg with her husband Alexei and their child Serozha, is pursued and conquered by Vronsky. She abandons both to go abroad with him.

A month or two later, Dolly and her five children come to spend the summer on Dolly's dowry estate of Yergushovo (or Ivitsy ...), not far from Levin's Pokrovskoe. She tells Levin that Kitty, now much restored, has returned from Germany and will spend the summer with her in the country. Levin realises that he still loves Kitty, but remains too hurt to visit her.

When he next shows up in Moscow, it is one year and some two hundred pages later, the novel having for some time pursued the vicissitudes of the Karenins. Stiva is giving another dinner party, but not until the men have left the table to join the ladies in the drawing room can Levin speak confidentially to Kitty, who is sitting at a small card table tracing circles on the green baize with a piece of chalk.

I was reading fast, with rising excitement. The next couple of pages continued:

'How can I live alone ... without her?' he thought with horror and took the chalk. 'Wait,' he said, sitting down at the table. 'There's something I've been wanting to ask you for a long time.'

He looked straight into her tender though frightened eyes.

'Please ask.'

'Here,' he said, and wrote the initial letters: w, y, a, m: t, c, b, d, i, m, n, o, t? These letters meant: 'When you answered me: "that cannot be", did it mean never or then?' There was little likelihood that she would be able to understand his complex sentence, but he was looking at her as though his life depended on her understanding those words.

She glanced at him seriously, then rested her knitted brow on her hand and began to read. Occasionally she glanced at him, as if asking: 'Is it what I think it is?'

'I understand,' she said, blushing.

'What's this word?' he said, pointing to the n that signified the word never.

'That word means never,' she said, 'but it's not true!'

He quickly rubbed out what was written, gave her the chalk, and got up. She wrote: t, I, c, g, n, o, a.

Dolly was completely consoled after the grief arising from her conversation with Alexei Alexandroich when she saw those two figures: Kitty with the chalk in her hand, looking up at Levin with a shy but happy smile, and his handsome figure bent over the table, his burning gaze directed now at the table, now at her. Suddenly he beamed: he had understood. It meant: 'Then I could give no other answer.'

He glanced at her questioningly, shyly.

'Only then?'

'Yes,' her smile replied.

'And n… And now?' he asked.

'Well, here you are, read this. I'll tell you what I would wish. Would wish very much!' She wrote the initial letters: T, y, c, f, a, f, w, h. It meant: 'That you could forgive and forget what happened.'

He seized the chalk with his tense, trembling fingers, broke it, and wrote the initial letters of the following: 'I have nothing to forgive or forget, I have never stopped loving you,'

She glanced at him, the smile staying on her lips.

'I understand,' she said in a whisper.

He sat down and wrote a long phrase. She understood everything and, without asking him if she was right, took the chalk and replied at once.

For a long time he couldn't understand what she had written, and kept glancing at her eyes. Happiness eclipsed all comprehension. He simply could not distinguish the words she had in mind; but in her lovely shining eyes he understood everything he needed to know. He wrote three letters. But even before he had finished writing she was already following what his hand wrote; she completed it and wrote the answer: 'Yes.'

'Playing secrétaire?' said the old prince, approaching …

I was swept by pride, admiration, amusement and extreme anger all at once. How clever and charming it was of Lyova to reproduce our sweet secret from the real Pokrovskoe. Out of the thousands of Russians who would read this novel, how many would realise that its famous author had courted his own bride-to-be in this way?

I blushed with pride and pleasure as I noted how adroitly Lyova had inserted the real-life incident into the fictional lives of his characters. He had transposed that magical exchange into a story that was and was not our own, and had done it with enormous skill. He truly was a brilliant writer.

My lips twitched with the thought that the whole book – well, at least the Levin and Kitty half – might be read as a kind of guessing game by people who knew us, or at least knew of us. My mental picture of their discussions was titillating.

'How much of it is true?' I could hear them asking. 'Do you think Sofya Andreevna really guessed what each of those letters stood for? Is it possible for love to sharpen people's intuition to such an extent?'

'Perhaps, if they are really in love …'

It was both entertaining and gratifying to think of going down in history – well, literary history – as a woman – no, I was just a girl, then – of such unusual perception. Lyova had exaggerated slightly, of course, he'd taken a little poetic licence … but the overall picture was correct.

It was a very different record of our courtship, however, from the way Lev told it in his diary ('She said yes'), but I preferred to forget what he wrote there. That account, unlike the novel in front of me, was of the most prosaic … In fact, the comparison forced me to face the harsh reality: no card table had been involved at the real Pokrovskoe, no chalk, and rather less divine intuition. The message had been in the *letter* that Lev had finally sent after failing to post it the first time, and he had stood by as I opened it, giving me clue after clue, until I was able to make a few intelligent guesses. Once I grasped how it was supposed to work, it was not beyond me to suggest that a capital 'T' might stand for Tanya.

He had trumped me again. Not only was his Kitty delightful in the way my little sister had been, with far more charm than I could ever aspire to, but nor had there been any mystical communion between myself and him, or not, at least, in regard to his proposal. He *had* loved me, I did not doubt that, and he *had* used initials to convey his feelings; but the passionate, tender, heart-on-sleeve exchange between Levin and Kitty was so romantic, so all that young love should be, it knocked the awkward communication between tense Lev Nikolaevich and anxious little Sonya into a cocked hat.

Of course, if we hadn't both been so on edge that evening, we could have been just as passionate and tender – *that* was what posterity had to understand. Like at Ivitsy, when I wore my white and mauve dress and Lev rode over on his grey stallion. His admiring gaze, his constant attention, his lover-like attitude could not have been clearer on that night if he *had* written messages in chalk on a green baize card table, as some of the young guests were doing.

Once again, it became clear to me that I must write my own little account of what happened, one that would make everything clear to the biographers and critics who would come after us, scavenging for information. It would not be false, because it would speak the inner truth that Lev's diary ignored. But I must do it now, and quickly. I took a piece of paper, headed it 'What the Chalk Wrote', and embarked on a description of a scene that I decided to set not at Pokrovskoe but at Ivitsy. There, my sisters would be less able to challenge me on my 'recollections'.

He brushed the games scores off the card table, picked up the chalk and began writing. We were both very serious but highly excited.
I followed his big red hand, feeling that all my mental powers and capability, all my attention, were focused on that bit of chalk and the hand that held it. Neither of us said anything.
'Y.y.&.n.f.h.t.v.r.m.o.m.a.&.i.f.h.'
'Your youth and need for happiness too vividly remind me of my age and incapacity for happiness,' I read aloud.

My heart was pounding so hard it made my temples throb, my
face was burning – I was outside time and reality; at that moment
I felt I could do anything, understand everything, grasp the
ungraspable.

'Well, let's keep going,' said Lev Nikolaevich and began to write
once more: 'Y.f.h.t.w.i.a.m.&.y.s.L.Y.&.y.s.T.m.s.m.'

'Your family has the wrong idea about me and your sister Liza.
You and your sister Tanechka must save me,' I rapidly and without
hesitation read from the initial letters.

Lev Nikolaevich wasn't even surprised; it was as if it was an
everyday occurrence. Our heightened emotions were so elevated
above the normal condition of the human spirit that nothing could
surprise us.

Reading over what I had written, I thought my version pretty
convincing, but perhaps not firm enough. What if that letter was lurking
somewhere, all ready to make a liar of me, its cryptic phrases giving an
unfair impression of the situation?

I took up my pen again and resumed writing.

Hearing Maman's cross voice summoning me to bed, we hurriedly
said goodnight, extinguished the candles and went out. Behind my
cupboard upstairs I lit the candle-end, and began to write my diary,
sitting on the floor, the notebook on the wooden chair. I wrote down
the words to which Lev Nikolaevich had given me the initials,
vaguely aware that between the two of us something serious and
significant had happened – something we were unable to stop. But
for various reasons I did not give way to my thoughts and dreams. It
was as though I were locking up everything that had taken place that
evening, keeping back things that were not yet ready to see the light.

There. That would do for posterity. Two could play at the writing game! I hid the pages in one of my shoeboxes, where Lyova would never find it.

11

Irony
1876

A year passed, during which my foray into literary reconstruction relegated itself to the back of my mind. It was not meant to disturb the here and now.

As soon as the summer ended, Lev escaped once more to Samara, intending to be away for two weeks. He was mad keen on setting up a horse stud there. With my nephew Nikolai for company, he left Yasnaya Polyana on September 3rd, arrived down south in Buzuluk four days later, and the same afternoon caught a train to the town of Orenburg, where he would buy the horses.

I took up my diary again, deeply resentful that he had torn himself away from me just when we were getting on rather well. His boisterous telegram announcing their safe arrival, assuring me that he was in excellent health, and congratulating himself at finding it all so exciting, did little to improve my mood.

I desperately wanted my husband back home for my name day, but the 17th dawned without a sign of him. After breakfast I excused myself and the children from lessons and sent them out to fly kites with Uncle Stepan Behrs, who had come for the celebration; as soon as they were out of sight, I ordered all of Lyova's papers to be fetched from the gun closet and sat down to immerse myself in his mountain of diaries and memoirs. I had for some time believed – again for the sake of posterity – that I should try to write a biography of Lev Nikolaevich. With public interest in the country's greatest author increasing every year, it was essential to prevent the promulgation of any mistaken ideas about his personal life. Hitherto I had put off embarking on such a daunting project, but today my sense of loss and resentment prodded me towards a task that would make his absence more bearable. I could at least be with him in spirit.

Why then did I find myself doing something quite different – scouring each notebook for those episodes that were bound to make me most unhappy? Not that this exercise delayed me very long. Coming across far too many confessions that I would have preferred not to see, I soon slammed the notebooks shut and gave way to a paroxysm of bitterness.

'What is he punishing me for?' I asked for the twentieth time. And answered, as always, 'Why, for loving him so much.'

To console myself, I turned again to the pile of paper that was the unfinished *Anna*, recalling how happy I'd been while copying out the romantic story of Levin and Kitty, based for all the world to see on *my* courtship and *my* wedding day.

Of course I had come to accept that Kitty and I were not identical. I'd been foolish to get upset over the differences. It was a novel, after all! And still a compliment to me. I began rereading from where I had left off.

Probably because I was so hurt by Lyova's failure to come back for my name day, I was struck by a slightly unsympathetic, almost mocking note in the voice of the narrator, a stern distancing of Lev from Levin, almost as if the author no longer sympathised with his hero. I began to read more rapidly.

After Kitty and her parents have left the dinner party, Levin is so elated he can't bear to be alone, and seeks the company of the always animated Stiva. But Stiva first teases him – 'So it's no longer time to die?' – then casually excuses himself to go off to another party. Deserted, Levin is rescued by his half-brother Sergei, who invites him to a meeting where Levin, for 'an hour, two hours, three hours', talks endlessly without noticing that he is boring everyone rigid. He thinks they all like him 'tremendously', looking at him 'tenderly and lovingly' – even the strangers!

Reaching his hotel at 1 am, he discovers that Yegor, the night porter, of whom he has previously taken little notice, is in fact an incredibly intelligent, good and kind man. Levin not only seizes the opportunity to tell him that the main thing in marriage is love, but registers that Yegor too is in a rapturous state, ready to share all his innermost feelings – until, unfortunately (or not) a bell rings, and Yegor makes his escape.

It was an amusing sequence, yet Levin in love was made to sound fatuous, as if Lyova was unwilling to indulge such a feeble state of mind. To put it bluntly, the ironic tone made Levin a figure of ridicule. It was Lev's way of indicating his disapproval of romantic infatuation.

I did not, could not, believe that he regretted falling in love with me, but, demoralised, could not help recalling the doubts that assailed him prior to our wedding. Were they more lasting than Maman or I realised? Her briskness seemed to have chased them away, but what if they had come back? What witness did my own diaries give of our early days together? Quickly I found the dusty volumes and began to turn the pages. I must have recorded some of his outbursts of love – but where were they?

I searched for much longer than I expected to, but here, at last, was one.

March 10th, 1865. Lyovochka has been much more affectionate today. He actually kissed me for the first time in days.

Written two-and-a-half years after our marriage, it was poor comfort. There must be other, more passionate entries from when we had just arrived at Yasnaya Polyana. Feverishly I leafed backwards through the pages, skimming each one. There were dozens of declarations of my love for him, but nothing in reverse – just a record of inadequate returns.

January 17th, 1863. I have been feeling out of sorts and angry that he should love everything and everyone, when I want him to love only me.

That was only four months after our wedding!

Feeling that the floor had dropped from under my feet, I thrust all the diaries onto their shelf and went back to the horrid novel. The mockery became more pointed in the next chapter, yet was also more affectionate, as if Lyova had regained some fondness for Levin, no matter how foolishly the man behaved.

Eager for his appointment with Kitty's father, Levin gets up so early next morning that when he emerges from his hotel he finds the streets deserted and the front door of the Shcherbatskys' house still locked. He goes back to the hotel, tries unsuccessfully to eat breakfast, and immediately strides out again, reaching the Shcherbatskys' soon after nine o'clock. Now at least there is a porter on duty, but Levin is still not granted admission. He cools his heels for another two hours.

But in the end all is well; at a civilised hour the old prince and his wife welcome him, bless him, and ask when the wedding will be. In a comic parody of himself, Lyova makes Levin answer: 'When? Tomorrow. If you ask me, in my opinion, the blessing today and the wedding tomorrow.'

They all think him entirely mad, but accept that it will have to be before Lent, which is five weeks away, because if they wait until afterwards, Princess Shcherbatsky's old aunt might have died and they will have to put off the ceremony until the mourning period is over.

I recalled that when I had first copied this section, I had wondered how, or even whether, Lyova would make Levin show his diaries to his bride-to-be. I'd got my answer almost straight away: he does, but Lyova had transposed his actions in this matter with a mixture of accuracy and dissemblance, and mine simply with brevity.

Having discussed the matter with Prince Shcherbatsky, who gives his permission (which Papa would never have done), Levin hands over to Kitty the volumes containing the full account of both 'his impurity and his unbelief'. The impurity makes her weep.

> 'Why did you give them to me! ... No, it may be for the best,' she
> added, taking pity on his desperate face. 'But it's awful, awful!'

He bowed his head and was silent. There was nothing he could say. 'You won't forgive me,' he whispered.

'No, I've forgiven you, but it's awful!'

It dawned on me now that although Lyova went on to write feelingly about Kitty's 'dove-like purity' and 'tear-stained, pathetic face', there was no trace of any effort to understand the impact such a confession would make on a young girl, or the gulf it must cause between any husband and wife. Moreover, as a writer, he had found an easy and self-favouring way of moving on from it that definitely did not spring from either his or my experience: 'She forgave him; but from then on he considered himself still more unworthy of her, bowed still lower before her morally, and valued all the more highly his undeserved happiness.'

He unworthy of her? In what cloud cuckoo land did this husband of mine live? Was it the same for all novelists?

I remained dejected until late the following morning, when out of the blue a telegram arrived from Lev in Syrzan, saying he would be home in a couple of days. My happiness was instantaneous: my diary records that 'I suddenly felt more cheerful, and the house was all happiness and light, the children's lessons went well, and they were adorable.'

Their tutor however, M. Rey, had a different impression. The children had been so naughty he had given them twos for behaviour, and I had to tell Seryozha that as punishment he would not be allowed to go hunting.

'*Peut-être ça te dira quelque chose*,' I admonished him.

'*Au contraire!*' he shouted rudely.

I did not speak to him for the rest of the day, but when I kissed him goodnight he asked so anxiously whether I was still angry, I had to forgive him. I was as glad as he was to be friends again, but an even greater exultation made me write in my diary: 'My heart leaps when I think that the day after tomorrow Lyovochka will be coming back, lighting up the house.'

In a much better frame of mind I spent most of the next day reassessing more of *Anna*. Skipping whole swathes centring on the wilful heroine and her tawdry love affair, I lingered again over Levin and Kitty's wedding plans. Princess Shcherbatsky is dividing the trousseau into two lots: some necessities to go with the newlyweds, the rest to be sent on afterwards. Immediately after the wedding the young people are going to the country, where the things in the larger collection will not immediately be needed. Meanwhile, 'Levin continued on in the same state of madness.'

I frowned. The first time I read that sentence, I had assumed that Lev was smiling indulgently at his character, but now I lost the note of affection. 'Madness', he'd written. Was that how my husband saw the elation that had made him propose to *me*? How could I not think so? It was becoming more than obvious that he regarded love as a temporary loss of reason that would come to be regretted only when it was too late.

It was the same with the advice everyone offers Levin: the princess advocates leaving Moscow straight after the wedding, Stepan Arkadyich recommends going abroad. Levin foolishly agrees to every suggestion. How stupid! Especially as 'abroad' is the last thing he wants. Kitty knows he is desperate to get back to his estate; it is her suggestion that they go straight to the country – just as we had done.

The satiric tone, the mindless agreement, both suggested that Levin in love had become a complete idiot. I read on, my lips pursed.

Before he can get married, Levin needs a certificate saying he has been to confession and taken communion. Not having done either for years, he is horrified.

But that hadn't been an issue for Lev, as far as I was aware. His religious doubts had come on much later, quite recently in fact, after Nikolai died at ten months and poor little Varya failed to live at all. There was no doubt that he'd questioned God's love then, and rejected belief in Him for some time; but then there had been another reversal. At the moment he was trying to revive his faith by adhering strictly to the laws of the Church. This had some reward for me – I could tell if his conscience was troubled or at peace by whether or not he went to communion. But because his ambivalence was preoccupying him *now*, he had passed it on to Levin *then*. Both of them, like so many of our contemporaries who had read the translated works of the English scientist Charles Darwin, and his explanation of evolution, found their belief in the Church's teaching shaken, yet were not firmly convinced that it was all incorrect.

Levin attends a liturgy, vigil and compline on one day, and goes to prayers and confession the next morning at eight o'clock. In the church there is no one except a begging soldier, two little old women and various priests. He goes through the motions of the service, and repeatedly mumbles the response, 'Lordamercy', thinking all the time of Kitty's dear little hand. After three roubles have been handed over, the priest asks him about his sins. Doubt is the only one that Levin comes out with, which the priest cheerfully agrees is common enough, but doesn't make any sense. The solution is for Levin to pray hard, and to think how he will answer his own little children when they ask him about God.

Levin leaves the church relieved he has not had to lie, but feeling like a dog that has been made to jump through a hoop.

On his last evening as a bachelor he dines, as Lyova had done, with some male friends. I was comforted to discover that Levin proclaims himself glad to be losing his freedom, but less enchanted by his sudden realisation that really, he hardly knows his wife-to-be at all! It is this shock that leads him next day, a few hours before the ceremony, to suggest calling the whole thing off.

'No, it's impossible!' he said to himself in despair. 'I'll go to her, ask her, tell her for the last time: we're free, hadn't we better stop? Anything's better than eternal unhappiness, shame, infidelity!' With despair in his heart and anger at all human beings, at himself, and at her, he left the hotel and went to see her.

He found her in the back room. She was sitting on a trunk …

Lyova had fleshed out charmingly that brief scene between the two of us, before we were interrupted by Maman. He had Kitty working hard at persuading Levin not only that she does love him, but that he is eminently worth loving. She tells him that she loves him because she thoroughly understands him, that she knows all that he loves – all of it – is good. Which seems perfectly correct to him.

When Kitty's mother comes in, they are sitting side by side amicably arguing over whether Kitty should give her maid the dress she was wearing when Levin proposed to her; he does not want her to.

I sighed. I could never have said that I fully understood Lyova, then or now; nor could I agree that everything he loved was good. Once again he'd rubbed my nose in the unpalatable knowledge that I fell far short of his ideal wife – always had and always would.

Yet it was truly wonderful to read his description of the ceremony that had been a chanting, glowing blur to me. He made it sound so beautiful – the gleaming gold, the glinting silver, the colourful banners, the old books, cassocks, surplices, and everything else all flooded with soft candlelight. The church is comfortably heated, and the people, dressed in their best, are talking in subdued but animated voices, waiting for the bride to arrive. I was enthralled to discover how the wedding guests had passed the time while I was still at home in my flimsy dress, waiting for Lyova's best man to arrive. How tense that time had been, how chilled and terrified I was, thinking that he would not come at all, that he had changed his mind entirely.

As the seconds tick past, the congregation becomes almost as concerned as the Shcherbatsky household:

Each time there was a creak as the door opened, the talking of the crowd hushed and everyone turned, expecting to see the bride and groom enter. But the door had already opened more than ten times, and each time it was either a latecomer who joined the circle of invited guests on the right, or a spectator who had tricked or cajoled the police officer into letting her join the crowd of strangers on the left ... The priest was constantly sending the usher or the deacon to see if the bridegroom had come and, in his purple cassock and embroidered belt, came expectantly out of the side door more and more often. Finally one of the ladies, looking at her watch, said, 'It is odd, though!' and all the guests became agitated and began loudly to express their astonishment and displeasure.

I skipped the next part, all the fuss about the missing shirt and the shops not being open, and let my eyes race on to the bride's arrival at the church. I was chagrined to read that she looked 'more dead than alive', and, at the altar, far less pretty than usual. Fortunately, to Levin, Kitty is exquisite, wearing 'her own special expression of innocent truthfulness'.

The description went on for several pages, everything sounding more familiar than not, and with many human touches – Stiva teasing Levin about the cost of the candles, Levin unable to grasp what the priest is telling him, the voice of the choir swelling, pausing, dying away, a muddle about the rings, and the chatter that goes on 'unceasingly in decently low tones' during the betrothal ceremony:

'Why is Marie wearing purple, almost black, for a wedding?' said Mrs Korsunsky.

'With her complexion, it's the only salvation ...'

After the betrothal came the marriage proper, with the priest putting gold crowns on their heads and giving them the flat cup of warm, red communion wine to drink, then at last the final prayer. After that, Levin still does not know what to do until the priest whispers to them, 'Kiss your wife, and you, kiss your husband.'

All that was perfectly beautiful, I thought, congratulating myself on the extraordinary luck no other woman in the world could claim – the amazing situation of reading a heightened, even romanticised account of her own wedding. There remained only one more thing to check.

After supper the young couple left for the country.

Correct. And then what happened?

A whole lot of stuff about Anna and Vronsky in Italy … When the main story was taken up again some twenty pages later, 'Levin had been married for three months.'

Nothing about the night at Birulevo, plenty about this being a surprise and that a shock, their quarrels both an enchantment and a disenchantment – whatever he meant by that. There were fewer pages on these crucial three months than there had been about the few lovely hours of the wedding; but as the chapter finished, my husband finally made mention of the honeymoon 'from which Levin had expected so much'.

It not only had no honey in it, Lev had written, but it remained in their memories as 'the most difficult and humiliating time of their life. They both tried in later life to erase from their memories all the ugly, shameful circumstances of that unhealthy time, when they were rarely in a normal state, rarely themselves.'

12

The Dead Mother
1876

Ilya did not try to guess the number of copies I made of *Anna Karenina*, nor was I counting, but the about-turns and bolts from the blue must have required at least six rewritings. Princess Betsy got off lightly, all things considered – shunted off the front page, but not entirely eliminated. Lyova was right, though, to defer her entry to the start of Part 2, Chapter 6. She might be a princess, but she was too lightweight a character to introduce such a truly splendid work. The public response to every instalment so far had been rapturous.

The unchanged opening line still referred not to a single individual, not even the eponymous heroine, but to collective 'happy families'. *All* happy families. Who, claimed the author, 'are alike in their happiness'. But are they? I was sceptical. The line had a clarion ring to it, but in my opinion was not borne out by the rest of the novel. Kitty and Levin had a long way to go if they were to emulate the Shcherbatsky parents – the Prince and Princess of Domestic Accord. Levin in particular seemed to struggle with the realities of married life.

'Levin is you, Lyova, without the talent,' I remember saying aloud as I read the first draft. He'd only grunted at the time, but he couldn't deny it; and I could easily have proved my point.

'Apart from the glaring similarity in names,' I might have said, 'Levin is a landowner like you, he has the same political ideas, he loves hunting, he's vitally interested in the peasants as well as in "the peasant question", and he hates leaving his estate – whose name, by the way, is filched from Papa's dacha, but looks a whole lot more like Yasnaya Polyana.'

And then I would add, 'And to cap it all off, Levin is a quite impossible man!' Indisputably a clone of my husband.

I said none of this, however, since he was not in a mood to receive either compliments or criticism; but after copying out certain passages three times – not that he ever changed the famous introduction once he'd hit on it – I found an opportunity to bring the matter up again.

It was late on a quiet morning following the excitement of a grand hunt the day before. Seven horses had been saddled to carry Lyova, the two Seryozhas (son and uncle), Ilyusha, a couple of servants and the boys' tutor, Monsieur Nief. This little band trotted after the pack of borzois racing ahead. Liza, who was staying with us, the older girls, little Lyolya, and the governess, Mademoiselle Gachet, all followed on donkeys. I remained behind to sort out some clothes for the baby I was expecting towards Christmas, but after a while, feeling left out and thinking I'd better make the most of my pre-baby freedom, I ordered the cart to be harnessed and set out to meet the children.

I found them at the boundary of the estate, but only Mademoiselle Gachet agreed to drive home with me. The girls preferred to amble back on their donkeys, arriving with hearty appetites but refusing anything to eat other than horseradish and sour milk, while they waited for the hunters to return. The posse turned up around seven o'clock, very pleased with a bag of six hares they'd strung up on a stick. We all dined together, and Monsieur Nief read aloud some Alexander Dumas until bedtime.

Next morning I slept in, using pregnancy as my excuse. The children crept into my room one by one to wish me good morning, and at last were followed by Lyova. I hoped so much that he would stay long enough for a real chat, but he shot out of the room the minute the nurse came in to discuss the day's arrangements.

I got up sighing; to lift my spirits, I decided to put on my new dress while it still fitted. Sergei Nikolaevich would appreciate it, even if Lyova didn't. Sergei seemed a little depressed in himself these days – I suspected he was still in love with Tanya – but he was always unfailingly nice to me. Indeed, before setting out for Pirogova, he said several sweet things about the children. Lyova had already ridden off to the Tula High School, where he was a trustee.

Left with no one to talk to and not even any copying to do, I could not avoid turning to the unfinished – unstarted! – biography. It always loomed as a problem, because it brought home to me that I, of all people, hardly knew anything about Lyova's life before I married him. That is, other than a few nasty details unfit for public consumption.

After sitting at my desk for half an hour without finding anything to say, I decided to look for direction in the biographies of other writers – we had tomes on Lermontov, Pushkin and Gogol on our library shelves. To my surprise, their contents were almost as shocking as Lev's diaries. The poetry and stories written by these gentlemen occupied a high place in the pantheon of Russian literature, but their personal lives were far from edifying. The tempestuous life of Mikhail Lermontov, for example, killed in a duel at the age of twenty-seven, almost undermined the pleasure I found in his work. However, the parallel was no excuse for Lev's youthful excesses. I continued to sit disconsolate, doodling and brooding.

Towards the end of the morning, Lyova rushed in from Tula. Taking no notice of either me or my mood, he drew up a chair to his desk and seized a pen. An hour or so later, as I passed by the door, he called out to me in rapt admiration, 'It's going to be so good!'

I stood hesitating in the doorway, encouraged even if not quite invited. I was determined to bring up the angry, muddled thoughts that *Anna* and the venality of men, especially writers, had churned up in me.

I replied, rather grudgingly, 'It will be marvellous, I'm sure. But I've been thinking that your opening line suggests there's only one way for a couple to be happy. But that way is only your personal ideal, and not many people live up to it, you know.'

Lev did not erupt, but the red, rough hand grasping the pen was arrested in its rapid movement across the page. His bushy, greying eyebrows drew together for a moment.

'It is important to state a universal ideal, even though in general it is bound to be betrayed by the human weakness of some individuals,' he pronounced.

'Most, not some,' I muttered, but not loud enough for him to hear. I went into the garden feeling dismissed. If I was really going to find out enough about him to write the biography, it was clear I would have to go to his writings.

Lev *was* Levin's alter ego, of that I was sure. Even if the courtship veered away from our personal history, there were plenty of details that came straight from real life. Levin's age, for example, in relation to Kitty's, and the fact that he had known the Shcherbatsky girls when they were younger, as Lev had known us. In fact, Levin calls Natalie, Dolly and Kitty the 'three bears', which was a rather nice pun, but also a direct give-away of his fairytale notions. Levin, we are told, had been briefly interested in both the older sisters; but Kitty was 'just right'.

Strangely, as far as the biography was concerned, *Anna* shed as much light on Lyova's early years as did *Childhood*. The poignant repetition of the line 'Levin could not remember his mother' was so touching it made me want to cry. But in the Shcherbatsky household 'he discovered for the first time the ambience of an old, aristocratic, well-educated and honourable family, which he had been deprived of by the death of his own father and mother ... He knew that everything that went on there was beautiful, and he was in love with its mysterious perfection.'

I was ashamed to be reminded that the deaths of Lyova's parents were a far greater loss than I usually allowed for. Of course he would like to warm himself at the Islenev and Behrs firesides, but did he realise that although those circles held a certain magic, even they were not perfect? No family is. After I left home some shocking rumours came to my ears about affairs my father was supposed to have conducted, which on the whole I chose not to listen to. But if they were true, his philandering must have been discreet, for certainly Maman never showed any sign of concern. And there *was*, there always had been, that lovely warmth and gaiety in our household, attracting many visitors besides Count Tolstoy.

The evening before, while I was looking at yet another passage lauding the Shcherbatskys, I could hear my own little boys, Ilya and Lyolya, giggling and splashing in the bathtub. For a while there was quiet, presumably while the nurse was drying them, and after that I heard them race upstairs to bed, Nurse stomping up behind them; then there was more suppressed laughter, more bouncing and romping, and finally Nurse's voice stern and firm, telling them to behave themselves or Sofya Andreevna would not come up and kiss them …

I went in to say goodnight before they fell asleep; they looked so happy and clean and splendid my heart melted, but they were already drowsy. I kissed them, smoothed their blankets, and made the sign of the cross over them; finally, unable to think of any more excuses, I crept out.

If poor Lyova had missed out on all that as a child, it should have been my sacred mission to make it up to him.

Deplorably, during this moment of tenderness, with guilt and affection softening my hard heart, selfishness again reared its rebellious head. After all, *I* had needs too, that he took no notice of, that were swamped by domestic chores, and copying, and this wretched biography that he didn't even want me to write. I never had any time to myself. Yet I had to admit that the last two tasks had turned into keys which helped me with the most difficult challenge of all – unlocking the heart of the man on whose unpredictable love I depended, without whom my life would be unthinkable.

Churning with contrary emotions, I sat down again in front of the pile of pages that had resulted from a recent burst of energy on Lyova's part, and began to decipher the tiny scrawls encased in balloons above thick, black erasure bars. The passage he had revised dealt with Kitty's initial rejection of Levin, to whom it seemed that 'Kitty was so perfect in all respects, a being so far above everything earthly that …' That what? I peered again … That it made Levin feel dreadfully 'earthy' – so earthy and base he immediately went back to nurse his shame in the country.

It is not until Stiva tells him about Vronsky's rejection of Kitty, and her subsequent illness, that a kind of energy of desperation comes over him, propelling him back to Moscow to try again …

By now winter has come, and Kitty has joined the flock of skaters on the large frozen pond below the snow-covered hills that skirt the city's southern edge. Levin's eyes rake the crowd of figures gliding across the ice. He glimpses Kitty straight away, 'a rose among nettles … more beautiful than he had imagined her', and thanks his stars that he is an excellent skater, though at the moment one without skates.

I pondered the impression that Kitty makes on Levin, trying to analyse how Lyova had conveyed it. For the first time I took a clean sheet of paper and copied out a paragraph for my own purposes. Then I read it through, and underlined several words.

They were all diminutives. Lev's feminine ideal was apparently a child rather than a woman: if Levin adored Kitty, it was …

the charm of that <u>small, fair</u> head, so <u>lightly</u> set on the shapely, <u>girlish</u>
shoulders, and the <u>childlike</u> brightness and kindness of her face. In
the <u>childlike</u> expression of her face, combined with the <u>slim</u> beauty
of her figure lay her special charm which he remembered so well;
but what always struck him as if unexpectedly was the expression of
her eyes – mild, calm, and truthful – and above all her smile, which
always carried Levin into a <u>fairyland</u>, where he felt softened and
filled with tenderness, as he remembered feeling on rare occasions in
his early <u>childhood</u>.

This meant, among other things, that Kitty was even less like Sonya

Behrs than I had realised. For a start, my greatest assets, or so it was said, were my black hair and dark eyes; and I doubt I ever projected the naïve, girlish quality that Lev was so taken with. Had he even wanted a *wife* when he married me? Or would he have preferred an enchanting child who would skate through life with him, clutching his arm in one glorious *pas de deux*? No wonder the location was fairyland.

Then it came to me that Levin's creator, my husband, was fixated on innocence and purity because for him a sexual relationship with a real woman implied lasciviousness on her part and degradation on his. But a sexless, underdeveloped child represented purity and salvation. Levin was not so much Lyova without talent as Lyova sanitised. Levin was amusing when he bristled at the polished fingernails and flashy cufflinks of sybaritic city dwellers, but very serious when he refused to endorse Stiva's shockingly winsome justification of the attraction of 'other women'. Even after a good dinner, he wickedly tells Levin, 'rolls sometimes smell so good you can't resist them'.

Levin delivers a priggish sermon on the superiority of 'platonic' over 'erotic' love, to which Stiva ripostes, 'You want all of life to be made up of wholesome phenomena, but that doesn't happen ... You want ... love and family life always to be one – and *that* doesn't happen. All the variety, all the charm, all the beauty of life are made up of light and shade.'

Stiva lived his life according to that philosophy, unconsciously persuading everyone except Levin of its truth. But Lev baulked at letting Levin approve of 'charm and variety'; he saw them as euphemisms for the wicked things in his diaries. No doubt Lev, like Levin, had 'first imagined to himself a family, *and then* the woman who would give him that family', and had thought of the life led by his dead parents as 'ideally perfect ...' Levin's future wife was supposed to be a reminder, a repetition of the 'enchanting and holy ideal of womanhood that his mother had been.' The mother whose death had made her life fleshless!

It hit me like a well-aimed kick in the stomach that I must utterly fail to remind him of the saint he had never known. That very day I had arranged to have my hair curled, and not only was I happily imagining how nice it would look, I kept wishing there was someone there to admire me. I even confessed to my diary, 'I adore ribbons. And I would like a new leather belt ...'

It would not do for Lyova to see that page, either.

13

White Boletus and Birch Mushrooms

1876-77

The morning following that revelation I awoke to a crushing sense of inadequacy. The fine spring mornings, fresh and invigorating even through the windowpane, did little to cheer my low spirits.

A few days later, my mood was no better. After breakfast, I went outside to throw crumbs to the hens. Usually I gasped with enjoyment at the bracing slap of cold air, but this day I remained stony, my resentment still building. Lyova must have spent far more time on his precious Kitty than he ever allocated to his flesh-and-blood wife.

Standing alone and motionless in the poultry yard with the tablecloth hanging in my hands, the crumbs already gobbled up, I was stiff with resentment over the important fact he seemed to have missed: he would have been quite incapable of writing his famous novels if he hadn't had the raw material of his own marriage to draw on. Yet he never acknowledged this – just filched basic details from *our* lives and covered them with a romantic gloss, as if icing an unappetising cake.

After Kitty's wedding he had the newlyweds spend eight weeks in the country and then make a trip to Moscow – exactly as he and I had done twelve years before. Moreover, when they came back to 'Pokrovskoe', Levin was in such a difficult frame of mind, Kitty felt that a gulf had opened up between them.

There was certainly nothing invented about *that*.

But my feet were getting chilled. Folding the cloth as I walked, I kicked off my muddy boots at the door, placed the cloth in the kitchen drawer, and went to look in on the children at their lessons. Then I sat down at my own desk. The coast would be clear until evening, Lyova having gone to Moscow the day before to correct some proofs and see a doctor. A month or so earlier, when there was still a good layer of snow on the ground, he had gone skiing and had a fall. He'd hit his head on a tree, and been left with a lump, a scar and severe headaches.

He needed to consult Dr Zakharin. *I* needed to do that skimming thing with the new Part Five I'd copied.

The ordered pages filled by my own regular handwriting could be read rapidly, which made it easier to pick up the – the what? The overtones perhaps? Or were they undertones? Something more than the mere words, anyway. It reminded me of when I taught the children that 'expression' in music lies somewhere beyond the actual notes. Perhaps that was what I was looking for.

One place I might find it was in the part where Kitty was doing some sewing, in particular making the little holes required for *broderie anglaise* with the points of her scissors. (Lyova was amazingly good at getting the hang of occupations you wouldn't expect a man to know anything about; he even had Dolly putting *gussets* in her children's clothes!) Levin is at his desk, bent over the book on agriculture he is writing.

Kitty raises her eyes and looks hard at the back of her husband's head, willing him to turn around. He does so, and they smile at each other. The work stops, and when the servant comes in to announce that tea is served, Kitty and Levin have to jump apart.

It was a charming scene, but there were definitely undertones. After it, Levin sits down beside Kitty, kisses her hand, and wonders why he has been given such happiness; but he also thinks to himself, 'It's unnatural. Too good.' Which wouldn't be terribly significant if the minute Kitty leaves the room he didn't take this criticism a great deal further, dwelling on the conviction that in his present life there is something 'shameful, pampered, Capuan' (Lyova's word for self-indulgence, which in itself was a euphemism for unmentionable behaviour). He reflects that he has never spent his time 'so idly and uselessly'.

And who is the cause of this state of affairs? Why, who else but Kitty! Levin tries to tell himself it cannot really be her fault, but he has to blame someone, and she is only interested in the house, her clothes and her *broderie anglaise*. She doesn't care for farm work, the peasants, music or books. She just sits around, leading Levin into frivolous flirting and kissing that he does not approve of.

But even Lyova knew in his heart that this was not the whole truth. Only a few pages before, he had written that 'Levin was surprised at how she, this poetic, lovely Kitty, in the very first not even weeks but days of married life, could think, remember and bother about tablecloths, furniture, mattresses for guests, about a tray, the cook, dinner and so on.' She has ordered new furniture from Moscow, rearranged rooms, hung curtains, supervised meals and filled the storeroom to an extent that Levin deems quite unnecessary – the same huge number of things for which I had taken responsibility in my efforts to make Yasnaya Polyana comfortable and civilised. Lev had not seen the necessity for these, either, until they proved useful to his novel.

Levin now cannot not make up his mind whether Kitty is too busy (in other words, too immersed in domestic trivia), or too inactive (that is, having the leisure and inclination to lead him astray). He does not approve of either alternative.

If I could resolve this paradox, I might have some hope of making him love me as I loved him. It was obviously something to do with the idea of the devil making work for idle hands. *Broderie anglaise* could be bought by the yard even in Tula, so when Kitty took up the pointless task of making it, she also became playful, provocative, and an embarrassment to Levin. Lyova, anxious to move her on, to ensure she outgrew her coquettishness (her waywardness?), had written:

Levin … did not understand that Kitty was getting ready for the period of activity soon to come, when she would be at one and the same time the wife of her husband, the mistress of her house, and would bear, feed and bring up her children. He did not imagine that she knew this intuitively and, while preparing for the awesome task, did not reproach herself for the moments of idleness and the happiness of love that she now enjoyed, while cheerfully building her future nest.

So these were Lyova's perceptions! All women, that is, women of our class, have one sole vocation – motherhood. Amongst the peasants, gypsies and low life of the city there are other women who are called whores; but there are no whores in society. In society there are only well brought up virgins who tempt men to think unsuitable thoughts but are saved by their own innocence, through which they channel the men into marriage. But as soon as possible they must become virtuous mothers, kept permanently out of harm's way by bearing babies. Between these two states, for a brief and dangerous time, they are playful young wives who think nothing of bringing the seductions of the marriage-bed into the drawing room. At this point they are neither virgins nor mothers, and hence a threat.

But a threat to what?

The answer was not entirely clear, but I suspected that part of it lay, as always, in the diaries. When I read them that terrible first time, I had inevitably fastened on the record of depravity and lust; but now I remembered that although Lev Nikolaevich fell frequently, he rarely did so without a moral struggle beforehand – however brief – and much breast beating afterwards. Didn't that explain why Levin was nervous when Kitty was 'inactive'?

I went again to the gun closet, making sure this time that no one was watching. In Lyova's school many of the younger servants had learned the rudiments of reading and writing, and I could not possibly risk any of them finding what was buried amongst the piles of journals and papers.

The dusty old exercise books were still lying higgledy piggledy on a low shelf. Pulling out the nearest few, I took them to a rickety table and arranged them in chronological order. The earliest was dated 1850, a time when for the third winter running the young Count Tolstoy was living in Moscow. I blew off the dust and opened the notebook with cold fingers, sick in advance at what I would have to look at. But although he began with the claim that the past three years had been spent 'dissolutely', the main thrust seemed to be a determination to return to a set of moral rules he had written out three years previously.

It was imperative to find those.

Scattering cascades of mouse droppings and silverfish, I searched for the 1847 volume and any in between. I kept drawing blanks and getting my hands so filthy I had to wipe them on my dress. It was looking disgustingly grubby when a sudden find justified all the effort and grime: I came across the notebook in which he had set down 'Thirty-nine Rules'. Most of them demanded a puritanical pursuit of industry, diligence and order, only one mentioning physical relations between the sexes – but in this he was adamant: 'Keep away from women. Mortify your desire by hard work. Sacrifice all other feelings of love to universal love.'

That was it. When he broke this rule, as he so often did, he seemed annoyed with himself rather than remorseful, and confident he would not fall again (except on certain occasions that he 'would not look for but would not let pass' …). Instead, he would busy himself with writing, practising music, and looking after his estate.

These minor objectives appeared to go to plan, but not the one crucial goal. In society his aim was to avoid getting drunk, and to play cards only 'in emergencies'; but, in the countryside 'women' remained a problem.

At a distance of twenty-five years these ambitions seemed immature and slightly precious, but they gave me a new view of my husband's commitment to high standards without his having formulated any real idea of how to achieve them. When it came to sexual sins, he was extreme both in his urges and in his shame, and thus blamed the woman. Marriage made little difference: he was similarly disgusted when he succumbed to the 'temptations' posed by his legitimate wife. My pregnancies should have provided a temporary cure, but even this condition could not be guaranteed to keep him from 'swinishness'.

I replaced the notebooks, dusted my hands and locked the door of the gun closet behind me. I knew that my reading of the novel would be irremediably altered in the light shed by the diaries.

Although Lyova was due home that evening, I felt obliged to delay going into the study. I had to fetch the children out of doors for a while. Cooped up in the schoolroom for such long periods, they deserved to feel the thin spring sunshine and see the trees sprouting their green and pink shoots. I requested the governess to release them, and watched them indulgently as they ran around like puppies on the new grass, begging not to have to go back indoors. I smiled as I shook my head, but promised them a game of croquet later on, if they studied hard for the rest of the day.

'We all have to work before we can play,' I adjured them. 'Even Maman!'

Whose task it was to forensically examine the passage in which Levin visits Nikolai, his dying brother. Nikolai was based on Lyova's brother Dmitri, whom I'd never met. I'd had to piece his story together from snippets the old ladies let fall, for even Lev had scarcely seen him since Dmitri left the Kazan house in 1847, at the age of twenty.

A total degenerate, Dmitri had been virtually lost to them long before he died of tuberculosis over twenty years before. Somewhere along the line he had rescued some woman from a brothel and taken her to live with him and look after him, but whether that was before or after he got sick was not clear. The woman had subsequently written from Oryol, where the pair were living, to tell the family that Dmitri was very ill. Aunt Toinette had immediately gone to visit him, taking a good supply of provisions. Soon there had come another letter saying that Dmitri was dying, and perhaps Lev Nikolaevich as well as Tatiana Alexandrovna might want to attend his death. The woman added she was not asking for money – not for herself – but Dmitri needed things, and they had nothing.

Lyova had reluctantly dashed off a note to friends in St Petersburg to apologise for missing some festivity he was invited to, and set off for Oryol.

In the sickroom he felt dreadfully nauseated by the smell of excrement, and irritated to feel himself completely useless. The two women, Toinette and the companion, knew instinctively what to do, but although he often philosophised about death, Lev had no idea how to handle it when it came to the point. He lasted only two days at the bedside, though Dmitri lingered on for some time before breathing his last.

In transposing the scene to his novel, Lyova did not spare either Levin or the provincial hotel in which Levin's brother 'Nikolai' is lying. A soldier in a dirty uniform, smoking a cigarette, does duty as a doorman; the waiter is wearing a filthy tailcoat, and there is dirt, dust and slovenliness everywhere. The sickroom is no better – in fact, it is a great deal worse, given the pungent odours. But none of this disturbs Levin – although he is extremely edgy – nearly as much as the fact that Kitty has insisted on accompanying him. Levin had not wished her to come. 'His wife, his Kitty, would be in the same room with a slut', he had thought, meaning Nikolai's companion and carer. The very idea caused him to shudder.

When I first copied out this passage, I'd done so without much reaction: its sensibilities were conventional, even if the moral balance was a little wanting. But now I saw Levin's disdain for the woman as unacceptable. Lyova had not treated Marya Shishkina like that; in fact he had behaved in almost the opposite way. He had disapproved far more strongly of the socially desirable relationship between Sergei and Tanya than the pseudo marriage with Shishkina. What was the difference?

The answer flashed up almost before I had posed the question. Shishkina had six children with Sergei. Lyova would have seen her as redeemed by motherhood, whereas Sergei and Tanya were in that dangerous, volatile and sensual state of being in love; and worse, the usual salvation could not in their case be counted on.

I went back to the deathbed scene with a mixture of curiosity and disapproval.

Kitty is newly pregnant at the time of the visit to Nikolai, but has not announced her condition (although Levin has his suspicions). In the interim, the sight of this emblem of purity performing the disgusting chores of the sickroom side by side with a woman tainted by carnality is a powerful assault on the mental barriers he takes for granted. Yet it is Kitty rather than the other woman who bears the brunt for breaching these exquisite standards – blamed not just for flouting Levin's wish to keep her away, but for threatening his own independence!

> He was displeased with her for being unable to bring herself to let
> him go [to Oryol, without her] when it was necessary (and how
> strange it was for him to think that he, who so recently had not dared
> to believe in the happiness of her loving him, now felt unhappy
> because she loved him too much!) and displeased with himself for not
> standing firm.

Unhappy because she loved him too much …

Here was the essence of my own plight in a nutshell, or rather, in a parenthesis. Lyova was not prepared to state it baldly, and had finished the paragraph apparently unaware that he had admitted the terrible truth about our own marriage. He had also landed himself in a dilemma: outside the brackets, Kitty – nurse and spiritual comforter *par excellence* – remains undefiled by her contact with Nikolai's companion, her virtue and purity symbolised by another retreat to the language of diminutives: she tidies with a *fine* comb the *soft* fragrant hair which grows from a *narrow* parting on her *round little* head, glancing the while at her *tiny* watch.

Kitty is temporarily made a child again in order to show she is not tainted. Yet, astonishingly, this child is carrying another one in her little womb (as the doctor will confirm). No wonder that with two such ethereally purifying states – child-like virginity and incipient motherhood – coinciding in his little wife, Levin is soon able to forgive her her moment of rebellion.

That night Lev Nikolaevich arrived back from Moscow in cheerful spirits because the proofs of the chapters for the *Russian Herald* had not been too badly done, and the doctor had said his head wound would gradually improve without treatment. But rather than being fired up to return to his writing, he seemed impatient to finish the novel and get it out of the way. For the next few months he worked in bursts on the final sections of Part Five, but only for a morning or an afternoon at a time, eagerly casting it aside at the slightest distraction.

I copied his output mechanically. Not caring to probe Anna's rather distasteful pursuit of seduction and adultery, I was impatient for the beginning of Part Six, when I could expect to encounter the Levins again.

Kitty's pregnancy was now public, and progressing normally. The thought of it never leaves Levin for a moment and he experiences a 'new and joyful delight', which he defines as a closeness to Kitty that is *completely free of sensuality*. I snorted with disgust. Kitty has time for only one pregnancy in the timeframe of the novel, but during the course of its writing I had had three real ones, and five before that (without counting one or two early miscarriages). Hardly a record that could be achieved by a husband free of sensuality.

Yet I also had the feeling that Lyova, through Levin, was moving away from his idealisation of family life. The following summer Dolly brings herself and her children to stay at Pokrovskoe because the house on her family estate has fallen into rack and ruin and there is no money to repair it. Levin feels utterly swamped by the Oblonsky clan and the various other visitors; the only guest he really enjoys is his unmarried half-brother Koznyshev, who, I noticed, always seemed to be around during the most significant events of Levin's life. The two of them discuss philosophical issues at great length, not offering Kitty any point of entry into their conversation – in fact leaving her quite out of it. She does not fail to notice the slight.

I wondered who in Lyova's own life was the model for Koznyshev. No one that I knew of. It was more as if – yes! surely that was it – Levin and his brother represented two different aspects of the same person – of Lev Nikolaevich himself! As if he needed two separate characters to express incompatible ideals – 'family happiness' on the one hand, and an austere ascetic life on the other. Delight at Kitty's pregnancy conflicts with his envy of his brother's capacity to rise above the weaknesses that beset him.

No wonder I was infuriated every time I had to transcribe a certain scene that was also a brilliant piece of writing, a simple but crucial passage so masterly it had floored me with admiration – and rage. Nothing much appeared to happen – in fact the outcome was negative – but the surface ripples betrayed profoundly significant undercurrents.

Kitty has invited an unmarried friend, Varenka, to spend the summer at Pokrovskoe. Varenka is a high-minded, spiritual girl who is attracted, and attractive to, Koznyshev. Delighted by the possibility of a match, Kitty manipulates the two of them into going mushrooming together. On the way to the meadow where the mushrooms are to be found, Koznyshev mentally rehearses the little speech in which he will ask Varenka for her hand; Varenka tremulously but joyfully awaits the declaration, preparing her acceptance. Her expectations and his intentions appear to be on the brink of fulfilment.

But the words that come out of Koznyshev's mouth are, 'What is the difference between a white boletus and a birch mushroom?'

And Varenka's lips tremble as she answers, 'There's hardly any difference in the caps, only in the stem.'

The moment has slipped out of their hands, as they both know; but, importantly, there is only one person who is genuinely disappointed, and that is Kitty. This non-marriage, the one that *didn't* happen because both Varenka and Koznyshev were above carnal needs, was clearly my cherished husband's true ideal.

14

Golden Days
1878

It was a great relief to turn from the discouraging results of reading between the lines to the resounding success of the novel as such. The *Russian Herald* published the final chapters at the end of 1877, by which time Lev Nikolaevich Tolstoy, already famous for *War and Peace*, had become a towering figure on the Russian and European literary scene.

But he was still my husband and the father of my six living children, and for more than one reason I needed to do all I could to encourage a sense of family.

On the night of December 31st, I let Seryozha (fourteen), Tanya (thirteen), Ilyusha (eleven), Lyova (eight) and Masha (seven) stay up to see the old year turn over to the new. Only my darling three-and-a-half weeks old Andryusha was asleep, tucked up in his crib. A snow-storm had been raging all the afternoon, the wind howling and the temperature dropping to seven degrees below freezing, but the tiled stove stoked with logs kept the dining room baking hot.

The children, determined not to give in to drowsiness, kept themselves awake by playing cards, but they were forever turning to look at the grandfather clock, willing the hands to crawl on to twelve. Lyova and Masha were drooping badly when at last it tolled twelve sonorous strokes. At the first one I jumped up and sent for two beaded bottles of champagne. Assuring the children that the wine was from the Don region, although the information meant nothing to them, I poured each child a small glass

Scraping snow off the roof was a regular chore after a prolonged snow-storm.

and larger ones for myself and the servants; the children were delighted when the yeasty bubbles fizzed in their mouths.

'It's like the champagne is laughing!' gurgled Masha.

Only their father refused to share the treat. He insisted on toasting the New Year with tea and almond milk, claiming he did not feel well. I suspected he had again succumbed to depression. Or religion. It was hard to say which was worse. The depressions, increasingly frequent during the past year, could be quite alarming, causing him to erupt into violent accusations against the world in general and me in particular. Astonishingly, he seemed to feel worthless both in himself and his endeavours – especially, of all things, in his writings. His inexplicable loss of self-esteem was accompanied by an overwhelming sense of guilt, and in consequence a paralysing fear of death.

As if to ward off these evils, he had been making a sustained attempt to practise religion, but the more effort he put into it the less comfort it seemed to bring him. If anything, it accentuated his anger, for inwardly he remained convinced that the precepts and rituals of Orthodoxy were neither godly nor appropriate. The gulf he saw between his own idea of a simple, basic faith and the self-righteous pomposity of the Church obsessed and infuriated him.

'Only the peasants are without guilt,' he thundered at me and everyone else within hearing, 'because only they have accepted the poverty preached in the gospels, and the humility shown to us by the saints.'

'And because they have little money and less choice,' I muttered, knowing it would be better if he did not hear. But, unable to stifle my point entirely, I added, a little louder, 'Once they get hold of a rouble, straight away they're swilling vodka. They mightn't love money, but they like what it buys. And there's worse than vodka, too,' I finished darkly.

Of course Lev caught my words. 'But their sins will be forgiven because they have faith!' he shouted. 'They are like little children, and of such is the Kingdom of Heaven!'

I held my tongue then, wondering about who waited on whom in Heaven. Lyova was much given to preaching the virtues of poverty, but he still expected Osip to polish his boots, Marfa to serve him at table, and his wife to anticipate his every requirement, whether in the farmyard, the kitchen or the study. Not to mention the bedroom. He regularly smoked cigarettes, hunted animals and ate meat, yet constantly denounced these practices as against his principles. I ascribed the contradictions to the crazily high aspirations to which he seemed driven, but which he could not attain. His maddening inability to live up to his ideals caused him to war with himself, and to take out his failures on the family. The psychology was simple, really, but that didn't make it any easier to put up with.

Nor did it fully account for the scarifying personal disagreements between us. These had lately become more and more frequent, inevitably ending in bitter acrimony and mutual recrimination. I searched constantly for ways around the problem, but found no answers; each time there was an outburst my despair edged me closer to the conviction that he must have done something that made him feel particularly guilty towards me, something really shameful. Yet for the whole of the previous year he had been busy finishing *Anna Karenina*. How could he have found the time or the opportunity to commit some – perhaps *the* – unforgivable sin?

Well, but hadn't there been many occasions when he couldn't write, and disappeared off somewhere without a word to me?

The minute I thought about those absences, frightful, jealous suspicions reared up to play havoc with my nerves. The secret sin that was making his veins stand out and his head pulsate with guilt could only be –

'No! That is the stuff of madness!' I anguished to my diary, appalled at how easily I could succumb to unnameable terror. 'God help me!'

I would go mad, I was sure, if such a thing were really to happen.

'It can't be,' I tried to convince myself. 'He has no opportunity to meet another woman. It's just the uncertainties of this age we live in that are upsetting him. Especially now that he hasn't got his novel to occupy him.'

Certainly it could be argued that Lev's anxieties were stirred by the vast social changes the country was undergoing. Was there anyone not touched by them? I was too busy to have much time for politics, but everyone knew that the disastrous consequences resulting from Alexander II's Emancipation were still with us, even though the legislation had been passed nearly twenty years ago.

'It is better to introduce reform from above than have it imposed on us from below,' Alexander had pronounced. But people still felt that when the old order went, dislocation and chaos had followed. The virtually impossible conditions imposed on the peasants had broken up thousands of rural families, whose sons and daughters and brothers and sisters had been forced to trudge to the cities to find work. All of a sudden there was something Russia had never had before – a whole class of urban workers drawn from the peasant hordes who had previously worked the land. These people laboured twelve hours a day in the new factories and at night slept on bare planks in overcrowded barracks, in which husbands and wives were split up by enforced segregation. Naturally the situation bred protest and talk of revolution. Hotheads urged workers to strike or rise up against their masters, even against the Tsar himself.

To my considerable alarm, many amongst this rabble claimed Lev Nikolaevich as their inspiration – and not, I have to admit, without a certain amount of justification. My husband had always held strong opinions on social justice, but now his views were becoming extreme. So bent was he on the urgency of reform that even before he'd finished *Anna Karenina*, he was decrying as useless and immoral the novels in which we all found so much to love. He'd churned out the final chapters with testy impatience, as though even thinking about them was distasteful, but kept dashing off with ferocious energy a stream of tracts and pamphlets denouncing the monarchy, the nobility, the hypocritical Church and the corruption that perpetuated the whole system. The acolytes who volunteered to distribute his secular sermons flocked by the hundred to Yasnaya Polyana, eager to hear the great man's words and carry his message to the external world.

I was supposed to find food and shelter for them all.

The effort involved in that enterprise would have been reason enough to put me off them, but there were plenty of other grounds for loathing these hangers-on. I usually referred to them as the 'dark ones', because they were poor, dirty and uncouth; I thought their idolisation of Lev Nikolaevich bad for both them and for him; and, most worrying of all, the changes they wanted to bring about were simply illegal, banned in advance by the Tsar. More than once the police came to check up on what was going on at Yasnaya Polyana, which was very frightening and awkward to explain to the children.

Yet religion seemed to be bringing about a few positive changes in Lyova's personal habits. He'd started getting up early, tidying his own room, pumping the water from the well and trundling it to the house in a barrel. He chopped the wood for the house stoves, made his own boots – very badly – and went off to work side by side with the peasants in the fields.

This last was so like what Konstantin Levin had done in the novel that he seemed literally to be taking a leaf out of his own book, leading me to wonder how normal it was for authors to imitate their characters. But admittedly, the scything scene was tremendously powerful, utterly transporting not only of Levin but also of the reader – as I can attest to.

It takes place soon after Kitty has rejected Levin and he is fretting his time away at Pokrovskoe, shooting game and entertaining the occasional visitor but unable to take heart from any of it. One summer morning he decides to help the peasants cut a huge meadow. He finds to his surprise that the heat and sweat of the physical labour are marvellously exhilarating, and that he is truly elated by his camaraderie with the men. He is utterly carried away, and the passage itself glorious to read.

Yet when Lyova did the same sort of thing, I had to make an effort not to dismiss it as pretentious humbug. Perhaps I wasn't being fair. It seemed important to find out where lay the difference.

Checking first that he was still busy in the barn conspiring with some of his dark ones, I scuttled into the library to find that particular instalment in the pile of *Russian Herald*s, and sneaked it off to my desk.

The repetition of certain words and phrases again leapt out at me, but this time they were not diminutives. This passage played a different tune.

> The sweat pouring off [Levin] cooled him down, and the sun, burning his back, head and arm in its rolled up sleeve, lent him strength and perseverance in his work; more and more often he had those moments of <u>unconsciousness</u> when it was possible <u>not to think about what he was doing</u>. The scythe cut <u>by itself</u>. They were <u>happy</u> moments ...
>
> The longer Levin mowed, the more often he felt those moments of <u>oblivion</u> during which it was no longer his arms that swung the scythe, but the scythe itself moving his whole body, full of life and conscious of itself, and, <u>as if by magic, without a thought</u>, the work got done properly and neatly <u>on its own</u>. These were the most <u>blissful</u> moments.

Of course the words were only underlined in my mind, but they added up to something rather staggering. Lyova could pontificate as much as he liked about universal fellowship and the brotherhood of man – the real reason he loved working alongside the peasants lay in that word 'oblivion'. Losing himself in a purely physical activity let him forget the guilt constantly stirred up by his nagging, driven conscience. The absorption in bodily exertion, the forgetting of all else, spelt for him as well as for Levin unqualified relief. Happiness. Bliss. Something approaching the Sublime. I wondered whether he also touched the Sublime when he galloped his horse over the grasslands, or gazed at the night sky, or, particularly, when he wrote. I had no doubt that that was what he was looking for, and not finding, in religion.

Well, it was a noble enough quest, except that *his* oblivion meant *my* being responsible for everything else that was mundane but necessary – the children's education and incessant general requirements, the management of the estate, the feeding of the hangers-on – not just the horrible dark ones, but the usual army of relatives, visitors, house servants and farm workers. Lev's insistence on making his own ill-fitting boots hardly contributed to the overall scheme of things. And when scything or whatever else failed to do the trick, he would simply take off.

In April, as soon as there was a little warmth in the sun, he went to Samara again, to buy yet more land. He certainly wasn't going to invite me this time, nor would I have accepted. I consoled myself with little Andryusha, now four months old. He was a truly adorable baby, a gurgling fount of joy. I also used the time to put the last touches to the L.N. Tolstoy biography, which for so long had hung over me like a dark cloud. It had thankfully become easier when dear Nikolai Strakhov saved me from doing what I first intended – a full account that did not baulk at anything. That fullness was the real reason the project had proved impossible. But Strakhov was preparing an anthology of selected extracts of Lyova's works, and had asked me to provide a short introduction to it. This option allowed me to write a lot less, avoid the difficult issues, and even complete it before

Lyova returned from Samara. It was an enormous relief to get it out of the way.

Moreover, Strakhov warmly applauded my efforts. The minute I finished it, he was able to include my Biographical Introduction in his manuscript and send the whole thing to the Russian Library for immediate publication. But even this emasculated version was too much for Lev. On his return he insisted on vetting it and reducing it even further.

In other respects his trip seemed to have been worthwhile, giving him a new sense of purpose. He made yet another start on his Decembrist novel, and we trundled on towards the end of the year without serious mishap.

By the time our wedding anniversary came around in September – Masha arriving to help us celebrate – I was grateful that everything seemed so pleasant and peaceful. The eve of the anniversary was clear and frosty, the day itself tranquil and glowing with autumn colours. There was no temptation this time to excuse either myself or the children from their lessons; on the contrary, my duties now seemed rather soothing, the routine almost precious. Andryusha had his smallpox vaccination and Lyova and Ilyusha went hunting with the borzois. They brought back six hares – a useful addition to the pot, although these days I was avoiding meat because it gave me indigestion. Lyova's diet depended on external factors. He was still punctiliously observing Church law and therefore practising abstinence every Friday, but thankfully he did not require anyone else to follow suit.

The day following the anniversary, a Sunday, he attended Mass and then went hunting again with Seryozha. I felt entitled to rise late, but once up and dressed and free of interruption, I started cutting out the jackets I wanted to make for the boys.

Just as I was about to leave that task in order to fetch the children from the village where they had gone to buy sweets, our old friend Prince Urusov, now Vice-Governor of Tula Province, called, his gun under his arm. I told him where he would be likely to find the hunters, and pressed him to come back with them for dinner.

We all enjoyed a chatty meal, and then played a twilight game of croquet, which lasted until the fading light made it impossible to knock the ball through the hoops. We trooped cheerfully indoors, where Lyova and the Prince set up the chessboard and the children sucked noisily on their sweets while I read a French novel by Octave Feuillet. Lyova had said he admired Feuillet, and I was keen to discover why. *Monsieur de Camors* told of a man who campaigns, successfully, to seduce the wife of his best friend; after the deed is done, the woman expresses her fear that Camors will no longer respect her. As he doesn't. 'Your charm should lie in your virtue,' her seducer tells her sternly. 'When you lose that, you lose everything.'

No wonder Lyova approved of it.

I snapped the novel shut somewhat savagely, but glancing at the beloved people and tranquil scene around me, I conceded that I had after all enjoyed *two* consecutively happy days. Dare I hope for more?

Reassuringly, morning after morning dawned clear and fine, the beautiful autumn weather enhancing whatever we chose to do. Masha invited her friend Anton Delvig to dinner with his two sisters and afterwards the company danced a quadrille, Lyova providing an accompaniment on the piano. When the dancers collapsed breathless onto sofas, the children's music teacher persuaded Masha to try a violin and piano duet with him, which in turn inspired Lyova to play some of his favourite Weber sonatas. The Delvigs stayed the night and joined in the next day's croquet. The harmony produced by that short visit was a balm to my bruised soul.

It almost seemed possible to believe that this lovely, happy interlude was going to last forever. There were a few incidental hitches, but only of the sort that could be coped with. I developed a headache and my usual inflamed nipples; the baby was sick and restless after another smallpox injection; Masha was irritable and out of sorts; and Lyova, whose writing – whatever it was – was not progressing, went out with the borzois and came back with no bag, a bad temper and a sore back. But on October 1st, the Feast of the Protection of the Virgin, things righted themselves again. Everyone had somewhere interesting to go, except for me, but I took up my sewing and later trailed contentedly around the garden. Life at Yasnaya Polyana, I assured my diary, was peaceful and happy and not at all dull.

Sometimes it could even be exciting! October 4th was Tanya's fourteenth birthday, and we celebrated it with a picnic. Leaves and branches were heaped up into four bonfires, and when the flames were dancing the French tutor, Monsieur Nief, cooked an omelette on one blaze while Seryozha roasted *shashlyks* at another. We ate a great deal, relished the superb weather, played games and had fun, eventually wandering home with the intention of setting up the croquet hoops.

But what should we see as we neared the house but a string of horses and donkeys coming up the road! Purchased by Lyova when he was in Samara, they'd been driven all the way to Yasnaya Polyana. The children were wildly excited, leaping immediately onto the donkeys' backs. The Delvigs and Masha's grown-up son Nikolenka arrived to wish Tanya a happy birthday and everyone drank champagne. It was yet another day of wonderful contentment.

Two days later I was suffering from a swollen cheek and rheumatism all over, but fortunately they cleared up in time for Nikolenka's wedding, at which Lyova was best man. It was a lovely, happy occasion, but two days later we had a terrible row about the Samara properties, which were not bringing in any money. The harvest down there had again been poor, but this didn't stop Lyova from renting some extra land without telling me, and even buying more cattle to put on it. I was furious, both the quarrel and the reason for it leaving me in the blackest of moods.

> I think I have been very ill-used, and I still don't think I have
> done anything wrong, but I hate everything: myself, my so-called
> 'happiness'. It is all dreary and disgusting …

I wrote in my diary. But two days later Lyova and I were such good friends again I vowed, in writing, always and forever to take the best care of him.

Some of our happiest times were in the evenings, when the whole family congregated in the dining room and I or Monsieur Nief read aloud from *Les Trois Mousquetaires*, making sure to omit anything unsuitable for young ears.

Masha had to leave at last, but then Sergei Nikolaevich came over from Pirogova for a few days, in search of a new bailiff. We were strolling through the kitchen garden, he advising me on how to get rid of aphids, when a casual allusion to the letter I had recently received from my sister Tanya elicited a surprising reaction. It seemed to me far more emotional than was called for.

'How is she?' Sergei asked eagerly. 'You know, I can't forget her – I never shall.'

'But Sergei, you made your decision,' I reproved him. 'And it was the right one for the children's sake, even though Marya Mikhailovna ...' I broke off, embarrassed. We still did not socialise with Sergei's wife.

'I know,' sighed Sergei. 'And it's fine as long as I don't see her, your sister I mean, but you know, I once ran into her at the station unexpectedly, and all my old feelings rushed back.'

Recalling how angry I had been with Sergei at the time he jilted Tanya, and how admirably my sister had behaved, though she was inwardly devastated, I felt it only just that the man should suffer a little too. Poor Tanya had never found complete happiness. Reciprocity in love was apparently elusive for everyone. I had experienced enough of it to know how wonderful it was, but I'd also learnt that such moments were fleeting and unpredictable.

It was also utterly unlike the love I felt for little Andryusha, which was unqualified and would, I knew, only grow stronger as he got bigger. But I wasn't in a hurry for that. Just now his happy, toothless grins were adorable, the source of my deepest joy.

Poor Sergei on the other hand remained depressed for the length of his visit, and finally rode off to Pirogova in low spirits.

The golden autumn, which had seemed to hold everything in an enchanted spell, at last began to fail us. In late October it rained, grew cold enough for a snowfall, and then turned warm again so that the snow melted into mud and slush. I conscientiously kept up my diary, but nothing seemed to deserve any special mention. Lyova hunted regularly and continued to plan his Decembrist book; I gave the children various lessons – Russian, French, German, music, scripture – and sewed clothes for them all, even making a christening gown for the baby recently born to Parasha, our cook's daughter. I was happiest of all working in the garden or walking in the forest, but when the dank November fogs came down even these simple pleasures were curtailed. The seasonal gloom brought on my usual pre-winter depression.

We were all longing for the soft, silent snow to blanket the land and a real freeze to ice up the pond so that we could go skating, but the weather remained sullen, humid and grey. For want of other news I recorded the coughs, colds and chills that riddled the family, various items of educational and domestic trivia, local outings, Lyova's daily bag, the children's games and the servants' transgressions. Small rewards and treadmill chores filled in the time without yielding any real joy. Even Lyova's spectacular fall from a horse at full gallop provided no great drama. The horse tripped and twisted its neck, and Lev flew over its head, but both were able to get themselves up and find nothing broken. Lyova walked home leading the horse, and applied a plaster to his side.

A fever, a toothache and a cough then laid me low for three days, but the weather remained the real oppressor. It was still too muggy to even think of snow, and I felt sick at heart – cold, dull, indifferent to everything. Only the arrival of winter with its sparkling frosts and crackling air would bring me back to life.

Sonya, seen here knitting, made nearly all her children's clothes.

Despite a year in which nothing really terrible had happened, and in which there had been some lovely weather and several happy events, my spirits were so low I again fell prey to gnawing suspicions about Lyova. They were far too horrible for me to spell out in my diary; but overall he showed me so little love, treating me to either cold indifference or outraged indignation, I was sure there could be only one explanation. This time he must have another woman.

'The stuff of madness!' I again scolded myself, again sick at heart; but what else could account for his constant, hurtful rebuffs?

15

Tatiana Pushkina
1877–80

Anna's devoted public was insatiable. Three years of greedily devoured instalments appearing every month in the *Russian Herald* had created an audience avid for the bound copy that would form part of the next *Collected Works*. The public appetite was only sharpened by the uncertainties: would the new edition be identical to the one they had read in the periodical, or might it be altered by revisions and add-ons, as *War and Peace* had been? In the case of *Anna Karenina*, it was desperately important for them to know

...

The last instalment of Part 7 reached its dramatic and tragic climax with Anna's suicide, when she threw herself under the wheels of an advancing train:

> And the candle by the light of which she had been reading that
> book filled with anxieties, deceptions, grief and evil, flared up more
> brightly than ever, lighting up for her all that had been in darkness,
> sputtered, grew dim and went out for ever.

Yet oddly, below this, editor Katkov had inserted a brief advisory: 'To be concluded', it said. This threw everyone into a buzz of anticipation, the resulting groundswell of vain hopes and maudlin sentimentality verging, in my opinion, on the hysterical. As the frenzy built up, the readers divided into two opposing camps.

A huge number clung to the hope that the *Herald*'s version did not necessarily constitute the final word on Anna. It seemed possible that the Conclusion might offer a reprieve. I could easily imagine the conversations.

'After all,' one lady might say, 'he tacked those two Epilogues onto *War and Peace,* and we weren't even aware of their existence until the *Collected Works* came out.'

'And when they did, I couldn't read them. They were so boring,' her friend would sniff.

'What he did to our Natasha wasn't exactly boring!'

'Well, no. She became a real drudge. But Anna is a different matter. I couldn't bear it when she died.'

'I wept for weeks! Wouldn't it be wonderful if ...'

On the other hand, the smaller, more prosaic group accepted that all was definitely over as far as Anna was concerned. No less affected by her death, they would cry their eyes out until there was not a tear left, then blow their noses and get on with their lives. They had no interest in a potential Part 8, whose aim could only be to tie up the less interesting ends. Who cared what happened to the minor characters? It was time to move on.

The first, more exercised camp, expressed their feelings in urgent petitions to the *Russian Herald.* The author *must* show that the heroine did not die under the train wheels, but had been saved by – by – well, the details were up to him. Admittedly it was difficult to see how he would manage such a feat, but they were sure that he could do it. And then the wonderful story would have a happy ending and everyone could put away their handkerchiefs.

Deaf to these pleas, my husband did produce a Part 8, but he wrote it the way *he* intended, which did not include restoring the heroine to life. Unfortunately, editor Katkov refused to print it. This decision however had nothing to do with Anna Arkadyevna. It arose out of Lyova's attitude to our government's recent declaration of war on Turkey. With very few exceptions, the country had worked itself up into a paroxysm of patriotism, Lev Nikolaevich Tolstoy being one of the minority who marched to a different tune, his anti-war views inflamed to near treason. He was completely unmoved by the government's Pan-Slavic belief that all Orthodox peoples, irrespective of country, were brothers under the skin. We had long given military support to Bulgaria's efforts to ward off Turkish incursions, and had backed with Russian money, volunteers and public prayers the various rebellions in Serbia and Montenegro, which were already under Ottoman rule. In April 1877 the situation had come to a head and the government, to the cheers of the vast majority of the people, had officially opened hostilities.

Lyova was deeply opposed to the heroics of nationalism. In the novel he let Koznyshev mouth some earnestly patriotic arguments, but made Levin speak firmly against them; however, their debate allowed him to claim an even hand and make use of the war in other ways, such as providing an exit for some of the male characters. Vronsky marches off to Serbia, his sabre at his side, while Levin stays at home shooting nothing but game birds. Volunteering may have been looked glamorous, but there was little doubt where Lyova's sympathies lay.

'That is the real reason why Katkov won't publish your Part 8,' I told him.

'You think I don't know that?' he answered crossly. 'He tried to make me remove what he called "the more virulent" anti-war passages! As if he has the right to censor me!'

'But a conservative paper like the *Herald* couldn't possibly run some of your views! That's obvious!' I pointed out.

Lev stalked from the room, but Katkov proved me right by setting out the situation in his May number:

> In the previous issue the words 'to be concluded' were inserted at the
> end of the novel *Anna Karenina*. But with the death of the heroine the
> novel proper finished. According to the author's plan a short epilogue
> of a couple of printer's sheets was to follow, from which readers

would learn that Vronsky, grief-stricken and bewildered after Anna's death, left for Serbia as a volunteer, that all the others were alive and well, while Levin remained in the country, angry with the Slavonic committees and the volunteers. The author will perhaps develop these chapters for a special edition of the novel.

Lyova, not at all pleased with Katkov's explanation or suggestion, wrote sarcastically to the editor of a rival periodical, *New Time*:

> The masterly exposition of the last unpublished part of Anna Karenina makes one regret the fact that for three years the editor of *The Russian Herald* allotted so much space in his journal to this novel. With the same laconic gracefulness he could have recounted the whole novel in no more than ten lines.

The impatient public knew that they would be unable to read the nineteen short but contentious chapters of Part 8 (rather more than a couple of printer's sheets!) until the fourth edition of the *Complete Works* became available; what they did not know was that this collection would not be printed until *I* had finished my new task of editing them. I was supposed to do this by Christmas 1879, two years after the last instalment in the *Herald* had appeared.

I had never thought of myself as a professional editor, but the prospect (mine alone!) of being able to trace the birth, development and final shape of my husband's brilliant creation was truly a thrilling one. It was not with myself in mind that I had kept every one of Lev Nikolaevich's drafts, amendments and passing thoughts, but with the biography now out of the way I could see no reason not to grasp this new opportunity to become part of Lyova's work. No one else had boxes full of scribbled pages and scraps of paper that would be precious indeed when it came to settling the kinds of question a definitive version would throw up.

Most surprising, and particularly fascinating, were the earliest versions of the character who finally became Anna Arkadyevna. Of course I'd copied these more than once the first time around, but I'd forgotten the earlier incarnations once Anna took her final, definitive form. It was enthralling to be reminded that this beautiful, elegant woman, whose name was inscribed in letters of gold in the hearts of thousands of readers, had started out very differently, as Tatiana Sergeevna Pushkina. She had also, briefly, been an Anastasia; but more extraordinary than the name changes were the dramatic transformations in the woman herself.

Lyova's jottings sketched an opening scene in a drawing room in which society people were discussing a notorious couple prior to their arrival. Reference was to be made to the wife's mocking eyes and diabolical (!) face. When this 'heroine' finally makes her entrance, she turns out to be very plain, with a narrow, low forehead, a short, snub nose, and a too-plump, dumpy figure – in fact so unappealing is she that 'a little more, and she would have been monstrous'! Even worse, her dress is bold and provocative, her neckline more décolleté than anyone else's, her voice loud and uninhibited. Far, far removed from the final Anna, she is not just 'vulgar', to use her creator's word, but actually 'disgusting'!

Where did this ugly creature spring from? Who were the potential influences for such an irredeemable character, a woman he'd claimed he intended to make 'pitiable'?

Three possibilities sprang to mind: the first was Lev's own sister Masha, whom we all loved, but who, it had to be admitted, had run away from her rightful husband and had an illegitimate child with a Swedish viscount. Masha had been obliged to remain in Scandinavia until the scandal died down. Then there was Marya Shishkina, an irreproachable mother to Sergei's children, but for many years a 'kept woman'. Finally, and most obviously, there was the wretched Anna Stepanovna Pirogova. But none of these women could fairly be called vulgar or disgusting.

And to all of them Lyova had shown genuine sympathy. In making

Tatiana so unattractive, the desire to repudiate her must have been stronger than he realised. If of course he was conscious of anything at all. It was impossible to guess what went through his mind. But something else came into mine. It was the recollection of a rather repugnant book by Alexandre Dumas *fils* (the less entertaining son of the man who had written the children's beloved *Three Musketeers*), about the relationship between men and women. Lyova had been reading it shortly before he began *Anna*. I had overheard him singing its praises to Strakhov, and seen their eyes bright with approval. Lyova even asked me to copy out a few marked passages from it that he was going to put into Levin's mouth. In the end he did not use them, but I knew the discarded drafts would be somewhere in the boxes, if I scrabbled for long enough.

The retrieved pages were even more judgmental than I recalled. In Dumas' view, woman was a weak creature whose only salvation lay in fidelity to family life. If she 'lapsed', her (morally superior) husband should try to forgive her, but only the first time. If she persisted in infidelity or remained unrepentant, his role was not only to judge her, but *literally* to execute justice. It was his duty to kill her!

I was horrified. I rushed outside and ran without thinking in the direction of the pond. It was an innocently blue day, with fleecy clouds gambolling like lambs in the sky. The water was clear and shining, as though it knew nothing of the black sludge that lay in male hearts. It took more than an hour of wandering about, of letting the breeze cool my hot cheeks and the sun dry my damp forehead, before my anger and disgust abated. I remained tremulous and shaken, but relatively calm, as I began to walk back to the house.

However, at the back door I still felt unable to deal with the nastiness that lay in the study. Instead of confronting my horrors, I snatched up plump little Andryusha from his perambulator pillows and buried my face in his warm neck, breathing in his milky, soapy fragrance; I peeped into the schoolroom and was consoled by the stumbling but clear voice of Ilyusha translating a pretty German poem by Heine; I walked through every room on the ground floor, taking comfort from the sturdiness of the familiar furniture, and the waiting chairs, sofas and cushions.

Only then did I reluctantly and lovingly replace Andryusha on his white pillows and make my way back to the desk.

One of the scraps of paper implied that Tatiana Sergeevna was what the French call a *jolie laide*, a woman not conventionally beautiful yet strongly attractive to men. Another, the one that mentioned the décolleté neckline, delivered a ruder shock. The dress in question was yellow with black trimming! Lyova had clothed the tainted Tatiana in a replica of what I had worn during my first visit to Yasnaya Polyana, at the picnic in Zaseka wood!

It was obviously no coincidence, yet I was nothing like Tatiana. The yellow dress *I* wore was completely suitable for a young girl. I would not deny or regret that in those days various young men had indicated that I was attractive, or that in our intimate relations Lyova found me physically irresistible, our relationship still charged with powerful carnal passion. But his attitude to me in bed and out of it were two different things. I was glad and grateful when he pinned me down and thrust himself into me because I'd been forced to accept that physical desire was the only love I would ever get from him. He never understood that I yearned for a union that was not crudely sexual – and would not result in another child. I had long regretted the lack of emotional fulfilment in my marriage, but never confronted the reason until the yellow and black dress threw it in my face. Now I saw that at some level Lyova identified me with vulgar, sensual Tatiana! He believed that all women were sisters under the skin, *in that way*!

It was a perverted and shocking idea, but not one that was going to stop me editing the Fourth Edition. For my sake, as well as for his.

The next revelation was that not only Anna, but also her husband and her lover were to undergo significant transformations. The original 'Pushkin', Tatiana's husband, was sensitive, generous, shy, and cultivated, the opposite both of his louche wife and of the future dried prune, Karenin; 'Gagin', her lover, enjoyed the same vividly handsome appearance as Vronsky, but was a victim rather than a seducer, a decent man unwillingly drawn into a shameful affair with a lascivious woman.

But, as the heroine shed her vulgarity and grew rapidly in brilliance, beauty and generosity of spirit, her male counterparts moved in the opposite direction. The more distinctly Tatiana metamorphosed into Anna, the more maddeningly did Pushkin/Karenin crack his finger-joints, and the more frequent were the references to his sticking-out ears. Similarly, every draft of the future Vronsky showed signs of increasing venality.

The Anna who makes her first appearance in Chapter 18, stepping off the Petersburg train onto a Moscow stage already well trodden by Stiva, Dolly, Levin, Kitty and Vronsky, is a luminous angel of mercy. The impression she makes on Vronsky, encountering her for the first time, is indelible:

He felt a need to glance at her once more – not because she was very beautiful, not because of the refined and modest grace that could be seen in her whole figure, but because there was something particularly gentle and tender in the expression of her sweet-looking face as she stepped past him. As he looked back, she also turned her head. The shining grey eyes, which seemed dark because of their thick lashes, rested amiably and attentively on his face, as if she recognised him, and at once wandered over the arrival crowd as though looking for someone. In that brief glance Vronsky was able to note the restrained animation that played over her face and fluttered between her shining eyes and the barely noticeable smile that curved her rosy lips. It was as if a surplus of something so overflowed her being that it expressed itself beyond her will, now in the brightness of her glance, now in her smile. She deliberately extinguished the light in her eyes, but it shone against her will in a barely noticeable smile.

Here was a woman endowed with more moral and physical beauty than 'Tatiana' or I, united by our yellow dresses, could ever lay claim to; yet no mention at all is made of what Anna is wearing. I whisked through several pages until I got to the ball scene, where I knew her clothing was described in detail:

> Anna was not in lilac, as Kitty had absolutely wanted her to be, but in a black, low-cut, velvet dress, which revealed her full shoulders and bosom, shaped as if from old ivory, and her rounded arms with their very small, slender hands. The whole dress was trimmed with Venetian guipure lace. On her head, in her black hair, her own, untouched, was a small garland of pansies, and another on her black ribbon sash among the white lace. Her hair was done inconspicuously. Conspicuous only were those wilful ringlets of curly hair that adorned her, always springing out on her nape and temples. Around her firm, shapely neck was a string of pearls.

I felt as though I had lost a race I had not known I was competing in. Once again the outfit was like a semaphore: black velvet, Italian lace, and the ivory bosom symbolising maturity, the artfully simple fresh flowers, inconspicuous hairstyle and single string of pearls, modesty. But the real point was those seductively escaping curls. It was but one step to that whole head of hair cascading down about the ivory shoulders and – yes – the naked breasts and belly. I saw vividly the seductive signal masked by the outward appearance of classical grace. Kitty wanted Anna in a prettier, lighter colour, mauve, but what would an *ingénue* like her understand of the simultaneous allure and restraint of black velvet? Of course, neither she nor many of the readers would grasp the significance of coded colours and wilful ringlets. It was left to me to divine that Tatiana, with her tawdry appearance and lack of morals, and Anna with her enviable elegance veiling unfulfilled desire, held the same sexual attraction for Lyova as did the gypsies and whores of his youth. As did I – at least in bed. We *were* a sisterhood, as far as he was concerned, although some filled the role more obviously than others.

But the 'monstrous' Tatiana had not been hard to get rid of. Lyova's savage pen and black ink relentlessly overwrote her, and replaced her by a woman of shining virtue called ... Anastasia? No, something more simple. Anna.

The work itself and the things I discovered in it forced me to neglect the children for several days, in a way that mere copying, necessarily done at night, never had. By the time the Christmas deadline loomed, they were constantly complaining. The final instalment of Papa's book had been published nearly two years ago, and still Maman didn't have enough time for them.

'Why can't you play with us *now?*' whined the little ones.

'We need you to take us to the shops in Tula,' complained the older siblings. 'We haven't been for ages.'

In the summer I was always trying to urge them out of doors, leading them down to the pond for a swim on a hot afternoon or organising games of croquet during the long, light evenings. But now, with winter already arrived and Christmas so close, it was impossible to make myself available, and they all, with the obvious exception of little Andryusha, grumbled that neither the bleak weather and short days, nor the fact that I was having another baby, were any excuse.

I told them repeatedly that although I had to edit Papa's famous books, the work was far less important to me than they were. It was just that I was in a big hurry to get it all over and done with so that I could enjoy Christmas with them. It was a bore, I said, but the only way to get it done was to shut myself in the study and stay there until I'd finished.

The children remained unimpressed and truculent. Sneaking out to stretch my cramped limbs, I would frantically hug any of them who crossed my path, and several times promised to set aside a whole afternoon for a treat. But they received these efforts coolly, making it clear that they were not taken in.

'What if she *is* tired out with editing Papa's book?' I heard Ilya complain to Seryozha. 'She doesn't have to do it. She's supposed to be a mother.'

'Well, she *is* having another baby,' answered Seryozha. 'That makes her extra tired.'

'And even worse for *us*! Don't existing children have any rights?'

Worse for *me* was the overdue baby's refusal to be born, the waiting exacerbated by my own mixed feelings. I deeply loved every one of my children, yet I was coming to resent each new baby until it was there, nestled in my arms. Before that all-forgiving moment, I would feel overwhelmed and depressed by the prospect of narrowed horizons and reduced activities. Privately, but deeply, I was also embarrassed by my rate of conception, as well as by what gave rise to it.

To add to it all, the weather was frightful; I stared out at the snow-covered wastes and tortured myself with the thought of abandoned infants left out in the deathly cold, the thermometer sinking to more than twenty degrees below zero.

Then, on December 20th, the new baby, a boy, slid out into the white world. We christened him Mikhail, Misha for short. The minute I tucked the tiny, swaddled mite into the crook of my arm, my heart melted, and I doted on the little love. Andryusha, who was now nearly two, might have to share his special role as the light of my life.

Certainly the advent of darling Misha could not possibly be held to account for any part of what had turned out to be another dark year. The quarrels with Lyova were the main cause of my despondency. I hated it when they came out of the blue, without rhyme or reason, but now I had a glimmer of an explanation that left me even more frightened. It seemed to me that Anna could no more quench that hot light shining out from her beautiful grey eyes *against her will*, than Lyova could control his pen. He could not resist making his morally beautiful Anna sexually irresistible, a powerful magnet *to his own lust*. As her unconscious desire escaped like the curls on the back of her neck, his leapt to meet it.

A terrible possibility struck me, yet one that touched on all my current despair. What if a husband were to fall *adulterously in love with a woman born of his imagination, one that he himself had invented?*

I was immediately convinced that it was not only possible, but had already happened. I was defeated by a chimera against whom I could mount no defence.

16

Terrorist Times

1879–82

Often mocked for my notorious stamina, I suddenly ran out of energy. Not only had I signed off and despatched the eleven volumes of the Fourth Edition while organising the Christmas and New Year celebrations for the family, the guests and the entire household, I had during that time given birth to our darling little Misha. He was quite adorable and no trouble at all – other than the usual problems to do with feeding. Many people congratulated me on these simultaneous achievements, and I suppose combining such different activities is something of a feat; but neither the editing nor the baby cost me anywhere near the effort I had to put into coping with my unspeakable suspicions about Lyova. But at least this *abstract* infidelity, if I can call it that, made me realise why the profound union I had so desperately longed for throughout eighteen years of marriage was riddled with underground tunnels, like a mine about to collapse. It was bitter knowledge.

Yasnaya Polyana, still deep in snow, was a world unto itself, but for once I was unable to meet its demands. I just wanted to rest, nurse the baby, and from my bed attend to the stories and entreaties of the children who trailed into my room. It was a comfort that they at least wanted to acquaint me with their day's activities or wheedle permission for some more daring exploit. But when the children were busy and little Misha peacefully asleep beside me, I brooded. I knew this was not healthy – that dwelling on Lyova's betrayal would only inflame my sense of outrage – but I had neither the interest nor the perseverance for sewing or reading. Tossing and fretting until I feared it might affect my milk, I realised I would have to find some distraction. Lyova was deeply absorbed in a series of religious articles, ranging from an idiosyncratic 'What I Believe' to a tub-thumping 'Investigation of Dogmatic Theology'. Neither was a topic I cared for.

Fortunately however, the weather and ten-year-old Lyolya came to my rescue. Like Seryozha and the book for Auntie, a child's simple question yielded unexpected results. Lyolya was one of the least complicated of our children, easy to get on with and good at his lessons. Though named for his father, the only similarity between them was the colour of their eyes; however Lyolya's, though grey, were not small but large and enquiring, under brows so light they were hardly visible, except in summer when his round face was tanned.

'Why don't some people like our Tsar any more?' he was now asking, after confessing that he'd tried to read Pushkin's *Boris Godunov* but found it too hard. I had an idea of what lay behind his query – no one could remain deaf or blind to the unrest in the country, including some recent acts of alarming aggression – but I didn't have a precise explanation. It made me realise how removed I was from life beyond our estate.

'I'd need to do some homework to answer that properly,' I confessed. 'But if you'd bring me up some of the newspapers I didn't have time to read when I was doing the Fourth Edition, we could talk about it tomorrow. There should be a whole stack in the library.'

Lyolya happily complied. With broadsheets all over my bed, I soon discovered that the life of the nation, bowling along towards some unknown destination, seemed to be a mixture of heroics and haplessness. Parts of it were so entertaining – at least from our comfortable distance – that I had to strive to keep a straight face when relating them to my son.

In February of the previous year, the Governor of the Province of Kharkov, Prince Kropotkin, had been assassinated. In March, there had been an unsuccessful attempt to kill the chief of the security police. In April, five shots were fired at the Tsar himself. (This was not the amusing part.)

All these acts led to savage reprisals. The execution of assassins was normal, but now any individual who voiced the slightest criticism of the regime could be arrested and, at best, beaten. In retaliation, a terrorist group had emerged, The People's Will, whose one goal was to rid the country of Alexander II. Dedicated and determined, but of insignificant numbers and woefully inexperienced, they were constantly afraid of being discovered, and thus tended to act too hastily.

Their first three attempts at assassination were a lesson in themselves, although not to Lyolya, who rolled about laughing when I related the story.

As the summer drew to a close, the Tsar was expected to be returning from his holiday down in the Crimea; the conspirators thus devised a plot to lay mines in three different places along the route of the imperial train. (I told Lyolya to bring an atlas so that we could trace its progress.) The chosen locations were Odessa, Aleksandrovsk and Moscow.

In Odessa, one of the plotters took a job as a railway signalman and on the appropriate day secretly placed a bomb on the line. However, the Tsar was either forewarned of trouble or smiled upon by fortune, for he ordered the driver of the carriage in which he was riding to make a detour; when the uninformed 'signalman' detonated the bomb, all he blew up were several wagons of southern-grown strawberries destined for the Imperial kitchens.

'A strawberry jam!' cried Lyolya, clutching his stomach and rolling his eyes in mock distress.

In Aleksandrovsk, another member of the group posed as a leather merchant seeking a new site for his business. Careless of their safety, he and his co-conspirators transported sacks of explosives in a jolting open cart to a hole they had dug near the railway track. According to plan, they joined the fuse wires as soon as the train approached – but the engine and wagons rattled on, unharmed and oblivious.

'So the Tsar was saved again!' I said, looking at Lyolya to see whether he was impressed.

'By a bung connection!' he giggled.

'It might have been divine intervention,' I reproved him, trying to sound severe. 'Anyway, the train was due to enter Moscow the following night. On the outskirts it had to go past a house which a man who called himself Lev Gartman had rented, along with his pretend wife. Her real name was Sofya Perovskaya.'

'Who was she?'

'Well, she was a girl of our class, but she'd been involved in revolutionary activities for a long time. She'd actually been arrested and put on trial, but she was acquitted – let off – and went into hiding for a while.'

'Really? Could a girl do that?' breathed Lyolya, more impressed by her than by the Tsar's escapes.

'Quite a lot of women are involved in that sort of thing these days. Anyway, Sofya came out of hiding in time to join The People's Will. She called herself Mrs Gartman, and she and her pretend husband started digging a tunnel that would end up directly beneath the railway track.'

'To put a bomb there?'

'Of course.'

'Did it work?'

'Wait and see! Before that they were almost discovered, not once but twice! The first time, a surveyor came to inspect the property, because they didn't have enough money to buy it outright and had applied for a mortgage. Sofya just stood there with her arms folded like this, deliberately looking like an idiot (I acted it out, which again made Lyolya explode with laughter) and refusing to let the man in, on the grounds that her "hubby" was not at home.'

'Good on her!' Lyolya cheered.

'Then a few days later a fire broke out in the neighbourhood and the neighbours rushed to help get the furniture out of all the nearby houses. Sofya stopped them from coming in to her house by lifting up an icon and crying, "Desist! Desist! Let God's will be done!"' (I was really enjoying my own histrionics.)

'Did it work? What's "desist"?' Lyolya was now open-mouthed.

'Yes! They did desist – it means to stop what you're doing – but guess what? If they hadn't, Sofya would have fired a gun at the bottle of nitro-glycerine they kept for emergencies. And if she'd done that, it would have blown up the whole house, along with everyone in it! Including her!'

'Phew! So did they get to plant the bomb? And did the Tsar's train come?'

'Yes, but not when it was expected. On the night, the "Gartmans" crept along the tunnel with the bomb, and set the fuse. Then they crawled back out and waited for the train which was due between ten and eleven o'clock. But just *before* ten they heard something coming. They thought it must only be an advance coach, so they let it pass and waited for the next one; when they heard it coming, they lit the fuse in good time, crept back, and waited for the explosion.'

'The Tsar got blown up?' breathed Lyolya.

'No. Just a whole lot of his servants. The Tsar was safe and sound in the first train.'

Not surprisingly, Lyolya adored these stories, and even I enjoyed relaying the chapter of accidents. It was a pity the newspapers took such a po-faced attitude.

By now the terrorists were desperate, and in the New Year they began to draw up their next plan. In February, a workman called Stepan Khalturin got himself employed as a carpenter in the Winter Palace and managed to place a large amount of dynamite underneath the Imperial dining room. Unfortunately it was not large enough. The floor shook but failed to collapse, while the Tsar, who was running late for his luncheon, missed the entire event. The only victims were several soldiers in the guardroom immediately below.

Lyolya looked rather stricken when I regaled him with this latest failure, but I explained that it was more important for God to protect the Tsar than to worry about his soldiers.

The succession of near misses led the government to establish a Supreme Executive Committee with wide-ranging powers. Throughout 1880 (we were now into current events), hundreds of people suspected of revolutionary aspirations or activities were arrested and tried.

The revolutionaries however were undaunted, still racking their brains to think up new tactics. I could not conceal from Lyolya my amazement when it was reported that they were now under the command of a woman. The new leader of The People's Will was Sofya Perovskaya!

'Sofya!' cried Lyolya delightedly, as though she were an old friend.

We did not of course find out about it until after the event had taken place, but Sofya had devised a two-pronged, fail-safe strategy, which she implemented the following year. The details came out in her trial, which Lyolya and I followed avidly – along with most of Russia.

The Tsar, who had been on the throne for twenty-five years, had formed the regular habit of reviewing the troops of the Michael cavalry barracks every Sunday, always taking the same route there and back. Sofya bought some gunpowder, selected four volunteer bomb throwers, and rented a suitably positioned shop into which moved a 'cheese merchant' and his 'wife'. Suspicious neighbours soon denounced the couple to the police, but an official search revealed nothing more than a lot of cheese and a small pile of newly dug earth in the corner of the storeroom.

'What is this?' asked the police.

'It is well known amongst cheesemakers that a little dug earth keeps the air damp and the product fresh,' answered Sofya, curtseying. The police departed.

The digging of the tunnel continued, but just before its completion another of the revolutionaries was arrested; cracking under interrogation, he told the police everything he knew about potential assassination plots. This made it essential to act before the police started rounding up suspects. The executive committee of The People's Will was panicked enough to make plans for the very next Sunday – March 1st 1881.

Early on the fateful morning, four bombs in brown paper parcels were delivered to a cafe located beside the Tsar's route, while the 'cheeseman' prepared to detonate a mine under the street. No doubt assuming he would perish in the explosion, he was observed making a hearty breakfast of wine, sausage and bread. The four young men who were to throw the bombs also expected to die, because only by hurling them from close range would they have any chance of hitting their target.

That morning the Tsar was warned of the possibility of a plot and urged not to go out. He retorted that he would not be kept a prisoner in his own palace. He even rejected the idea of a police escort, insisting that he had full confidence in the armed Cossack who sat beside the sleigh driver, and the other six Cossacks who trotted after him on horseback. Behind them, nevertheless, came a group of police officers in sledges. And Alexander was persuaded to alter his route, agreeing to take the road beside the Catherine Canal.

The change of plan immediately rendered the cheese shop manoeuvre useless. The 'couple' told the neighbours they would be leaving the next day, and deposited a few coins on the counter to pay for the cat's meat they had ordered.

'They must have been good people, Maman,' said Lyolya, his eyes shining. 'They were honest.'

'Up to a point,' I replied.

Sofya Perovskaya, informed of the new route, assumed, correctly, that the Tsar would also return along the Canal. Reverting to her fallback plan, she planted her bomb throwers, with their brown paper bags, at intervals along the canal embankment. She herself crossed to the other side of the road, from where she could see the cortege approaching. At the appropriate moment she would wave a white handkerchief.

At 2.15 pm the Tsar and his retinue came into sight and Sofya gave the signal. However, the first bomb was thrown a few seconds too late, exploding a little behind the Tsar's sleigh. Against all advice, Alexander got out and walked to the spot where a passer-by had been wounded. 'Thank God I am safe,' he murmured. At that moment the second bomb was thrown, which hit him and killed the man who launched it. The Tsar was wounded in the stomach and legs, his blood gushing into the snow.

'It's cold ... cold,' he whispered. 'Quick ... to the palace ... to die there.' As he did, that same night.

Deeply shocked, the whole country went into mourning and was put under an official state of emergency. The existing widespread police powers were extended to military tribunals and administrative officials. An all-out attack was launched on the assassins in particular, plus anyone else who might be considered a conspirator; five terrorists suspected of involvement, including Sofya Perovskaya, were arrested and accused of regicide.

While we were awaiting the outcome, I became fascinated by a couple of side issues that I did not share with Lyolya. Apparently Sofya and one of the men, Andrei Zhelyabov, had managed against all odds to achieve a brief spell of personal happiness. Falling in love while in custody, they were permitted to live together as man and wife until April 3rd 1881, when they were publicly hanged with three other conspirators. Sofya was twenty-seven; Zhelyabov had been her only love.

Most of the remaining members of The People's Will were either sentenced to death or imprisoned in the cells of the St Peter and Paul prison, below ground level, in darkness and freezing damp, lying on rutted floors swarming with rats. You couldn't help but pity them.

I was even more distressed by another rumour, which claimed that at least two of the female detainees were pregnant when arrested. In one case the baby was taken away as soon as it was born and put in a foundlings' home where it survived no longer than its mother, who died in prison. In the second case, the mother refused to give up her child, clutching it fiercely to her body so that neither rats nor guards could get at it. But I also heard that when prisoners were being moved from one prison to another, the wretches were always shackled, and often so weak they could hardly stand; I did not hold out much hope for either the mother or the child, wherever they were.

These accounts disturbed me profoundly. Much as I longed for a more expansive life, I realised I could never pay that price – the possible sacrifice of my own child – simply in order to take part in political events, no matter how noble the cause. And in any case, contrary to Lyova, I did not agree with them. I was a monarchist.

His views were now getting very worrying. He personally wrote to the new Tsar, Alexander III, begging him not to hang the assassins; and although the famous Tolstoy name lent him some protection, he and I both knew that he was viewed with disfavour in official circles. Oddly, his thirst for religious conformity increased noticeably that year. He gave up hunting and smoking, and constantly criticised the rest of us for being too worldly; in June he made another pilgrimage to the Optina Pustyn monastery. And perhaps he did learn something there, for at the end of the summer he reluctantly agreed to engage in a difficult conversation that I had long wanted to have. It was about necessary changes to the older boys' schooling.

'No doubt we should consider the situation,' he conceded. 'It's probably not very suitable for Sergei and Ilya, or even Lyolya, to go on being taught at home.'

'They should certainly be at a proper high school,' I quickly agreed. Then I hesitated. Lev had conceded my point, but I could not find the courage to spell out its ramifications. Luckily he anticipated them.

'Isn't there someone they can stay with in Moscow?' he asked.

'It's difficult. We can't expect Maman to be responsible for two great boys, especially without Papa to help,' I observed. 'And in any case, I would have to be with them, to supervise their progress. The only solution is for us all to live in Moscow over the winter.'

'You surely don't expect me to buy a house there?' Lyova bristled.

'Not in the first instance,' I quickly conceded. 'I'm sure we could rent a decent enough flat.'

He did not answer, but I knew the battle was won. Later he grumpily accepted the compromise of a rented flat in Prince Volkonsky's house in Denezhny Lane for the coming winter months. The older children were delighted. Sergei, now eighteen, became a student at the university and Tanya enrolled in an art course. With somewhat less enthusiasm, Ilya and Lyolya started at the secondary school a few doors along from where we were renting.

I revelled in the temporary migration. Now, whenever I had a free moment – and without a large house and estate to attend to, there were many more of these – I could visit Maman, socialise with friends, or get hold of tickets for concerts and exhibitions. And having recovered my strength, I found I could also relegate to the back of my mind the horror of Lyova's (abstract) infidelity. After all, the woman *was* dead! In any case, by making her so hateful at the end he had clearly repudiated her, even if the Russian public refused to give up their rose-coloured spectacles. More fools they, from one point of view; from another, their permanent love affair with Anna assured me that the book would bring in royalties for a long time to come.

Being in Moscow unquestionably contributed to a new deterioration in our relationship; the more I enjoyed myself, the greater was my awareness that the move was a serious factor (although not the major one) in our profound disagreements. Coming back together from a play at the Maly Theatre one frosty, freezing evening, when during the interval I had earned Lyova's ire by accepting a glass of champagne from a gushing fan of *Anna Karenina*, I forced myself to broach the whole awkward issue.

'Can't you see, Lyova,' I began carefully, 'that although we're only doing this for the sake of the children's education, Moscow has a great deal to offer all of us? It's still the cultural and historical heart of Russia. Petersburg has always seemed cold and bureaucratic to me.'

I thought that this *aperçu* might mollify him, given that it derived directly from his characterisation of the two cities in both *War and Peace* and *Anna*. Moscow was ancient and warm-hearted, full of old wooden buildings and upright families; St Petersburg, only founded in 1703, was a cold and calculating, Western city, built appropriately of stone. It was where the court and the bureaucracy were housed. Both the Rostov and the Shcherbatsky families lived in Moscow, while Vronsky and Alexei Karenin came from Petersburg, which made the point. The only place that was more wholesome and ethical than Moscow was the countryside.

But Lyova would have none of my cajoling.

'No doubt I'll have to adjust to it for the children's sake,' he growled. 'But you should know that this first month here has been the most agonising of my entire life!'

I dropped the subject. How could I not appreciate the domestic comforts, the opportunities for social life, and the rich cultural activities, especially the concerts, that Moscow had to offer? Any woman would. Why did he have to disapprove of everything I enjoyed with every fibre of his rigid, Christian body? Christian! When to his long-suffering wife, this man who had already betrayed her by falling in love with a fictional heroine was increasingly distant and mean, interested only in promulgating an idiosyncratic notion of religion and a dangerous brand of politics! Latterly, in his sympathy with the radicals, he'd been leaning perilously towards socialism!

In the bedroom, of course, nothing changed. On the last day of October 1881, I gave birth to little Aleksei, whom we called Alyosha. To my embarrassment, I had to chalk up my eleventh confinement and eighth living child. But in himself the baby could not have been sweeter.

I avoided my diary: the discord between Lev and myself, although it preoccupied most of my waking thoughts, reflected too badly on both of us for me to want to spell out the problems. All the time we were in Moscow he simply looked for excuses to hive back to Yasnaya Polyana, where, with no one looking over his shoulder, he used his own diary (as I later discovered) to work through various contingency plans. They all

Summer of 1887, Yasnaya Polyana.

anticipated the moment when he would announce that he could no longer bear to stay one more minute in the family home.

I also learnt that he intended as soon as possible to distribute the income from his Samara estates amongst the poor, give the Nikolskoe land to the peasants, and drastically reduce the amount of money available for his own family to live on. He was going to train us to live without servants, and persuade us all to agree to radical new domestic arrangements – the males living in one room and the women and girls in another.

'Sell or give away everything superfluous', he had added. 'The piano, the furniture, the carriages.'

The piano was, oddly, the worst shock of all. Playing or listening to music had always been one of the few pleasures we loved to share. Even the children enjoyed music, especially Seryozha and Tanya, whose squabbles ceased the minute they sat down to play duets. Had my husband no heart? No concern for his own family's innocent enjoyment?

By the end of May 1882, when we were all back at Yasnaya for the summer holidays, glad to relax under a full sun and cloudless skies, it was not too difficult to ignore Lyova's crazier ideas. So far he'd done nothing to implement them. And the late spring weather was so glorious it almost made up for the fact that not much else went right. The minor difficulties of readjustment to country living were swallowed up in the alarm of Ilya's falling

Lev wanted the family to live without servants such as the cook,
Nikolai Mikhailovich, and the older children's nurse, Maria Afanasievna.

terribly ill, with typhoid fever! I was hysterical with anxiety, and furious with Lev's apparent indifference. He seemed hardly to notice, let alone care about, the danger; certainly he did nothing to help me look after the child. He just continued on, cold, distant, and totally absorbed in his own affairs. When, desperate to get some kind of attention, I goaded him into a quarrel, the result was predictably disastrous.

'Don't you want your son to get better?' I reproached him, grabbing him by the arm as he headed unseeing into his study.

'All I want,' he shouted, shaking me off, 'is never to see any of you again! My dearest wish would be to leave you all!'

I still did not believe that he would truly do such a thing, but the fact that at that moment he meant every word was enough reason for terror. How could I continue to exist without his love, without *him*? Why did we have so many problems when all I wanted to do, and did do, was to love him? For the last three years the intensity of our marital disharmony had been extreme, and now, at four o'clock in the morning, after tossing restlessly most of the night in my own bed, to which Lev had preferred the cot in his study, my diary was my only resource. I got up, found it, and taking care to avoid looking at any prior entries expressing foolish love and hope, turned to the blank pages towards the end. There I began to blacken their whiteness with the fears I tried so hard to keep at bay.

August 26th, 1882. 20 years ago, when I was young and happy, I started writing in this book the whole story of my love for Lyova: there is virtually nothing other than love in it. 20 years later, here I am sitting up all night on my own, weeping over that love. For the first time in my life Lyovochka has gone off to sleep alone in his study [this was not exactly true, but who knew who might one day read my confession?]. We were quarrelling about trifles – I accused him of taking no interest in the children and not helping me look after Ilya, who is sick, or make them jackets. But it has nothing to do with the jackets, it's about his growing coldness towards me and the children … I cannot show him how deeply I have loved him for twenty years. It oppresses me and makes him fed up ... I cannot sleep in the bed my husband has abandoned ... The clock is striking four.

I have decided that if he doesn't come in to see me, he must love another woman. [Pause.] He has not come.

But then he did. My spirits soared instantly, but we did not discuss anything.

As morning dawned after a night in which I had had virtually no sleep, I left his warm side to get up and walk through a heavenly cool, clear morning, across grass sparkling with silvery dew, into the woods and down the path to the bathhouse. There I sat for a long time in the icy water, exulting in the miracle of natural beauty all around me.

I truly hoped I might catch a chill and die. It would be the perfect moment, before anything ruined those few hours of bliss. However, it was to no avail; and anyway I had to go back and feed Alyosha, who chortled with joy at seeing me.

The sole entry for the rest of that year, 1882, read:

> September 10th. Aunt Tanya and her family have left for Petersburg.
> And Lyovochka has taken Lyolya to Moscow. Today was the last
> warm day. I went for a swim.

The last warm day meant that it was time to think about the return to Moscow. Rather than go on paying rent, we bought a house in Dolgokhamovnikheskii Street, near the beautiful little Church of the Weavers. With familiarity, we shortened the impossibly long name to Khamovniki Street; and there we continued to lead our up-and-down lives.

17

Publishing 'L.N.'

1883–88

To me, a home of our own made wintering in Moscow doubly attractive. Upstairs there was a sunny little study that I used for my work, but I was happily distracted by social activities both in and outside the house. Visits from old friends of mine were one pleasure, but I was even more delighted when Tanya's lively fellow students from the art school came and went. Feeling gayer and more youthful than I had in years, I threw myself into anything that was offering.

'I shouldn't really spare the time for this frivolity,' I sometimes told myself – but went out anyway, to tea or a concert. It was one way of ignoring the residual shudders over Lyova's 'betrayal'. What else could I do when I still loved him? He did however seem calmer this year, a little less prone to violent rages. Was it because in Moscow I was less dependent on him?

The baby, Alyosha, was a greater worry. I breastfed him for longer than usual, partly in the hope that it might defer another pregnancy, but more because he was not very strong. The backlash came when he turned two, and I could no longer put off weaning him: the pangs of separation I experienced then were almost as painful as my old problems with mastitis. And the contraceptive effect ceased immediately. By the end of the summer that we were of course spending at Yasnaya, I discovered to my shame and embarrassment that I was pregnant for the twelfth time. People would think us worse than rabbits.

It was all the more galling in that Lev was again becoming morose and withdrawn. When he wasn't writing religious tracts or pamphlets extolling the virtues of celibacy(!), he was forever seeking the company of his new and favourite disciple, Vladimir Chertkov, the handsome, sanctimonious son of a rich general, whose one goal in life seemed to be to suck up to my famous husband. The more Lev saw of this man, the more he quarrelled with me, often threatening to leave in order to embark on some kind of ascetic life far away. His clumsy boots planted firmly in the moral high ground, he insisted on signing over into my unwilling hands a full power of attorney regarding everything to do with the estate. Not only did this leave me with the onus and tedium of responsibility for all our financial affairs, the more I delved into the accounts the angrier they made me.

Even the pains heralding my next delivery were preceded by a major quarrel.

'Why do you have to maintain so many horses on the Samara estate?' I asked. 'They yield nothing, and they're terribly expensive to keep.'

This was the truth, and Lev had no answer to it. Furious, he strode out of the house. Outside, he hesitated a moment – I was watching through the window – then turned towards the stables, saddled up, and rode off towards Tula, angrily kicking his horse into a gallop. I went to sit on a bench in the garden; given the circumstances – the contractions had already started when we began arguing, and were now coming more and more strongly – I naturally expected him to relent and ride back to me.

Stung by remorse, he did come up the drive before too long, but on the way he passed two of our sons playing cards with some old peasant men.

'Where is your mother?' he asked.

'Near the croquet lawn,' answered Tanya, who was watching the game. 'Didn't you see her?'

'No, and I don't want to,' he retorted.

Tanya went to find me. After one glance she led me inside, then ran for the midwife. As I went into labour, Lev was packing his bags in preparation for an immediate departure to America. Fortunately, at five in the morning, he returned to round off the altercation, just before our third daughter, Alexandra, came into the world.

'Not one kind word did he say to me,' I recorded after the event. 'I gave [the baby] straight to the *wet nurse*.'

No gesture could better demonstrate my anger and defiance.

After a few weeks of lying in, however, I was itching to resume my professional role in Lyova's life. I begged him to let me bring out a new edition of his novels.

'Novels!' he growled. 'There is nothing good in any of them. Besides, you need money to do that.'

'If you would give me a little to start with, it would soon double!' I retorted. I was keenly aware that our main source of income was not the estates, nor the properties in Samara, and certainly not the religious pamphlets, but his fiction. Its ability to generate roubles was staggering.

Lev knew this too, but he just glared at me, wary and silent.

'All right then, I'll borrow it elsewhere,' I told him. 'The returns will pay off the debt in no time, and after that it will be all profit.'

Lyova still said nothing, but I could tell from his sullen attitude that he was in two minds. 'Making a profit' was in his book a sin, yet he knew how much money was required for the immediate family to live, not to mention feeding the retinue. I decided to take advantage of his silence, going ahead as though there were no objection. As soon as we moved back to Moscow, I found an empty shed near Khamovniki Street and had it converted into a warehouse and office; before long I was going there daily to deal with the editing and proofreading of a Special Edition.

This forced Chertkov to show his true colours. The scoundrel set up a rival publishing house not far out of town, which he called the Intermediary. He deliberately set his prices to undercut mine, on the sanctimonious grounds that he wished to make the works of the great man more available to the masses. I was very angry, and could not refrain from gloating when the police turned up at the Intermediary. They pounced on the printing machine and seized all the copies of Lev's tract 'What I Believe', his radical and idiosyncratic reading of the gospels.

The raid was hardly surprising. Lev's pamphlet was based on the firm conviction that he alone, out of all the commentators in the nineteen hundred years since the Bible was written, understood their true meaning, while the Church, in particular, did not.

Chertkov of course supported him in this – thus shoring up my deluded husband's conviction that the two of them were kindred spirits. Lyova became utterly reliant on the odious, oily fellow, even appointing him his executor and secretary, as well as taking him into his confidence about all sorts of other things. With me, on the other hand, my husband reported himself engaged in 'a struggle to the death'. Before Christmas we had another terrible argument, in which he again threatened divorce, and then went off with Tanya to stay at the house of some friends.

This was hard enough for me to bear; it was as well that I did not at the time see the letter he wrote to Vladimir Chertkov, which read: 'I would terribly like to live with you, and if we are still alive, I shall live with you. Never cease to love me, as I love you.'

My work in the publishing warehouse was a welcome antidote to the resentment and anxiety that haunted me, but the foothold in Moscow was also valuable in keeping me alert to national events. An interest in the political situation had come to my rescue once before – why not again, at a time when I needed any distraction I could find?

We were at Yasnaya for the coronation of Alexander III in the summer of 1883, but friends of Seryozha and Tanya who were staying with us regaled us with tales from the capital. They reported that every single member of The People's Will was now dead, behind bars, or in exile, but many students and intellectuals were forming small groups to discuss the radical ideas of the German Karl Marx. Seryozha was very up in arms when a law was passed in August 1884 abolishing the independence of the universities, and requiring all staff to be appointed by the Ministry of Education. We also heard that fees would rise at the start of the next academic year, and that women's entrance, already highly selective, was to be further restricted. As for the workers, or as Herr Marx apparently called them, the proletariat, their dissatisfactions led to huge strikes in the mills near Moscow.

Two years later my own husband was denounced by the Archbishop of Kherson and Odessa as a heretic! But the Archbishop was a long way away, and Lyova simply shrugged. It certainly didn't stop him writing pamphlets.

Far worse were the personal tragedies with which that year began and ended. In January poor sweet little Alyosha, aged four, died of quinsy, and in November my dear mother, Liubov Andreevna Behrs, passed away in Yalta, where she'd gone to escape the Moscow winter. The intervening months were little better.

As well as coping with the misery of losing Alyosha (or perhaps in an effort to keep busy), I exhausted myself attending to the unwanted responsibilities that Lev had loaded onto me. I was supposed to supervise every aspect of the housekeeping, servants, farm workers, estate and finances at Yasnaya Polyana, but found it all inordinately demanding and difficult. Peasants, for example, would ask me for the use of a horse, but I would have no idea whether an animal was available, because that depended on the requirements of the farm. If I refused the request, though, they would not grasp my dilemma, but scowl and mutter imprecations against me. I protested to my diary:

> It is not my job to manage the farm, I have neither the time nor
> the aptitude for it ... Everybody in this house – especially Lev
> Nikolaevich, whom the children follow like a herd of sheep – has
> foisted on me the role of <u>scourge</u>.

By the time we moved back to Moscow, the government had become so despotic that some of the things they did were deeply distressing. One

Yasnaya Ployana. The estate for which Sonya had 'unwanted responsibilities'.

event was so shocking I had to write it down in my diary: five students in St Petersburg had made some bombs, which they intended to throw at the Tsar on his way back from a memorial service for Alexander II. They were arrested that day, and several more the next morning. *All of them were executed two months later without a proper trial.* (One of those picked up was Alexander Ulyanov, the older brother of the man who was to lead the Revolution under the name Vladimir Ilyich Lenin.)

My personal unhappiness was still so acute that *I* now became the one desperate to leave. Once, nursing Lyova through a serious illness lasting some weeks when a leg injury turned septic, I enjoyed the pleasure of feeling wanted again; but the minute he was well, though walking with a slight limp, he resumed treating me as a milch-cow, constantly demanding money to give to the scroungers that hung around him. In my view, many of them were not even poor, but had learnt that making brazen demands was an easy way of filling their pockets.

Inevitably I retreated whenever possible to Moscow, where I could lose myself in the publishing and see a few congenial friends. But then Lev began dictating to me his new play about peasant life, *The Power of Darkness*. I was thrilled to be creatively involved with him again, and even thought it a good piece, if a little flat. It was certainly a great deal more interesting than his *Critique of Theology*.

Then an influential friend brought *The Power of Darkness* to the attention of the Tsar, who deemed it excellent and ordered that it be performed in all the Imperial theatres. This put Lyova in such a good mood that the winter was on the whole peaceful, though he complained frequently of stomach pains, and our daughter Masha was also ill. Reading *King Lear* to her in bed, I told her how much I loved Shakespeare, even though, I admitted, 'he sometimes does not know when to draw the line – all those brutal murders and innumerable deaths.'

I was also worried about Ilya, to whom drawing any line was an alien concept. He was in Moscow, drifting – drinking vodka, keeping bad company, and hiding most of his doings from me. Without knowing much about them, I was sure that if they were so mysterious, they could not be right.

I even felt out of touch with the younger children, having lost confidence in my ability to teach them anything; and Chertkov, sly and malicious, remained a constant thorn in my side. It did not help that he claimed to enjoy an inspiring spiritual communion with his own wife, whom to our Tanya's chagrin he had recently married, and loudly pitied Lev Nikolaevich for missing out on comparable joy. But Lyova's stomach pains were not abating, and as was so often the case, we were harmonious for as long as I was allowed to look after him.

When the pains failed to improve, he took himself off to the doctor, returning with several injunctions which I wrote down in order to be sure of getting them right:

1) Wear warm clothes.

2) Wear a piece of unbleached flannel around the stomach.

3) Avoid butter.

4) Eat little and often.

5) Drink half a glass of fresh Ems Kanchen or Kesselbrunn water, heated up, three or four times a day i) on an empty stomach, and ii) a quarter-of-an-hour after lunch – and the third an hour before dinner. He should follow this regime for three consecutive weeks, then stop, and repeat again if necessary. It should be as hot as he can drink it without burning himself, hotter than fresh milk.

6) Fight fondness for smoking.

I made sure that he kept drinking the waters as prescribed even when the summer holidays brought us back to Yasnaya Polyana; but privately I thought his anti-Orthodox resumption of meat-eating – suddenly growling a request for meatballs on a Friday! – a more significant factor in his improved health. He was also in a remarkably good mood, having received a letter from an American traveller and writer, George Kennan, who had visited Yasnaya Polyana and published an article about us. Kennan enclosed both the article and some highly favourable reviews of the *Complete Works*, now translated into English. I noticed that Lyova was looking radiantly happy, and frequently heard him exclaim, 'How good life is!'

Meanwhile, to my surprise, I found myself busy with patients other than the family. Hordes of sick peasants with nowhere else to go were knocking at my door, and I could not turn them away. I had considerable qualms regarding my competence as a doctor, but thanks to regular consultations of a manual for home medicine, my reputation grew alarmingly.

There was so much to do I hardly saw the children, yet the feeling of having lost the older ones made me try to keep a close eye on the youngsters. I couldn't ask them to do regular lessons during the holidays, but I insisted they keep up their music and made sure as often as I could that I had time to read the classics with them. Luckily they listened happily to Lermontov's novel *A Hero of Our Time*, a favourite of mine, and exciting enough to keep them all interested. In fact the story was so enjoyable I quite forgave the author his youthful debaucheries, feeling almost ashamed of the disapproval I'd expressed long ago when I was researching biographies. These days I found Lermontov's ideas remarkably mature.

'Apparently as a person he was unpleasant and bilious,' I told the children, 'yet he was so clever, and so *very* far above the average human being. Everybody misunderstood *him*, but *he* saw through everybody.'

I rather felt I had something in common with him.

On midsummer's day the weather at last became warm, enticing me down to Middle Pond for my first swim of the season. The trees around its edge were in full leaf, and the water gaspingly refreshing. Yet I did not enjoy it as much as I expected to, and asked myself why. The answer came swiftly. I was too haunted by maternal concern for Ilya, idling his life away without supervision back in Moscow. I could not enjoy the summer until I had checked on him in person.

It was a relief to find him perfectly friendly towards me and relatively happy, thanks largely to the kindly landlord and his wife who owned the hovel in which he lived; but he was wasting on snacks and sweets – and not eating proper dinners – the money I'd given him to pay off his many debts. Still in love with a girl called Sofya Filosova, who had broken off their relationship, he was living on memories, letters and hopes (at least this was my interpretation). I carted him back for a few days of healthy air and good food at Yasnaya, but he left straight after a brief but successful hunting excursion, when he shot three snipe.

I knew I had to accept that the fledglings had 'flown the nest', but I did not find it easy.

At least there were always visitors, some welcome, others less so. A regular amongst the former was dear Nikolai Strakhov, who was both amusing

The Middle Pond, where Sonya loved to swim.

and engaging, even if his book attacking spiritualism was heavy going and completely unconvincing. His presence could be counted on to make everyone more cheerful, including Lyova, who was drawn into the dining room one evening by the strains of a waltz that Seryozha was playing. My unpredictable husband advanced towards to me.

'Shall we take a turn around the floor?' he asked, to my delight and the children's merriment.

The next day, before dinner, when the air was mild and calm after a morning storm, Seryozha went to the piano again. This time his choice fell on Beethoven's *Kreutzer Sonata*. With the children's music teacher, Iulii Lyassota, on the violin, the two played the piece right through to the end. The rest of us were arrested by its power and beauty, even though we had just sat down to an excellent meal; in silence, without lifting a fork, we gave ourselves up to each richly melodic movement, while the sweet perfume of the vase of roses and mignonette in the centre of the table wafted around us.

'What power!' I breathed when the music finally ceased. 'It expresses every conceivable human emotion.'

Fortunately, I could not foresee that within two years Lyova would write a novella under that very same title, nor that its publication would cause me rage and humiliation. For the time being I revelled in the beauty of the still innocent piece of music, for once appreciating my own life, and thanking God that I had found true *goodness* and *happiness*. After dinner I was able to record some of that in pictures as well as words, making sure to adjust my newly acquired camera to the bright sun.

The stream of visitors remained unceasing. In the less welcome category I placed a former revolutionary called Butkevich, who was invited to tea but stayed for two days. Very dark and very silent, with a squint, a fixed expression and blue-tinted spectacles, he earned my intense dislike by epitomising all I most loathed about my husband's disciples. The effort of being polite to Butkevich soon made me retreat to my diary.

> What unattractive specimens Lev Nikolaevich's disciples are! There
> is not one among them who is normal. And most of the women are
> hysterics. Like Maria Alexandrovna Schmidt, for example, who has
> just left. In the old days she would have been a nun – now she is an
> ecstatic admirer of Lev Nikolaevich's ideas …What peculiar and
> disagreeable people they are, and what a strain they put on our family
> life. And what a lot of them there are too!

Nevertheless, I pasted into the book a flower that Lyovochka had brought me; it withered, dried, and remained stuck to the page, where I found it decades later.

I consciously and thoroughly enjoyed that summer in the country, not only because Lyova was nice to me most of the time (particularly when he heard that *The Power of Darkness* was to be produced in Paris!) but also because its pleasures contrasted so positively with the news from the capital, which was of an unrelieved gloom.

The government crackdowns were getting harsher with every year that passed. Many offences, such as murder and the assassination of officials, were now tried by juryless courts; Justices of the Peace had been dismissed and replaced by Land Captains appointed by the Ministry of the Interior; Jews could only go to the bar by special permission of the Ministry of Justice; a law allowing factory inspectors to lift the ban on night work for women was passed; and the previously independent *zemstva* were brought under state control, and Jews excluded from them.

Yasnaya Polyana managed for a whole summer to seem like a grateful haven, untouched by these outside horrors; but the idyll was about to be shattered by something I could never have predicted.

18

The Kreutzer Sonata
1889–91

On the last day of February 1888, our second son Ilya, whom we feared had lost his way, wed Sofya Filosofova, for whom he had been pining when I visited him in Moscow. She was a sweet-natured girl, and marriage, I believed, was exactly what Ilya needed to settle him down.

One month later, on the last day of March, I gave birth to our ninth son. Ivan, or Vanya as we called him, was my thirteenth pregnancy (not counting the miscarriages) and, thank God, my last baby. I was forty-four, and He was at least going to spare me the embarrassment of having a child and a grandchild of similar ages.

After the exhausting joy of the two events, Lyova retreated to his study, preoccupied with another kind of gestation, a new work of fiction. Within twelve to fifteen months it took shape as a novella he called *The Kreutzer Sonata*. Throughout the process, he asked his daughters rather than me to do the copying.

Unable to see in this slight anything but a deliberate wish to keep me out of his life (I knew nothing about the story's contents then), I was bitterly hurt; the girls were now so much closer to their father than to me that I suffered atrociously from loneliness *within* the family. All the older children were dispersed – in Moscow, Nikolskoe or Grinyovka, Ilya and Sofya's home; and to make matters worse, Lyova again broke off all relations with me. I wished he would fall ill so that I could look after him again and make him feel grateful, but he remained obstinately healthy.

Excluded, I tried to regain some closeness by reading and rereading his diaries, but he came along and discovered me at it. He snatched up the ones I had taken out of the gun closet and put them away where I could not find them, and for some time afterwards spoke to me in a querulous and grudging manner and then only when it was strictly necessary.

'How can he treat me like this,' I asked my diary, 'when I am so open and cheerful with him, so eager for his affection?'

Kept at a distance, I could not then see any connection between his behaviour and what he was writing. It is only now that I have begun to understand that it was the very act of writing that radically disturbed Lev Tolstoy's relationship with me. Writing forced him to plumb his subconscious, where seethed his detestable sexuality, his unforgiving conscience, and the misogynistic conflicts that were the result of this warring combination. Most of the process, I am sure, went on without his being aware of it, even though the subjects he chose, like Anna Karenina, could be guaranteed to throw up emotional turmoil.

As for the novella he was now engaged with, it was clearly triggered by two apparently different, yet connected, experiences. One was a half ludicrous, half unpleasant anecdote related to him by an acquaintance, who, while travelling in a railway carriage, had been forced to listen to an unknown man pour out a crazy, histrionic story about his wife's infidelity with a musician. The other was the far more enjoyable effect of regularly hearing Seryozha and Lyassota play *The Kreutzer Sonata*. The music softened his hard carapace, moved him to tears, and released deep-seated tides of anguish and self-hatred.

The anecdotal germ and the churning human emotions were thrown together as if in a crucible and heated with the fire of his personal frenzy. The result was a white-hot tirade against women, lust, sex, marriage and music. Its loathing and contempt were devastating.

The Kreutzer Sonata begins with a garrulous man, whom he called Pozdnyshev, announcing to a compartment full of train travellers that

Self-portrait with daughter Sasha and daughter-in-law Sonya, married to Ilya, at the Khamovniki house in Moscow.

some years previously he had killed his wife. Before the passengers have had time to recover from this shock, they are held captive to a lurid account of Pozdnyshev's *fiançailles* and marriage: attracted to a girl in a too-tight jumper, he courts her, weds her and takes her away on a honeymoon, which he dubs 'horrid, shameful and dull'. By the time children are born, life has become a regular hell (his word). A violinist visiting the house offers to accompany Pozdnyshev's pianist wife in duets, and the two begin playing together on a regular basis. Pozdnyshev convinces himself they are having an affair, and one day, after pretending that he is going to the country, returns early in order to surprise them. When he bursts in, the two are sitting decorously on the sofa, conversing; nevertheless, Pozdnyshev seizes a scimitar hanging on the wall and brings it down on his wife, killing her; the violinist manages to escape.

Finishing this lurid tale in the autumn of 1889, Lev Nikolaevich remarked that he had felt very happy to be writing fiction again!

'The awareness of life through the recovery of my talent has been restored to me,' he exulted.

I was stunned. I was always glad when he wrote something other than pamphlets, but that story, dramatic though it was, was riddled with outrageous generalisations and sweepingly exaggerated accusations, which, although they came from Pozdnyshev's mouth, were not much different from the most extreme views of its author.

Pozdnyshev shouted: 'As long as mankind exists the ideal is before it, but not of course the ideal of rabbits and pigs, to breed as fast as possible, nor that of monkeys and Parisians – to enjoy sexual passion in a refined manner – but the ideal of goodness attained by continence and purity.'

Lev Nikolaevich wrote in his diary: 'If men were not so bound to women by sexual feeling and the indulgence which results from it, they would see clearly that women (for the most part) don't understand them, and they wouldn't talk to them. Except for virgins.'

What about the example of his own life, I muttered as I caressed the soft cheek of my adorable, sleeping Vanya? I loved both my husband and my child deeply, inordinately even, but I had not sought this last confinement, and the attitudes struck in *The Kreutzer Sonata* became highly embarrassing to me long before the novella was finished.

Its content was not the only offence. I was also irate that Lev had given permission for 800 copies of it to be lithographed in the offices of Chertkov's Intermediary Press, now set up in St Petersburg. Not only did he do this without the work having been passed by the censor, I was about to bring out the latest edition of the *Complete Works,* including a Volume 13, which was supposed to contain *The Kreutzer Sonata.* Now I would have to exclude it until it received an official imprimatur, and then issue that volume separately.

Government approval was finally granted in November the following year, but in the interim I continued to brood over the story's strident and objectionable message. In fact I was so incensed, I wrote an indignant riposte to it. I called my story *Who Is to Blame?* in imitation of the novel by Alexander Herzen, which forty years earlier had also questioned the patriarchal role of husbands. My friends persuaded me not to publish it, which was probably just as well, but I continued to smart with personal humiliation. Yet the readership for *The Kreutzer Sonata* continued to grow, while I resumed my attempts to copy Lyova's diaries in case he removed the rest of them. Unfortunately the exercise only revived the agonising pangs of jealousy, the horror of that first appalling exposure to male depravity, that had shocked me when I was eighteen. Time and distance allowed me a little objectivity, but overall it was a dismal picture.

'A woman wants marriage and a man wants lechery, and the two can never be reconciled,' I wrote in my own diary.

Convinced that men only 'love' women when they are moved by physical need, their affection turning to disgust the moment they are satisfied, I wondered that my own marriage had survived at all. In some ways Lyova's attitude to me was paralleled by the way he behaved with the children. On the rare occasions he happened to feel like it, he would throw himself into playing with them, and enjoy every minute of it. But he never looked after them when they were ill, and habitually sent them packing when he was busy.

To add to my miseries, the public reception of *The Kreutzer Sonata* was becoming distasteful. Readers were quite sure that the story was based on our own private life, and all, even people close to us like Lyova's brother Sergei, and his best friend Dmitri Dyakov, felt horribly sorry for me. According to some Petersburg friends, rumour had it that the Tsar himself had expressed his sympathy! Ashamed and enraged, I decided to have it out with Lev.

There was no difficulty in initiating a confrontation, but as usual it flared up into vicious personal attacks which achieved nothing but mutual bitterness.

Until we managed to patch things up. The usual way.

However, although I was so angry, I was even more displeased to hear that, thanks to our oppressive censorship, the public life of this obnoxious piece was likely to be cut short. I might have my personal reasons for disliking the work, but they in no way encroached on my pride in the man I was married to – Russia's most revered writer, whose fame was spreading well beyond our shores, beyond Europe, even to America! I was therefore outraged when on February 25th the whole of Volume 13 of the *Collected Works* was seized by the police, then banned by the censor. Lev was less upset than I, his interest at that moment having been caught by an article about a vegetarian diet of bread and almonds in a German magazine.

'I am sure that the man who wrote that keeps to his diet in much the same way as Lyovochka practises the chastity he preaches in *The Kreutzer Sonata*,' I noted, rather tartly.

But while making a quick dash to Moscow to investigate the situation, I discovered that eighteen thousand copies of the banned volume had already been printed – so who was supposed to bear the costs for that lot? And at the same time, some articles in Volume 12 had also been queried. Such impudence! Such totally unwarranted interference! But Lev would do nothing about any of it, of that I was sure.

Gradually a plan began to hatch in my head that refused to be dismissed. For the second time in my life I would go to the Imperial Court in St Petersburg and plead mercy for my cherished Lyova. My previous venture, in 1885, an attempt to defend his banned profession of faith, 'What I Believe', and other similar works, had failed because I only succeeded in gaining an audience with the Tsarina. This time I would make sure of seeing the Tsar himself, in person. My husband's writings were above being judged by ignorant, hidebound clerks.

I began to make some enquiries and contact people of influence, but the replies were slow in coming back, and I lost patience. I sat down, composed and despatched my own letter to His Imperial Majesty. But even then, I still heard nothing. No doubt the weather was to blame: it was so cold, windy and snowy that only sledges could be used, making communication difficult.

Finally a letter arrived from the Countess Alexandra Andreevna

Tolstaya, an influential member of the extended family, with whom Lev was in regular correspondence. Alexandra advised that the Tsar did not normally receive ladies, but told me to be patient for another week or ten days in case he agreed to make an exception in my case. The waiting period was made tolerable by Lyova's good humour, which had little to do with my plans to save his work, as my diary recorded.

Lyovochka is in an extraordinarily sweet, cheerful and affectionate mood at the moment – for the usual reason, alas. If only the people who read *The Kreutzer Sonata* so reverently had any idea of the voluptuous life he leads, and realised that it was this that makes him happy and good-natured, then they would cast this false god from the pedestal on which they have placed him!

But not wanting to let it appear that I had criticised him too harshly, I added judiciously,

Yet I love him when he is kind and normal and full of human weaknesses. One should not be an animal. But nor should one preach virtues one does not have.

By the end of March I had still not received my reply from the Tsar, but with the weather improving slightly – the temperature had climbed to seven degrees above freezing – I decided to set off anyway, travelling second class to St Petersburg.

The Kuzminskys having settled in the capital on their return from the Caucasus, I was able to stay in my sister Tanya's house; and it was there that I received the wonderful news that well-connected acquaintances lobbying on my behalf had miraculously succeeded in getting me my audience with the Tsar! I was presented with a document already written in the language of the Court, but above my name, requesting that His Imperial Majesty should allow the banned works to be published, and he himself take over the responsibility of censoring the works of Lev Nikolaevich Tolstoy. I so disliked the tone of the letter I rewrote it my own way:

Your Imperial Majesty,

I make so bold as to enquire very humbly about the audience Your Majesty has so graciously granted me in order that I may bring to Your Majesty's notice my personal petition on behalf of my husband, Count L.N. Tolstoy. Your Majesty's gracious attention gives me the opportunity to specify the conditions under which my husband would be able to return to his former artistic and literary endeavours, and to point out that some of the very grave accusations that have been made against his work have been unfounded, and have stolen the last ounce of spiritual strength from a Russian writer who is already losing his health, but who might still bring some glory to his country through his writings.

Your Imperial Majesty's faithful subject.

Countess Sofya Tolstaya
March 31st 1891

My venture was now looking fairly promising, but most unfortunately the very next day one of the Grand Duchesses died of pleurisy. The court was immediately plunged into mourning for two weeks, wearing black and receiving nobody. Fuming at the delay, I used the time to make an appointment with the censorship committee.

'Why has the whole of Volume 13 been suppressed?' I demanded collectively of this body. 'Some of its contents have already been published in magazines, and there have been no complaints, official or otherwise. Excuse me, gentlemen, but it leads me to wonder whether any of you have even looked at this volume! I cannot help suspecting, my good sirs, that you have all been acting on hearsay!'

I succeeded so well in embarrassing Censor Feokistov that within two days he brought me Volume 13 in person, accompanied by the news that it had now been passed for publication.

Part of my mission had been accomplished, but I was still determined to see the Tsar. In the interim I visited the Theatre Board to argue about royalties, attended two picture exhibitions, went shopping with Tanya, and socialised with several acquaintances. I declined to attend a stage performance by the famous Italian actress Eleanora Duse, pretending I could not afford it, but the real reason was that I felt too impatient to sit through a whole play. I admit that anxiety about whether the audience with the Tsar would or would not come off had me on tenterhooks. Everything now depended entirely on His Imperial Highness.

By Friday April 12th, with Holy Week approaching and no word from the Palace, I could wait no longer. I paid a round of visits to the people who had helped me, and began to plan my departure for Sunday, two days hence. At eleven o'clock that night, just as I had gone to bed, a note arrived informing me that the Tsar invited me to see him at 11.30 next morning, in the Anichkov Palace. Relieved and elated, I started packing, wrote various notes, and went back to bed at 3 am, although I was far too agitated to sleep.

At 10.45 I set off, dressed in my homemade black mourning dress, a veil and a black lace hat.

Arriving at the door of the Palace, I enquired of the young footman in his bright red and gold uniform and a huge three-cornered hat, 'Do you have instructions from the Tsar to receive Countess Tolstaya?'

'I should think so, Your Excellency,' replied the man heartily. 'The Tsar has just returned from church, and has been asking about you.'

I followed sedately as the footman ran up an ugly green-carpeted staircase, bowed deeply, and left me sitting on a couch outside the reception room. My heart was pounding; I was half dead with fright. Reminding myself that the thing to do with a horse driven too hard is to lead it about quietly, I rose from the sofa and walked up and down the antechamber. As this manoeuvre had no effect, I loosened my stays, massaged my chest, and thought of the children.

At last the footman returned, saying, 'His Majesty begs Her Excellency the Countess Tolstaya to enter.'

I followed him into the study, where the Tsar – very tall, somewhat stout, and almost bald but with kind eyes – came to meet me. He gave me his hand and I bobbed a small curtsey, before he apologised for keeping me waiting and moved straight into a conversation about Lev Nikolaevich, enquiring as to the exact nature of my request. I began to recount the history of the banned works, but as soon as I mentioned *The Kreutzer Sonata*, the Tsar interrupted.

'Surely you would not give a book like that to your children to read?' he asked, raising his eyebrows.

'This story has unfortunately taken a rather extreme form, but the fundamental idea is that the ideal is always unattainable,' I replied in a firm voice. 'If the ideal is total chastity, then people can be pure only in marriage. It would make me so happy if the ban was lifted from *The Kreutzer Sonata* in the *Complete Collected Works* ...'

The Tsar replied in his pleasant, melodious, slightly shy voice, 'Yes, I think it might very well be included in the *Complete Works*. Not everyone can afford to buy them, after all, and thus it will not have a very wide circulation. But could he not alter it a little?'

'No, Your Majesty,' I answered decisively, adding only half truthfully, 'He can never make any corrections to his works, and besides, he says he has grown to hate this story and cannot bear its name to be mentioned.'

There followed a more wide-ranging conversation about Lev Nikolaevich's attitude to religion, many questions about the children, and even an enquiry about Lev's disciple Chertkov! This was a difficult moment. One could hardly share one's feelings of disgust and animosity with the Tsar! I moved on quickly to the second issue.

'Your Majesty, if my husband should start writing works of fiction again, and I should publish them, it would be a very great pleasure for me to know that the final verdict on his work rested with the person of Your Majesty.'

The Tsar replied benevolently, 'I should be most happy to do that. Send his works directly to me for my perusal.'

With a further exchange of niceties, a discussion of childhood chickenpox (my excuse for leaving St Petersburg that same day), and an invitation to meet the Tsarina before I departed, the interview drew to a gracious close.

I cooled my heels in another anteroom for a further twenty minutes, then was ushered into the presence of a slim woman, quick and light on her feet, with chestnut hair piled artfully on top of her head and wearing a high-necked, narrow-waisted black woollen dress. The conversation, mostly about our respective children, was conducted in French. It was all very charming, but I was impatient to be off so that I could impart the good news to Lyova.

Back at Tanya's house, I flew up four flights of stairs, prattled to everyone about my success, despatched two telegrams, had lunch and set off to catch the 3 pm train at the Moskovsky Voksal.

Lyova and Dmitri Dyakov came to meet me at the Kursk Station in Moscow on Sunday morning, but unbelievably Lyova was not at all pleased with either my adventure or my 'ingratiating' meeting with the Tsar.

'You've made us take on all sorts of responsibilities that we can't possibly fulfil,' he fumed. 'The Tsar and I have managed to ignore each other up until now; all this could do us a lot of damage, and might have some disagreeable consequences.'

We travelled home in silence, but our mutual hostility was diffused by the arrival of some friends. After dinner everyone went out for a walk, and in the evening we had music. The guests' heartfelt appreciation of my hospitality made me wonder why so many people were warm and charming to me, while my family treated me with contempt, coldness and jealousy.

No one, family, friend or member of the public, had any idea of the real reason for my trip to St Petersburg. It was less about saving Lyova's works than a blow struck for myself. Ever since I was told that the Tsar had said, 'I feel sorry for his poor wife,' I had felt riled and humiliated by the report; the real reason for the journey was to test my personal powers to impress and persuade. I felt quite confident of success, both vis-à-vis the Tsar and in the eyes of the public, calculating that people would think that if I had felt diminished by the story, I could have not pleaded for it. But I had both pleaded and been granted what I asked for; no one could have any excuse for dubbing me a victim.

The other thing the public did not know was that not only had the mission been successful, but the Tsar told Princess Urusova, who told me, that he had found the Countess Tolstaya sincere, simple and sympathetic; he would like to have had more time to spend with her!

Nor was that all. The Tsar had also said he had not realised that she was still so young and pretty.

Much indeed had been achieved.

Sonya believed that Ilya, shown here with three of his children, needed marriage to settle him down.

19

Famine and Finances
1891–94

The summer of 1891 was exceptionally hot and dry. Without rain, harvests failed and thousands died of starvation.

Yasnaya Polyana was parched, but here at least no one went hungry except for its skin-and-bone owner, who kept by choice to an ultra-strict vegetarian diet consisting mainly of bread and fruit, and drank ersatz coffee made from rye. I could understand his rejection of table meat, given the slaughter involved, but why did he refuse the eggs I gathered, whose production it was my job to ensure?

'Our hens are well fed and happy. It's natural for them to lay,' I argued crossly, but to no avail.

The more serious differences between us revolved around two major issues. Although Lyova had passed on all responsibility to me, he still detested being a landowner and was determined to be relieved of everything he possessed; he thought he'd start by giving away all his estates. Secondly, he wanted to release Volumes 12 and 13 of his works as 'public property', so that anyone could print and distribute them.

To both of these notions I expressed objections based on financial concern for the family. I tried to persuade Lev Nikolaevich to simply divide his properties among the children, but Masha, for one, schooled by her father, had no more desire to be a proprietor than he did. And her objection was the least of the complications that I foresaw. As for releasing Volumes 12 and 13, it was a crazy idea. It would only mean that thousands more readers would slaver over *The Kreutzer Sonata* without us getting so much as a kopek. The altercations drained me of the energy to fight.

'Do what you like with them,' I said wearily, in the end. 'Print whatever you want to.'

But given permission to go ahead, Lyova seemed to lose interest; instead, he produced an alternative topic for contention.

He absolutely, point blank, refused to live in the Moscow house ever again. That was final. Dread of his threat being carried out revived my failing resistance.

'How am I supposed to give the boys the education they need here in the country?' I protested. 'And Tanya stands a much better chance of getting married if we are in Moscow.'

Neither of these was the right argument to use on Lyova, as I should have known. But he was more irritated by my threat that if he didn't go, I would also stay behind. In revenge, he made himself sick eating green peas and watermelon. A week later, he told me that he was sending a letter to various newspapers definitively renouncing the copyright on all his latest works.

'But it's so unfair on your family,' I argued, anger again fuelling my opposition. 'It's simply another way of publicising your dissatisfaction with all of us. Especially me!'

'You're only interested in money! I've never met such a stupid, greedy woman!' shouted Lev.

'I have to be interested in it. I feed and keep us all!'

'Yes! Using my money to spoil your children.'

'*My* children! What about your role in that? All you've ever done is humiliate me! You have no idea how to behave to a decent woman! And in any case, you're just as greedy in your own way – greedy for fame, you are, because it feeds your insatiable vanity.'

'Get out! Get out!' shouted Lev, ending the argument.

I ran outside, intending to go to the ravine to throw myself in, but on the way I encountered my brother-in-law, Tanya's husband Alexander; the

Kuzminskys were staying with us for their daughter Masha's wedding. In shirtsleeves and looking uncharacteristically rumpled, Alexander was most surprised to see me wandering around in the dwindling light of an early summer evening. He made haste to explain his own presence.

'I was coming back from Koslovska,' he said, 'intending to take the route through Voronka, but I was attacked by a great swarm of flying ants! I had to run for cover in a thicket and take off my clothes. I waited a while till they were gone, and then set off again. I did not expect to meet you!'

I knew, but did not say, that I was there because God had made it clear that I should not commit the sin of suicide that evening; meekly I accompanied Alexander home. However, when we got there I could not make myself enter the house, deciding instead to stay out and go through the Zaseka wood towards the river, where I could either have a swim or drown myself. I was still half inclined to put an end to it all.

In the forest it was very gloomy, and I was startled by a wild beast

The river in which Sonya could either have a swim or drown herself.

suddenly leaping across the path. Dog, fox or wolf, I still do not know. But I screamed at the top of my voice. The animal ran away, making a great rustle amongst the leaves, and I, my courage deserting me, ran home. But Lyova was not there. I rushed straight up to little Vanya's room. After a frantic hug and a comforting kiss, I went to my own bed but could not sleep. I was far too anxious about Lyova, who must be out there somewhere in the gathering dark.

I went down into the garden and lay in a hammock until I heard him returning. Reassured, I stayed where I was, dozing, until Masha came to call me for evening tea, after which we all read aloud a play by Lermontov titled, appropriately, *A Strange Man*. When everyone else had left the room, Lyova kissed me and promised he would not print the renunciation statement until I understood why he was doing it.

'I will never understand, Lyova,' I answered wearily. 'Just as I shall never understand what you meant by *The Kreutzer Sonata*, that you want everyone to read for nothing.'

'What has *The Kreutzer Sonata* got to do with it?' he asked, tensing.

'*I* thought we were finished with it, too,' I answered, 'but it's been haunting me ever since you talked about your renunciation. I will be humiliated all over again.' I drew a deep breath and resolutely delivered my ultimatum. 'Lev Nikolaevich, I feel I can no longer live with you as your wife!'

'But that's exactly what I want!' he cried jubilantly.

I did not believe him. About anything.

And not without reason. Two days later the renunciation of copyright was definite. I voiced my opposition, but feebly; already crushed by the thought of the new demands that would be foisted on me if our income was drastically diminished, I was ready to give it all up.

'Were it not for the flying ants that attacked Kuzminsky,' I reflected bitterly, 'I might be in the happy position of not being alive on this earth today. I was never so calmly determined about it as I was then.'

Yet I had to ignore the stone on my heart while I organised a game of charades for all the children – our own plus several others – as part of the celebrations for the name day of my niece Masha Kuzminsky, the girl about to be married. As well as sundry parents and relatives, the grown-up audience included some Bashkirs up from Samara, the coachmen, and all of the servants. It was a great success.

Two days later, my diary proclaimed my still volatile emotions, and the deep, unsatisfied longing at the heart of it all.

> July 27th. Terribly dissatisfied with myself. Lyovochka woke me
> up early with passionate kisses … Afterwards I picked up a French
> novel, Bourget's *Un Coeur de Femme* [A Woman's Heart], and read in
> bed till 11.30, which I never do. The most unforgivable debauchery –
> and at my age too! …
>
> Ah, what a strange man my husband is! The morning after we
> had that terrible scene, he made passionate love to me and told me
> that I so overwhelmed him he had never imagined such a feeling was
> possible. But it is all physical – that was the heart of our quarrel. His
> passion dominates me too but I reject it with my entire moral being,
> I never wanted that. All my life I have dreamed sentimental dreams,
> aspired to an ideal union, a spiritual communion, not that.

I was strung out and exhausted, which caused me to keep myself frenetically busy and feel spasmodically suicidal. I had to make all the arrangements for the Kuzminsky wedding, which was to be held at our place, keep my eye on the preparations for the proposed divisions of property, run out into the fields now that it was raining again to gather the copious crops of mushrooms, harvest a colossal number of apples, and get the boys to the tailor to be measured for their new suits. At the same time I assiduously kept up my diary; I felt it particularly necessary to record my occasional flashes of genuine joy unrelated to Lyova.

August 15th. Marvellous weather. The children lured me outside
to pick mushrooms and I was out for 4 hours. How beautiful it
was! The earth smelt heavenly and the mushrooms were so lovely:
shaggy-caps, sturdy brown-caps and wet milk-caps glistening in the
moss. The soothing silence of the forest, the fresh dewy grass, the
bright clear sky, the children's happy faces and their baskets full of
mushrooms – that is what I call real enjoyment!

But such moments had to be set against my resentment of the estrange-
ment between me and my mercurial husband. Outbursts of passion would
be followed by periods of prolonged coldness, then more passion, and more
coldness. When I tried to talk about it with him, it was always the same
reply: 'I live a Christian life and you cannot accept this.'

The end of summer brought to a head the standoff over the transfer
to Moscow. I was adamant that we had to go for the sake of the boys'
education; Lyova could not bear the thought of it. I agreed, icily, that in
that case we would stay, and I would immediately start looking for tutors.
To my considerable distress, Lyova was insistent that I go by myself.

'But that means a complete separation – you wouldn't see me or your
five children all winter!'

Even Lyova did not quite have the heart to retort that that, precisely,
was the idea.

I compromised by accompanying the boys to the house in Khamovniki
Street, getting it cleaned, papered and painted, the furniture reupholstered
and the rooms rearranged. Then I installed a tutor and returned home to
Yasnaya Polyana.

Lyova immediately set off with the two older girls, Tanya and Masha,
to the distant Epifania district, which had been particularly hard hit by the
famine. They intended to spend the whole winter on the steppe, dispensing
potatoes and beetroot. Before I had a chance to decide what I would do, I
received a letter from young Lyolya, assuring me that there was no need

Vanya in Moscow.

for Maman to even think of coming back to Moscow – I would only disturb their studies.

Alarmed at the implications, I immediately started packing for an extended stay in town.

In December Lyova and the girls returned twice to the town house; at the end of the second visit, I decided to leave Tanya to look after the boys while I accompanied my husband back to the starving people in the desolate areas on the Don River.

The weather was so bad we had to transfer from the train to sledges. At our destination, Begichevka, where we lived in one room, we set up a canteen with two other volunteers and doled out food to the starving peasants: a slice of bread with cabbage soup, followed by potato stew or peas, wheat gruel, oat porridge or beetroot. This was repeated in the evening. I heard that there were about a hundred such canteens in the area.

Sonya with Tanya, then thirty-one and still unmarried.

One day, noticing the village priest haranguing his flock, I crept nearer to hear what he was saying. His message was that none of them, no matter how hungry they were, was to accept bread from that infidel Lev Nikolaevich Tolstoy! My husband's public criticism of the government, including letters sent as far as London, had thoroughly incensed the authorities, who were threatening to order us both into exile. In a brief moment of solidarity, we shrugged our shoulders and held our ground, our only reaction being to write letters of self-defence to government ministers and official gazettes.

Nothing came of the threats, and Lev's banned articles circulated widely, if unofficially, but the government continued its campaign of general oppression. They passed a law denying peasants the right to a passport – a document necessary in Russia for any move, however temporary, away from one's place of birth – without the consent of a household elder or a land captain. Non-Orthodox sects were harassed and imprisoned; Jews were forbidden to use Christian names.

Lev Nikolaevich appeared to thrive on his notoriety, but I was profoundly disturbed. I had come to the conclusion that my husband, a basically good man, had been taken over by evil spirits who were making him destroy his children and exert a pernicious influence over those he came in contact with. Above all, they urged him to alienate his wife, while he remained oblivious to his own failings and inadequacies. I resorted to my diary ...

What about his life? He walks, he rides, writes a little, does whatever
he pleases, never lifts a finger to help his family, and exploits
everything to his own advantage: the service of his daughters, the
comforts of life, the flattery of others, my submissiveness, my labours.
And fame, his insatiable greed for fame drives him on ...

Meanwhile, in the capital, on November 1st 1894, Alexander III died of nephritis, one of the very few of our Tsars to expire of natural causes. He was succeeded by his eldest son, the twenty-six-year-old, equally conservative but sadly weak Nicholas II.

20

Vanya and Taneev
1895-98

For the first two days of the New Year a howling snowstorm raged without let-up; the temperature fell to seven degrees below freezing. Most of the children were spending the holidays at Yasnaya Polyana with the result that, incredibly, a scattering of minor complaints amongst them diverted my attention from a real downturn in the health of my frail six-year-old, our darling Vanechka. He and his sister Sasha, four years older, were showing distinct signs of the flu, but both chose to ignore their symptoms, gleefully running around the house and taking no notice of my orders to rest. In contrast, Masha, who was twenty-five and her own mistress, had silently taken to her bed and was refusing to get up.

On New Year's Eve the healthy ones took themselves off to various celebrations. Lev Nikolaevich went with Tanya (then thirty-one and still unmarried) to visit friends at Nikolskoe. Lyolya, twenty-six and suffering from a chronic nervous illness for which he had begun electrical treatment, had been invited to the Shidlovskys. Andryusha (eighteen) was in the country with boisterous, married Ilya, who was probably leading him astray; and Misha (fifteen) had been asked to play his violin at another party. It occurred to me that the lack of an invitation for Masha might have had something to do with her indisposition.

Lyova's absence made the time particularly restful, although I only admitted this publicly in regard to meals. He was now such a committed vegetarian that two dinner menus had to be prepared every day, which was time consuming and annoying. More generally, his preoccupation with the ideals of love and goodness had rendered him even more indifferent to the family, while his lofty renunciation of worldly goods made him critical and disapproving of our perfectly normal requirements.

By January 3rd the older boys had come back, and Vanechka's flu was turning feverish. Already stick-thin, he was rapidly losing even more weight thanks to a stomach upset which prevented him from eating. On the 8th, instead of going to a children's party with the others, he agreed to stay at home, sitting listlessly on my knee. For a while I had to settle him under a blanket on the couch so that I could get the chores done – paying the laundress, giving the labourers in the workshop their orders, receiving a group of servants who wanted leave to attend a wedding, signing documents from the police station about a theft that had taken place while I was in Moscow, and dealing with estate wages and overdue passports. When all was finally in order, I went back to Vanya, giving him and Lyolya a history lesson on the Egyptians, and reading to them from Grimm's fairytales.

The usual crowd of visitors kept coming and going over the festive period, but soon I was devoting my attention solely to Vanya, who still could not eat. He even refused the soft caviar that I went to the market to buy especially for him. But he loved it when Sasha and Misha tried to entertain him by playing a waltz on the mouth organ and violin, his sunken eyes lighting up.

'I would so like to do something very, very well,' he said to me in his shrill, hoarse voice. 'Will you teach me music, please, Maman?'

Of course I promised that I would – but where would I find the time, and he, the strength?

The snow turned to rain, making a sea of mud around the house. Tired of being cooped up, I put on my boots and went outside to check whether the ice on the skating pond had melted. To my horror, coming back, I glanced through a window to see Vanya running about without a stitch of clothing on – just when he had developed a frightening, rasping cough! I stormed inside and shouted at the nurse, who screamed back at me, our angry cries making Vanya burst into tears. Making an effort to calm down, I salved my conscience by giving Misha ten roubles for his name day, and sending the older boys off to the circus in Tula.

Vanya's temperature went up every day around noon now, and he had grown frighteningly pale as well as thin, although I was treating him with quinine. The weather was occasionally beautiful and bright, but always well below freezing, and the frigid nights regularly brought a hoar frost. I added arsenic drops to Vanya's regime and for three days he ran no temperature, which allowed me to dwell on my dissatisfaction with Lev Nikolaevich and his indifference towards his wife and children. I was also irritated with myself – meaning my uncontrollable but stupid outbursts of sentimental passion for my infuriating husband.

One night, as we were going separately to bed, a violent quarrel erupted about whether I could make a copy of his excellent new story 'Master and Man', before he gave it to a publisher. Lyova forbade me to take so obvious a precaution.

'But we must keep a copy, Lyova. Be reasonable! What if the publisher loses the manuscript?'

'It would be no great loss in the overall scheme of things. You just want it for yourself. I can't write anything without you hoarding a copy of it!'

'True! It's a safeguard, and in any case I need a copy if I'm going to do the editing.'

'Which I never asked you to! You just want to take over everything! You suffocate me! I tell you, I can't stand it! I'm going to leave!'

He really sounded as though he meant it.

Frenzied, I ran out of the house in my nightdress, dressing gown and slippers and tore off down the drive. I was the one who needed to leave, not him! Lyova came after me in his pants and waistcoat but without a shirt.

'Come back! Please come back, Sonya!' he bellowed. 'You'll freeze to death!'

'That's what I want,' I sobbed over my shoulder. 'Let them take me away and put me in prison! Or send me to the mental hospital!'

As I ran, I kept falling over in the slush, slowing myself down. Lyova soon caught up with me and dragged me back to the house.

Somehow we smoothed things over, but the next day we were quarrelling again over 'Master and Man', with me getting wild-eyed at his unreasonable stance when I was only trying to protect his interests. Three times I left the house, determined to freeze to death in the woods on Sparrow Hills, but by now everyone was watching me like a hawk. Each time I escaped I was hauled back. I attributed the whole maddening situation to my *limitless* love for Lyovochka, and my restless, passionate temperament.

In the end Lev Nikolaevich gave the story both to me and to Chertkov's hateful Intermediary. I had won a partial victory, but at what price!

During these parental spats, Vanya kept himself amused by putting little labels on his possessions, and writing in his childish hand, 'With love to Masha from Vanya', or 'To Simeon Nikolaevich our cook, from Vanya'. He took down all the pictures from the walls of his nursery, and asked me for a hammer and nails so that he could hang them in Misha's room. Misha was his favourite brother.

Resting a while after his exertions, he asked, 'Maman, is our Alyosha an angel now?'

'Yes,' I replied. 'It's said that children who die before the age of seven do turn into angels.'

'Well, it's my seventh birthday soon,' said Vanya reflectively. 'I had better die before then, so that I can be an angel too. But if I don't, Maman, will you make sure that I die fasting, so that I don't have any sin?'

Next day, when he seemed no better, Masha and Nurse suggested taking him to Professor Filatov's clinic. All three came back in high spirits, saying that the doctor had told Vanya he could eat whatever he liked, and go for walks or even drives. Vanechka immediately took advantage of these permissions, walking a little way with Sasha and afterwards eating a hearty dinner. The relief in the house was palpable.

In the evening Masha settled Sasha and Vanya on the couch and read them *The Convict's Daughter*, a children's version of the English story *Great Expectations*. Then it was time for bed. Vanechka came to kiss me good night. Thinking he looked rather dispirited, I asked him about the book.

'Oh, don't talk about it, Maman,' he burst out. 'It's terribly sad. Estella doesn't marry Pip in the end.'

I took him downstairs to the vaulted room, which we were using as a sickbay. Vanya yawned with exhaustion, then, with tears in his eyes said, 'Oh, Maman, it's back again. That – that – *temperature*.'

I put the thermometer under his tongue, and after a minute read 38.5 degrees. Vanya said his eyes were aching. Realising he was still very ill, I burst into tears.

'Don't cry, Maman,' said Vanya wearily. 'It's God's will. Why don't you read me the fairytale about the crow, the one we didn't finish?'

The next day Vanya developed a sore throat and diarrhoea, and we sent for Doctor Filatov. He diagnosed scarlet fever.

Vanya's temperature went up to forty degrees, and then forty-two; the pains in his stomach were excruciating, and he was barely conscious. We all took it in turns to sit with him, day and night.

Doctor Filatov came again after supper, wrapped him in blankets soaked in mustard water, and laid him in a warm bath, but nothing did any good. The child's hands and feet were cold, and his head lolled.

He died that night, February 23rd, at 11 pm.

'My God! And I am still alive,' I wrote in utter despair.

Lev Nikolaevich described the funeral as 'A terrible – no, not a terrible, but a great spiritual event. I thank Thee, Father,' he wrote, 'I thank Thee.'

But, as he predicted in his next line, I could not see it that way.

It was not only the gaping hole felt by everyone who missed the sweet-natured, lovable child that so badly undid me. I also found utterly unbearable the thought that his absence meant the final end of the dear little nursery world that had been a vital, merry, hopeful undercurrent to the fractured life in our discordant house.

By spring Lev Nikolaevich was able to resume work on a new novel he'd been planning. It was called *Resurrection*. He had more than once vowed never to write any more fiction, repudiating *Anna Karenina* in particular in scathing terms: 'What's so different about describing how an officer got entangled with a woman? There's nothing different about it, and above all nothing worthwhile. It's bad and it serves no purpose.'

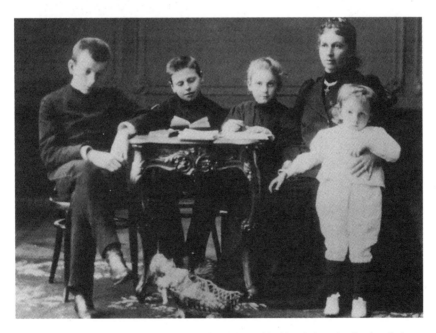

Sofia Tolstoya with her younger children, left to right: Mikhail (Misha), Andrei (Andryusha), Aleksandra (Sasha) and Ivan (Vanechka).

Sonya grieving over a portrait of Vanechka.

But, as with *The Kreutzer Sonata*, an anecdote from out of the blue proved irresistible. His lawyer friend, Koni, had told him a true story about a violated peasant girl turned prostitute, who by coincidence came up for trial before her original seducer, an aristocrat. He, ashamed, offered to marry her ... Once again my husband was seized with the desire to make a gripping story out of a tiny snippet, but his anti-fiction vow stood in the way. He salved his conscience by promising to give the proceeds to the Dukhovors, a banned religious sect who were trying to migrate to Canada.

In between stints of dedication to the new work, Lev Nikolaevich learnt to ride a bicycle and was soon wobbling enthusiastically around the estate. I however was still grieving for Vanya; Tanya took me off on a holiday to Kiev before the summer set in and the southern climate got too hot. I was very pleased to spend time with her, the only one of my daughters I felt close to; but as soon as we got back the usual flock of visitors descended on us, obliging me to look after them rather than nurse my loss.

In August Anton Chekhov, whose country place lay between Tula and Moscow, visited us for the first time. I happen to know that the gentle doctor–playwright with the signature pince-nez had until now avoided

LN learns to ride a bicycle.

a meeting with my husband, but this time he agreed to come to us for a day and a half. On the first afternoon he had what he later described as an audience, rather than a conversation, with Lev Nikolaevich; next morning Lyova read him some chapters of *Resurrection*, but, disappointingly for Lev, Chekhov made little comment.

He came again in September, when a larger audience was treated to a further instalment: as well as Chekhov, there was a neighbour's wife and a musician called Sergei Ivanovich Taneev, who for some time had claimed his place as a family friend. The reality did not quite bear out his presumption. I was fond enough of him, a short, chubby, red-bearded composer and performer with small eyes, a turned-up nose and a high voice, and greatly enjoyed his musical ability; but except for when they were playing chess, he got on Lyova's nerves. And unlike Chekhov, whose visits were never prolonged, Taneev was intending to spend the whole summer at Yasnaya Polyana. Moscow was almost deserted, with no demand for concerts and few pupils requiring lessons, while country houses were full of families and their visitors. Taneev was quartered in one of the wings as a paying guest.

It was I who suggested this arrangement. I was discovering that music was the most effective of all antidotes to grief, and Taneev the best musical companion I could imagine. Although he was only forty, twelve years younger than I, his presence was a balm to the pain I suffered through loss and neglect; he soothed my sadness with gentle sympathy and provided musical distraction to any guest or child who asked.

He returned to Moscow for the winter season, but I of course was there too, with the boys, and saw no reason not to attend as many of his concerts as I could manage.

The next two summers I invited him to stay at Yasnaya Polyana free of charge, in return for regular piano lessons for myself and those of the children who chose to avail themselves of the wonderful opportunity.

However, the situation made Lev Nikolaevich fly into a jealous rage, which was perfectly ridiculous. Regardless of what he might suspect,

Sonya's fondness for the composer and pianist Sergei Taneev caused ructions.

there was no impropriety between Taneev and myself. Sergei Ivanovich simply did his best to make me, a bereaved mother and neglected wife, feel comforted and appreciated.

Lev Nikolaevich, however, wrote in his diary:

> Taneev ... disgusts me with his self-satisfied, moral and, ridiculous
> to say, aesthetic (real, not outward) obtuseness and his 'coq du village'
> [cock of the walk] situation in our house.

When autumn came Taneev returned again to Moscow, and so, of course did I. I attended all his winter concerts, but when he left for the capital to play in their spring music season, I too went to St Petersburg. I could always find a bed in my sister's house, and Lev well knew how much I enjoyed staying with darling Tanya.

Yet this latest visit was apparently more than he could stand. He wrote me a highly aggrieved letter.

It is terribly painful and shamefully humiliating that a total outsider, an unnecessary and quite uninteresting man rules our life and poisons our last years: it is humiliating that one has to ask when and where he is going, and when he is playing at what rehearsals.

This is dreadful – dreadful, painful and disgusting. And it is happening just at the end of our life – a life spent purely and well, just at the time when we have been drawing closer together in spite of all that could divide us.

At the start of the following summer, Lev Nikolaevich baldly announced that this year Taneev was simply not welcome at Yasnaya Polyana, but I failed to pass on his edict. My excuse was that I was preoccupied with another important event, the marriage in Moscow of our daughter Masha to Prince Nikolai Obolensky. Kolya was a long-eared lazybones as far as I was concerned, but we were thankful that Masha had at last found someone who loved her.

I hoped, and feared, that Taneev would simply turn up at Yasnaya. I knew very well that his unannounced arrival would cause Lyova to erupt into fury and rudeness, yet I took no steps to prevent it. And so, what I both dreaded and desired was exactly what occurred. Arriving by prearrangement, as he imagined, to give young Misha a music lesson, Sergei Ivanovich innocently took it for granted that he would stay on for at least a night or two. Lev Nikolaevich was thunderstruck. Amazingly, he contained himself at the time, although rage was written all over his face, but next morning when he confronted me, he was quite out of control.

'I demand that you have nothing more to do with that parasite!' he shouted like a classic stage husband.

But I had secretly resolved that nothing, not even Lyova's anger, would ever make me break off altogether with Taneev. After all, the relationship was guiltless. I answered him with icy reproof.

'You are being ridiculous and unjust. My friendship with Sergei Ivanovich is pure, and far more peaceful than my life with you. You have nothing to reproach *me* with, whereas *you* … and those diaries of yours …'

I was haughty enough not to finish, and Lyova, for once, wise enough to swallow his retort. He took himself off in a huff, while I seized possession of the even higher moral ground by working assiduously on the proofs of his play, *The Power of Darkness*, which was to be incorporated in the next edition of the *Complete Works*. But after a while I decided to go for a swim, and *quelle surprise!*, down at the pool I encountered my friend.

Dinner was as usual at two o'clock. Lyova appeared, but his seat at the far end of the oval table allowed him to confine his conversation to those on either side of him. After the meal Taneev played some of his songs to Tanya, while I listened ardently. I did so adore his calm and noble demeanour. For the rest of the afternoon I divided my time between copying for Lyova and feeling transported by the distant piano, its strains released by Sergei Ivanovich's caressing touch.

Next morning I read some more proofs, then took my mid-morning coffee out onto the balcony, complacently waiting for my friend to join me. After all, he was planning to leave later that day; of course he would want to see me alone before he went. But to my utter chagrin, Sergei Ivanovich failed to show up.

Deeply disappointed, I went out into the garden to communicate with my little saint in heaven, my Vanechka.

'Is there anything wicked in my feelings for Sergei Ivanovich?' I asked him soundlessly. I sensed that in answer Vanechka urged me to draw away from Taneev, no doubt in order to protect his father. But neither did he judge his mother. Vanechka would never do that. After all, it was he who had sent Sergei Ivanovich to comfort me in the first place.

Everyone met again over dinner – Lyova, the older children, Sergei Ivanovich (who had in fact turned up for the coffee session, but a little late), and myself, plus two other guests. The adults followed the meal with a pleasant walk, during which Lyova, aware that Sergei Ivanovich was leaving immediately afterwards, forced himself to converse civilly with him, about art.

Tanya for a while nurtured a secret passion for Anton Chekhov, pictured here with LN.

The wedding of Masha and Kolya Obolensky, which should have been a happy family event, was, I confess, somewhat overshadowed by these dramas. They were married on June 2nd 1897, in Moscow; Seryozha and Tanya attended the ceremony but not Lev nor I. The bridal couple arrived at Yasnaya Polyana the next day, but regrettably I had little to say about them in my diary, compared with everything I needed to pour out about myself, Lyova and Taneev. No doubt Lyova would have been surprised to see the letter that Masha wrote to her friend Leonila Annenkova, on May 8th, giving her interpretation of our attitudes:

> Maman was at first opposed to my marriage, as he is very poor, which is to say that he has nothing, and is slightly younger than me; Papa likes my future husband very much, however, and thinks he is the best person I could have chosen. But he pities me and feels sorry for me, although he will never say what's on his mind, never gives me any advice, and just avoids me ...

Lyova's extraordinary views on marriage were more clearly explained in another letter that he wrote to Tanya a few months after Masha's wedding. Tanya had for a while nurtured a secret passion for Anton Chekhov, whom she had met only twice. But he of course was far too poor, as well as of lowly birth, for us to consider him. Then, at the age of thirty-three, our eldest daughter became involved in a platonic but romantic relationship with Mikhail Sukhotin, a fat middle-aged man, who was charming and witty but saddled with a wife and six children. The wife however was ailing, and when she died two years later, Tanya and Mikhail were able to marry. Both Lev and I regretted rather than celebrated the occasion, because we were sad to be deprived of a daughter we had had to ourselves for thirty-five years. But the letter that Tanya received from Lev during the time she still yearned to be united to Mikhail must have been thoroughly alienating – at least that's what I thought, when she showed it to me.

> I have received your letter, dear Tanya, and I simply cannot give you the answer you would like. I can understand that a depraved man might find salvation in marriage. But that a pure girl should want

to get involved in such a business is beyond me ... As far as being in love is concerned, for either men or women – since I know what it means, that is, an ignoble and above all unhealthy sentiment, not at all beautiful, lofty or poetic – I would not have opened my door to it. I would have taken as many precautions to avoid being contaminated by that disease as I would to protect myself against far less serious infections like diphtheria, typhus or scarlet fever ...

Fortunately this did not put Tanya off, and she and Sukhotin were happy enough together.

But when Sergei Ivanovich went back to town, I could not conceal from myself how acutely I missed him. Trying to shake him out of my thoughts, I busied myself with proofreading, swimming in the pond – sometimes as often as three times a day – tying back the rampant roses, and playing pieces on the piano that I associated with my dear friend. They rekindled the sense of his presence in the room.

At night the moon was bright and stately, its brilliant light making sleep difficult until it faded with the flush of the early dawn. One morning, waking out of a doze, it came to me that life is like a piece of cloth which has to be stretched over something. Sometimes it is too big, and there is a surplus; sometimes there is exactly the right amount to be happy; and sometimes there isn't enough, so that when you stretch it, it tears.

I continued to have dreams about Sergei Ivanovich, and was irritated when Lyova banged away on the piano, in cacophonous contrast to the sweet and delicate music my friend had delighted me with. But mostly there were too many demands and obligations for me to give myself up entirely to my longings.

He of course continued to enjoy all the benefits of ownership – the lovely open stretches where he rode his horse or bicycle, the beautiful garden, the orchards and vegetable beds, and the forests in which he had once hunted. The hard physical work was still done by a bevy of servants, but someone had to oversee them and make responsible decisions, and that person was not their master. It even fell to me to handle rather unpleasant matters, such as dealing with some peasants who had cut down estate trees and used the wood to build their huts (I decided not to tell the village policeman, but to make the peasants pay for the wood with their labour). I was even asked to help an activist woman who'd been exiled to Astrakhan for giving some banned books to a clerk in Tula, although Tanya had expressly warned her not to. I was willing enough to do what I could to help, but had no idea where to start.

Copying, which I always imagined I would make time for, was nowadays less a pleasure than a chore. A nasty, irascible tone had crept into many of Lyova's articles; he was always attacking something or somebody. And when one day I came back from a visit to Nikolskoe, he was so cross at merely seeing me he was outrageously rude – I was mortified by the blatant proof of his complete lack of consideration for me.

'For him to pay me any attention and value me, he has to feel he is in danger of losing my love, or sharing it, even in the most chaste and innocent way, with another man,' I thought. Lyova could not grasp that neither the presence nor the absence of others could ever destroy the affection I had for them in my heart – or do anything to diminish my love for *him*.

A couple of nights later he awoke with an agonising stomach ache. Hearing his fearful groans, I rushed in with linseed poultices, soda water, rhubarb, and clean shirts. Later, when I was finally back in my own bed, I realised how lonely I would be without the man who was my only husband. Even though his love for me was so ruthlessly physical, entirely lacking the emotional intimacy I craved, he was integral to my life, and I knew I simply couldn't live without him.

This mood lasted until I received a cool little note from Sergei Ivanovich, saying he would come on the following Sunday to give Tanya some songs he had written for her. He planned to stay a few days. Lyova's stomach was much better, but I was terrified that rage would make him ill again if I mentioned Taneev's visit. I therefore kept quiet about it, but at dinner,

Sonya and Lev's 40th wedding anniversary, shortly before Sonya finished the proofs of the 14th edition.

Misha gave the game away.

'When Sergei Ivanovich comes, will he be playing any songs?' he asked.

'What? Is he coming again? It's the first I've heard of it,' shouted Lev Nikolaevich, flushing crimson. But he did wait until we were alone before accusing me of lying, and insisting that I absolutely break off all relations with my friend.

'That would constitute an admission of guilt where there is none!' I retorted, turning my back on him.

Lev Nikolaevich was angry, unforgiving and sullen with all the guests in the small group who happened to coincide with Taneev. In the evening Sergei Ivanovich took himself out of the way, pleading a bad headache and making me wonder whether Lyova knew how much upset he was causing with his boorish behaviour. The next day my friend was recovered enough to play two Mozart sonatas exclusively for me. What a special joy that was!

Later that evening and again the following morning he played for everyone, but I alone was moved to tears. 'What nobility, what integrity, what a sense of timing!' I confided to my diary. 'His playing reduces me to sobs.'

When he was not occupied with music, Sergei Ivanovich and I went for several long walks – in Zaseka wood, through the lemon groves, down by the river. At these times Lev Nikolaevich went off on his bicycle.

I suppose he would have been glad to know that a few days later, when I was in Moscow to attend the dentist (I was getting false teeth fitted) I spent an evening with Sergei Ivanovich which did not go at all well. He seemed a little cold, and I was suffering from remorse over the torments I had caused Lyova; perhaps there was also a hint of embarrassment at our being alone together without anyone knowing. At least in the country our walks and talks were on public view.

Then something truly mortifying happened. Ilya told me that my 'intimacy' with the composer Taneev was the talk of the town! Even serious, loyal Seryozha teased me: 'Maman is in her second childhood,' he grinned. 'I shall give her a doll and maybe a china tea set too.'

After that shock, I continued to attend concerts when in Moscow, and Sergei Ivanovich naturally called at the house, but our friendship, which I admit had been intense on my part, began to peter out. Thank the Lord. The good, calm man had been a wonderful help to me after Vanechka's death, and had given me much spiritual consolation. But it was high time to relegate his role in my life to that of concert performer and music teacher.

Meanwhile I had to draw on every ounce of strength to cope with the ongoing strains of life at Yasnaya Polyana. My cranky husband was mostly sleeping in one of the lower rooms, in order, he claimed, not to have to climb the stairs; the bedroom next but one to mine held nothing but a deathly emptiness.

Luckily there was plenty of work to do – we were up to the Fourteenth Edition of the *Collected Works* – but underlying every task to do with my husband's writing there was always my desperate need to come to terms with his determination to estrange himself from me. The half-guesses I'd made during the editing of the Fourth Edition regularly came back to undermine me as I worked on successive printings; each time it happened it became more obvious that in 1879 I had been closer to the full truth than I had been able to acknowledge. Now I was fully convinced that the suspicions I'd once pushed to the back of my mind were perfectly accurate. He had been in love with another woman, who lived in his mind, in his book, and in the sentimental hearts of thousands of readers. It required an effort to accept that I had never really got over this revelation, but once the shock wore off, I felt thoroughly ashamed of my stupidly persistent urge to reach out to him and try to *make contact*. What a fool I'd always been.

And still was.

LN and Sasha on tennis court with visitors.

21

The *Anna Karenina* Proofs

1903

For forty-one years I had wanted only to love my husband and be loved in return. In contrast, the one thing he wanted, or had since he wrote *Anna Karenina*, was to get away from me – even if, to date, he had only threatened to do so.

Yet in my own head I had made some progress. Amongst the huge public who to this day still mourn and adore Anna, there are many, I know, who mock or pity Sofya Andreevna, but not a single person, other than me, has detected the direct link between their beloved heroine and the fissures in the notorious Tolstoy marriage. Perhaps some astute reader or searching critic will one day make the underlying truths of the novel clear to everyone. In the meantime, I, as usual, had no confidante other than a blank-faced diary.

On March 6th 1903 I recorded: 'I have finished the proofs of *Anna Karenina* ...'

Next morning, when a bright sun glittered on the glassy rounds of frozen puddles and the twittering of birds gave hope of an early spring, I reread my brief sentence, decided it was too bald, and dipped my pen to add: 'By following the state of her soul, step by step, I grew to understand myself and was terrified ...'

Terrified of following the same path as Anna? Hardly.

I might have cast myself into various ponds and been rescued from a few snowdrifts, but never had I gone so far as to throw myself under the wheels of an oncoming train.

The real terror was of living with a knowledge almost impossible to swallow, of confronting the unacceptable reason for the fractures in my marriage.

The horror I glimpsed during the Christmas of 1879, when the children were so put out by my absorption in the Fourth Edition, had visited me on and off ever since, for nearly a quarter of a century. There had been times when lovely weather, or family pleasures, or the joys of music had lulled me into a brief forgetting; but then would come that incessant, wearying to-and-fro, as if I were playing a game of tennis from both ends of the court.

– Why did he start with a fiendish Tatiana, then replace her with an angelic Anna, only to turn her into a virago?

The answers were lobbed gracefully back.

– That's easy. He set out to show magnanimity – pity – to a 'fallen' woman, but to his horror he was magnetised by her very sexuality!

– But that is not Anna's defining quality.

– Certainly not at the beginning. He reworked Tatiana like an artist using a lewd model as the basis for the portrait of a well-born lady. He made her increasingly beautiful and good, yes, but that fusion of moral and sexual beauty was even more irresistible.

– And he was not proof against it ...

– No. He fell passionately in love with Anna Arkadyevna, lusting after her with all his usual lack of restraint. But then, furious at his helplessness, he took the only escape, making her hateful, vilifying her. The usual pattern. You know.

– But were the readers supposed to hate her too?

– Oh, yes. But that didn't quite work. Because they always want to remember her as she was at the beginning – elegant, charming, beloved by all.

– Which is why her suicide remains such a tragedy in their eyes?

– Of course. Except that it was no suicide.

– What? She deliberately threw herself under the train! That is made perfectly clear!

– By the author who held the power of life and death over her! The power to make her beautiful or ugly, good or bad, alive or dead. He chose to push her under the train. He murdered her!

– What? Ah! I see ... Because she forced him to 'break his resolution'?

– Of course. Vronsky was his stand-in, but Lev Nikolaevich made sure she perished. She paid the price, but it was *his own sexuality* he was trying to kill. He never understood that. Not that it worked, of course. How many pregnancies were there after Anna? Five!

When I had this conversation with myself, I had been overcome by a hammering in my chest. I had stood up and taken some deep breaths. I had paced around the room – I was in Lyova's study – cluttered though it was. But there was no way I could sit down again at his desk – just looking at it plunged me back into the nightmare. Perhaps I should not after all avoid the children. Their bright faces and inconsequential chatter were probably my best salvation.

It was a dank afternoon, the evening fog already making the unlit passageway dark and chill. But when I opened the door to the dining room, I found it glowing with light and warmth. The lamps were lit, the tiled stove was giving out its ever reliable, baking heat. I drew the dark red curtains and turned around to embrace with outstretched arms the warm and comfortable room, which spoke so eloquently of my dear, cherished family life.

Going back to the door, I called through to the schoolroom, 'Ilyusha! Mashenka!'

Masha appeared in the corridor, her face and pinafore both white in the gloom.

'Come in here where it's warm, *solnichka*! Tell the others to come too. And bring your work,' I urged. 'I want to see you all, and hear what you've been doing.'

I ordered some tea and waited for them to clatter in. Lyolya arrived first with his German textbook, then Masha with a poetry collection.

'Will you hear my poem, Maman?' she asked, pushing past Lyolya. 'It's the one with, "Snow has veiled the sky in mist…"'

'Yes, of course, *solnichka*. And perhaps saying it will make the snow come!' I smiled encouragingly at my daughter.

Ilya came last with his best drawing to show me, but it seemed that Seryozha, who must have been sixteen then, was still out with Lyova; at that time they hunted together nearly every day. Tanya was also absent, spending a few days at the Delvigs, but I heard the poem, admired the drawing and went over the simple German passage with my ten-year-old. Nothing could have been more reassuring. By the time Seryozha rushed in, red-cheeked from the cold and chattering with excitement because he had shot a hare, my black thoughts were banished. They could be ignored until night time, when no doubt they would pinion me again.

The evening, cosy and domestic, was dominated by the children, who made much of the opportunity to criticise their absent sister.

'Why is she always invited to the Delvigs?' pouted Masha. 'They never ask any of us.'

'That's not true,' I demurred. 'They always ask all of you to their parties. It's just that Tanya is old enough to be company for Nadezhda and Rossa.'

'But they're ladies, like you,' objected Ilya. 'Tanya's only fourteen.'

'But they're not married and they don't have any children of their own. They enjoy borrowing her.'

'Well, she needn't give herself such airs about it,' sniffed Masha, flouncing over to the bookcase.

The clock struck nine. Lev Nikolaevich, who had been reading in an armchair, announced that he felt a cold coming on and would go to bed straight away for fear of infecting anyone. For once I felt relieved.

I stayed up with the older children a while longer, reading aloud a sketch I thought might do for their Christmas play; but after they had gone to bed I lingered on in the quiet room. Once I was alone, the thoughts

I had banished would be released like a flock of black bats and I could not bear the thought of dealing with them in my cold, solitary bedroom. Here, with the children's things left untidily about, and the imprint of their little bodies in the cushions, I felt as though they were still with me; certainly the room continued to glow as if with my love for them. Safe in its embrace, I cautiously let a few of the smaller bats circle in my brain.

Whether people realised it or not, the dark side of Lyova's novel began casting its shadow long before Anna's death. It loomed from the moment her seducer, pale, and with trembling jaw, stood over his conquest, 'feeling what a murderer must feel when he looks at the body he has deprived of life'. Even Vronsky, careless and sensual, had felt let down by his seduction of Anna, the spoils of victory yielding only 'one grain of the mountain of bliss' he had anticipated.

The pallor and the trembling jaw were repeated later in the novel, in the heart-wrenching episode of the horse race in which Vronsky was riding Frou-frou, his favourite mare. He genuinely adored this 'gentle, spirited creature', but for the sake of the race, he forces her to gallop beyond her strength. She falls and breaks her back.

Vronsky is devastated. The crash has put him out of the race. Savage with disappointment, he kicks the suffering mare in the belly. The doctor and men from his regiment arrive at a run, but after one glance at Frou-frou an officer draws his gun and shoots her.

It is the second time Vronsky has destroyed a being he treasures.

Was that how Lyova felt at Birulevo? On that night in 1862 my eighteen-year-old body had been awakened by a powerful frisson of sexual response, and even now I surrendered every time to my body's shuddering ecstasies. But hadn't I also, at Birulevo, been terrified of the man standing over me at the bedside? Had Lyova felt like a murderer then?

If so, he would never admit it. It was always his way to pass the blame onto the female, exonerating the male predators in his novel with one excuse. Levin's mother had died, like Lev's, before he was two; Vronsky's was never there, being too involved in the intrigues of the imperial court;

Anna and Stiva were brought up by an aunt. Not one out of the four had been moulded by a proper family life. Levin at least longed to learn about such things, but Anna was the worst of them all – putting on a false front while remaining impervious to the obligations of motherhood. 'For most of her adult life,' Lev had written, 'she had played the partly sincere but greatly exaggerated role of a mother living for her son.'

She was not even interested in the love child she had with Vronsky: 'Everything about this little girl was sweet, but for some reason none of it touched her heart.'

Reliving these chilling *trouvailles*, I sat for a long time in the cooling room, rousing myself only when Misha's hungry wails made my nipples prick. I heaved myself up, unbuttoning my dress as I went along the corridor.

While Misha was sucking, his little hand convulsively massaging the swollen flesh, my thoughts roamed to the part of the novel where Lyova had viciously catalogued the ways in which Anna's inadequate mothering was shown up. It was not simply that she abandoned Seryozha, but that Vronsky rather than she had ordered the fashionable toys and English furniture for Annie's nursery, where the little girl was cared for by a slovenly wet nurse (I smiled grimly at that); that Anna exploited the baby in order to manipulate her lover, but it took Dolly to notice that the child had two new teeth; and, finally, that Anna used contraception to avoid any further pregnancies.

Anna's adulterous brother, on the other hand, with his brilliant looks, feckless charm and wonderful empathy, was surely the secret envy of a creator so 'ugly' that as a boy he had tried to hack off his own eyebrows. I thought about Stiva arriving late at his own party, only to find the guests stiff and awkward, the conversation refusing to flow. Instantly sizing up the situation, he begins to knead 'all that society dough in such a way that the party took off, and the drawing room was filled with animated voices.'

Lyova could occasionally be jolly – I would never forget the name day party in 1866, with lanterns on the veranda and me in a white muslin dress dancing with the officers from Yasenki – but Stiva's unstinting bonhomie flowed without restraint. The dinner following that party was also the one at which the card table courtship took place – without his social lubrication and innate kindness there might never have been a marriage between Kitty and Levin! More significantly, Stiva and Dolly stayed together, where the Karenins broke up and the Levins floundered in the shallows of misunderstanding. Really, naughty Stiva stood charged only with peccadilloes. Like Tanya Behrs when she was young, he got away with the unforgivable simply because everyone loved him; Lyova himself was incapable of painting him black, even when Stiva openly enjoyed good dinners *and* rolls. In fact, I realised, Levin's disapproval of him was a blind, hiding Lyova's envy of other men's freedoms, ones he could not condone because they were also part of himself. They included not only Stiva's foibles, but also Vronsky's voracity and even Koznyshev's asceticism.

No wonder Lyova had been so desperate to finish the novel. It stirred up conflicts he found unendurable. But strongest of all was the compulsion to get rid of the woman who lived out (his own) uncontrollable sexuality. For that, he killed her.

22

Flight
1910

It had never occurred to me that a rival could be anyone but another woman, but finally it became obvious even to my distracted self how far Vladimir Chertkov had insinuated himself into my husband's life. He was now not only the most favoured follower, but my husband's self-appointed publisher, which infuriated me. *I* had always been his most dedicated copier, editor, proofreader and publisher. But Chertkov, motivated by a cold determination to rival me, had founded his own printing press, The Intermediary, and undercut my prices. Moreover, it was to him that Lev now handed over a decade's worth of his diaries, so that Chertkov could publish some of the choicest extracts.

At first they kept these activities secret, but after a few days Lev's conscience forced him to confess what he had done. The news – a bombshell to me – made me take to my journal:

> June 26th: Lev Nikolaevich, my husband, has given all his diaries
> since the year 1900 to Vl. Gr. Chertkov, and has started writing a
> new diary at Chertkov's house, where he has been staying since June
> 12. In that diary, which he started at Chertkov's and which he gave
> me to read, he says amongst other things: 'I want to fight Sonya
> with love and kindness.' Fight?! What is there to fight about when
> I love him so passionately and intensely, when my one thought, my
> only concern, is that he should be happy?... My life with Lev. Nik.

becomes more intolerable each day because of his heartless and cruel behaviour towards me. And it has all has been brought about gradually and very consistently by Chertkov ... Yes, if one believes in the devil, he has been embodied in Chertkov and destroyed our life.

Chertkov should have been the interloper in the relationship between my husband and myself; yet I knew and recorded that 'both Lev Nik. and Chertkov regard *me* as having come between *them*'.

I kept on hammering Lev Nikolaevich to get the notebooks back, but he claimed not to know where they were; finally he admitted that they were 'in the bank'.

'Which bank? Where?'

'Why do you want to know?'

'Because I am your wife, the person closest to you.'

'Chertkov is the person who is closest to me, and I don't even know which bank they're in. Anyway, what does it matter?'

It mattered hugely, because I had always registered in what deeply unfair and totally unfavourable light my husband's entries would cast me:

> Lev Nik. has always deliberately represented me in his diaries –
> as he does now – as his tormentor, someone he has to fight and not
> succumb to, while he presents himself as a great and magnanimous
> man, religious and loving ...

I was forced to lower myself to approach the detestable Chertkov in person, and implore him to return the notebooks. But my plea was not only fruitless – it escalated the whole situation.

'You're afraid I'll use them to unmask you!' Chertkov shouted at me angrily. 'If I really wanted to, I could drag you and your family through the mud!'

A little later I heard him say to my own son, Lev Lvovich, as the two of them came downstairs together, 'A woman like that is beyond me. She spends her entire life murdering her husband.'

'A slow business, this murder,' I commented to my diary, 'considering that my husband has already lived to be nearly eighty-two.'

As usual we made it up, but this did not stop me from wondering how long the reconciliation would last.

The answer: long enough for me to go to meet Lev with some porridge, coffee and milk when he returned late from being out all day; and long enough to slip into his bedroom as he was going to bed that night.

'Promise me you won't ever leave without telling me,' I urged him.

'I would never do such a thing,' protested Lev Nikolaevich. 'I'll never ever leave you. I love you.' But a furtive look in his eyes belied his words.

'I'm so frightened of losing you,' I hiccupped through a torrent of tears. 'I have never stopped loving you for a moment! Even now I love you more than anyone else in the world!'

'You have nothing to fear,' he offered, unconvincingly. 'The bond between us can never be destroyed.'

Only partially reassured, I went to my own bedroom. My true comfort followed when Lev Nikolaevich came in after me.

Despite our reconciliation, Lyova had no intention of getting the diaries back from his toady. And that was enough to drive me mad. I was not even ashamed to use melodrama. 'The diaries or my life!' I cried – and the gambit proved at least half successful. Lev Nikolaevich did get the notebooks back; but he refused to pass them on to me! He gave them to Tanya, who sealed them up and deposited the package in a bank in Tula, dragging me along as a witness. I, reluctantly, handed the receipt over to Lev Nikolaevich, who would have the sole right to take them out.

'What an insensitive, distrustful attitude,' I fumed. 'And how unkind to his wife!' Why should I still love him to distraction when these days all he ever gave me was his cold heart?

That night even the elements raged against us, a terrible thunder storm followed by roaring winds and pounding rain preventing any possibility of sleep. In the morning the weather suddenly cleared and the July sun came out, but I was only half conscious of its consoling warmth. It had suddenly struck me that if Lyova went to such pains to keep the diaries from me, there must be something in them that he didn't want me to know.

He must have reverted to the debauchery of his youth.

I dwelt on this likelihood for a day and a night before confronting him. But when I did, he flew into a temper and said that he could not conceive of such a thing. Betray me? After all these years?

'I have given everything away!' he shouted at me. 'My property! My works! The only thing I had left was my diaries, and now it seems I shall have to get rid of them too! I wrote to you saying I would leave, and if you go on tormenting me, I shall!'

Leave! That was my great terror. He mustn't go! He must not!

I placed a phial of opium on my bedside table, but inwardly I knew I wasn't really ready to give anyone the pleasure of my death. Lyova of course could easily have relieved me of that temptation, but he did not want to … Our five remaining sons, all married and living elsewhere, would be genuinely saddened if I killed myself, but not the girls, who always took their father's side. Sasha often had friends over to play cards, but never did she invite me to join them, although that would have been a pleasant and relaxing thing to do. Tanya, when she was recently ill, asked Lev Nikolaevich to visit her, but not her mother.

On the 22nd of August I turned sixty-six, and Lev eighty-two on the 28th. I gave myself a birthday treat of an utterly delightful early morning walk around our park, revelling in the avenues of trees, the brilliant wildflowers, the saffron milk-caps, the silence, the solitude. I prayed to God that I would recover Lyova's love before either of us died.

He, in contrast, seemed to ignore the bright birthday weather that nature turned on for him, remarking during the course of the day that the Christian ideal was celibacy and total chastity. This was too much for a wife who had endured thirteen pregnancies! Deeply offended, I spoilt the occasion by arguing furiously with him.

On my name day, September 17th, he was away. On the first of the month he'd been summoned to St Petersburg, to stand trial for a pamphlet he'd published five years previously called *The Construction of Hell*. He returned late at night on the 22nd – the eve of our wedding anniversary. On the day itself there was no celebration, but he was a little nicer to me – until the following morning, when he shouted at me again.

By mid-October the weather had turned frigid. I went for a long walk and, tortured by thoughts of Lyova's exclusive love for Chertkov, I stretched out on the freezing ground, which was deliberate, and dozed off, which was not. One of the servants found me and brought me inside, where I sat on my bed, not moving, until Lev Nikolaevich came.

'Will you be going to see Chertkov this evening?' I asked through numbed lips. He didn't answer my question, just shouted at me: 'I want my freedom! I won't submit to your whims and fancies, I'm eighty-two years old, not a little boy, I won't be tied to my wife's apron strings …'

Later that night I went to his room, and we made up. Twice.

The truce was maintained for more than a week, because Lev Nikolaevich grudgingly refrained from any contact with Chertkov. Things were quiet, peaceful and happy until the 26th.

On that cold, still night I slid out of my bed and crept into Lyova's study. There were no papers on his desk, and although I distractedly opened one or two drawers, I really had no idea what I was looking for. I picked up the candlestick and went into my husband's bedroom next door. He must have been less agitated than I was, for when I held the candle above his face, his eyes remained fast shut. Finally I went to my own room, and the house was quiet for about an hour.

Then I heard rustlings from Lyova's room, and saw a light in it. I went in and asked quite loudly, 'How are you feeling?' Lyova refused to answer me, just gasped as if for breath and started counting his pulse. Angry, I returned to my own room, having no idea that he was making up his mind to leave me!

The following account derives from notes I put together after interrogating all those concerned. I need to relive everything, just as the tongue cannot keep away from a sore tooth.

Before dawn, Lev Nikolaevich went to the outhouse, but in the dark he lost his way back and fell into a thicket. Pricked by thorns, he extricated himself, fell over, and felt his cap fall from his head; his fumbling hands failed to locate it. (One of the servants came across it a few days later.) He made his way back to the house, found another cap, took a lantern, and went to the stables. There he ordered the boy to harness the horses.

Lyova and Dushan Makovitsky, the gentle Czech doctor resident at Yasnaya Polyana, were ready with their luggage by six o'clock. Dawn had still not broken. Sasha, standing by, jumped inside the carriage for a second to give her father one last embrace.

As they rolled along the shadowy road to the station, he must have wondered how I would react to the words he had left me:

> I cannot go on living in the luxury which has always surrounded me
> here, and I am doing what most old men of my age do: leaving this
> worldly life in order to spend my last days in solitude and silence.
> Please understand this, I beg you, and do not come and fetch me,
> even if you should discover where I am.

At Shchyokino station, they found they had an hour to wait. Lev Nikolaevich was in great trepidation, Dushan confessed, expecting every minute that I would arrive before the train. But it came at last and Lev remarked that I must not yet know. In keeping with his views on social equality, they climbed into a third-class compartment, the whistle blew and the wheels began to turn. He was safe. It is clear that he allowed himself to feel some pity but no remorse, remarking to Dushan, 'I wonder how Sofya Andreevna is now? I am sorry for her.' But he never entertained any doubts about his intentions.

In fact he felt so jaunty at being on his way that he tried to engage the young peasant sitting next to him in a discussion of the ideas of the American Henry George (who held that land should belong to society in general and not to individuals). Lev Nikolaevich was in entire agreement with this, but the only response from the peasant being a look of incomprehension, he turned to the whole carriage and began to harangue them on the virtues of pacifism. They didn't take in much of that either, but word spread through the train that Russia's most famous writer was amongst the travellers.

He had no notion that the news of his departure had already been telegraphed to Moscow and St Petersburg. Even as he lectured the bemused passengers, a headline was appearing on the billboards of the major cities:

LEV TOLSTOY LEAVES YASNAYA POLYANA

He was astonished and vexed to be told at the end of the exhausting six-hour journey that a small crowd had gathered on Kozyolsk station, waiting for him to descend.

The doctor cleared a way through the throng to where a cab stood waiting, and the two of them were driven off to Optina Pustyn, where Lev hoped to spend the night before visiting his sister Masha, now in a convent.

When the grill in the monastery guesthouse was slid open, Tolstoy announced himself: 'Lev Nikolaevich Tolstoy, excommunicated by the Church. I have come to talk to your elders, and tomorrow I shall go to my sister at Shamordino.'

The grill clanged and the door was opened; a monk showed the two of them to a guest room. Before falling asleep, Tolstoy wrote a letter and a telegram saying where he was, which he asked to be sent to Chertkov and Sasha.

Next morning a fellow arrived with messages from Chertkov, who declared himself overjoyed that Tolstoy had finally extricated himself from Sofya Andreevna. But my husband apparently showed some dismay at the rest of the letter, which told him in full how his wife had reacted to his departure. In the small hours of the night of the 27th–28th, I had

had to resort to a sleeping powder, which rendered me oblivious to Lev's movements, and all else, until 11 am. The moment I was awake, Sasha gave me Lev Nikolaevich's letter. I read it quickly, screamed, and rushed outside.

'Goodbye, Sasha,' I was calling as I ran. 'I'm going to drown myself!'

It was the middle pond, of course, that I flung myself into, the one where I had always swum, and where the little bathhouse was erected. The water was very cold, but I managed to swallow a good deal of it; and it was hard not to flail my arms, but I was determined to avoid swimming. After all, I had set out to drown myself. I should have remembered the water was never any more than waist deep; the peasant women often did their washing there.

Sasha came running after me, bringing Valentin Bulgakov, Lyova's secretary, and yelling to a manservant to come and help. Between them they pulled me out, ignoring my protests and strenuous resistance.

My survival, which upon learning of it later my husband apparently deemed entirely predictable, undid the brief concern he had held for me.

'If anyone should wish to drown,' he wrote to Sasha, 'it is certainly not she, but I. Let her know that I desire only one thing – freedom from her … and from the hatred which fills her whole being.'

Sasha was waiting for Seryozha and Tanya to arrive to take care of me before she too set out. Meanwhile, she was consulting a psychiatrist, probably one of the doctors her father had called in a few months earlier to examine me. Their diagnosis had been paranoia and hysteria. But what does that signify, when Lev Nikolaevich had at the same time rewritten his will, leaving everything to Tanya should Sasha die before him, and giving Chertkov sole power to change or publish anything after his death? Sergei and Andrei had at that time contemplated having their father certified and restoring the will to something more sensible.

After seeing Masha and telling her everything, Lev wrote me what he imagined to be a more compassionate letter:

Do not think I went away because I do not love you. I love you
and am sorry for you with all my soul, but I cannot act otherwise.
Farewell dear Sofya. May God help you. Life is not a plaything, we
have no right to throw it aside on a whim ...

Sasha and her friend Varya now arrived, which pleased Lev, but
also gave him the feeling that everyone was crowding in on him; when
Sasha checked on his room, it was empty. According to the porter, Lev
Nikolaevich and Dr Makovitsky had been gone about an hour.

Sasha and Varya caught up with them at Kozyolsk station, arriving a
second before the train pulled out. Sasha asked her father where they were
going, but he seemed unsure. Maybe to the Caucasus. Maybe to a Tolstoyan
colony in Bulgaria ...

Between four and five o'clock, Tolstoy began to shiver, and his
temperature went up to forty degrees. Dushan felt that he should be taken
off the train and put in a hospital, or at least a comfortable inn, but the
wheels kept clacking inexorably. Lev Nikolaevich's skin was flushed and
dry; he seemed hardly conscious.

The conductors moved the small party to a better compartment, where
Lev Nikolaevich rallied briefly, squeezing Sasha's hand and murmuring,
'Don't lose courage, Sasha. Everything is all right, very much all right.'

The train slowed and Sasha saw that they were stopping at a small
station: Astapova. She went to get some hot water to make her father a
drink, but walking down the platform she realised that she was being
followed by two men. Turning around, she asked them sternly who they
were. They showed their police badges.

'Who sent you?' she asked.

'The Countess Tolstoy,' answered one.

'Can you tell us, Madame,' asked the other, 'whether Lev Nikolaevich
Tolstoy is travelling on this train?'

'How should I know?' Sasha snapped. 'I'm too busy looking after my
elderly uncle, who is not well.'

She returned to the carriage with the hot water, but it was apparent that her father was seriously ill. She and the doctor began to haul the luggage down from the rack. The two of them virtually had to carry Lev Nikolaevich onto the platform.

The stationmaster, on seeing that this was an emergency involving a famous personage, put his simple house at their disposal. Sasha and the doctor held Lev Nikolaevich up on either side as the crowd doffed their caps and respectfully let the little party through. My husband managed to shuffle into the house and was put straight to bed.

He slept soundly through the night, and next morning felt so much better he was all for resuming the journey. When this was vetoed, he dictated a letter to Tanya and Seryozha, in which he explained that he could not let them come when he had banned their mother; he also asked that Chertkov be sent for.

At Yasnaya Polyana, I was utterly demented. I had had no idea of my husband's whereabouts for five tortured days. During that time I ate nothing. At 7.30 in the morning of November 2nd, I received a telegram from the editors of the Moscow newspaper, *Russkoe Slovo*: 'Lev Nikolaevich in Astapova, temperature 40°.'

Astapova! What could he be doing there? And why did everyone except me know where my husband had gone? I had to leave immediately. No matter what Lyova said, he needed me.

I drove into Tula and ordered a private train to run from there to Astapova. As soon as it was ready I climbed in, with Andryusha and Tanya, plus a doctor, a nurse, and a couple of servants. Seryozha had already gone on ahead, without specifying his destination. How could my eldest son do that to me?

A contingent quite separate from mine had also set out from Yasnaya Polyana, inevitably including Chertkov. Hordes of newspaper correspondents and photographers were also descending on the little town. Pathé Movie News had despatched a cameraman to the town and cabled him their orders: TAKE STATION, TRY TO GET CLOSE-UP, STATION NAME. TAKE FAMILY, WELL-KNOWN FIGURES, CARRIAGE THEY ARE SLEEPING IN.

Naturally the cameraman was not allowed into the bedroom where Tolstoy was barely conscious, in pain and receiving injections of morphine, but outside he was able to shoot what must have been a desperately heartrending picture. It shows a woman (me) who has rushed from the station, but is not allowed into the stationmaster's house. She has wailed at the door and implored them to at least take the special pillow she brought, because it was 'Lyova's favourite'. The pillow is accepted, but not me. I had then run around the house to where there was a window – was it even the right one? – which I tried to push open. Finding it stuck fast, I was rubbing the pane with my handkerchief, trying to peer in. I looked utterly distraught, and the cameraman no doubt felt quite sorry for me. But he would have been chuffed that it made such a great shot.

Self-portrait of Sonya at Tolstoy's grave.

It was just after midnight, on November 7th, when it was clear that Lev Nikolaevich had very little time left, that they finally allowed me in to see him. Chertkov had been sitting by the bed, but he rose and left the room, which still seemed very crowded. Six of our seven children were there, Ilya being abroad, plus the doctor and several Tolstoyans – anyone, in fact, who imagined they had some claim on Lev Nikolaevich. But they did clear a way for me to get through. I knelt by the bed and, weeping, whispered, 'Forgive me, forgive me.'

'She's disturbing him,' someone said accusingly.

I was taken out of the room. But I refused to go any further than the porch of the stationmaster's house, where I stood in the freezing night air from 3 am until 5.30. The door then opened again and Seryozha led me back inside.

The slight figure under the blankets was still breathing, but Lyova had already gone somewhere else.

'I have never loved anyone but you,' I murmured, then leant down and put my head on his chest.

Nothing.

Epilogue

After the initial horror of my discovery that I had been the wife of a genius who, for all his loathing of French novels, had immersed himself body and soul in a *crime passionel*, I slowly settled into a rather dour kind of acceptance. I knew I would survive whether I wanted to or not; I always had. After he died, I was busier than ever with his papers, his works, and the estate. And also, thank God, with his grandchildren.

Watching some of the children playing together during an Easter visit, I recalled a jotting I'd read in Lev's diary of 1879, two years after he finished *Anna Karenina*, and twenty-four years before I completed my work on the Fourteenth Edition. At the time it had been a mere flicker of illumination that I soon forgot, but now, after his death, a conversation that he recorded with two of our own children leapt into my mind.

'Ilya and Tanya have been telling me their secrets,' he had written. 'They are in love. How terrible, nasty and sweet they are.'

Remembering it, my heart contracted. Even Lyova's innocent children, who must have been twelve and fourteen at the time, were to him tainted by carnality – 'terrible' and 'nasty' despite their very sweetness.

At that moment I was swamped by a huge wave of the emotion that he had tried but failed to extend to his tragic heroine. From the bottom of her ardent heart, the Wife pitied the Husband.

Author Note

After Lev Tolstoy's death in 1910, Sonya continued to live at Yasnaya Polyana, working on her own and her husband's papers, and his literary and philosophical heritage. She died in 1919.

I worked from the diaries of Sonya Tolstoy in both the original Russian and the translation made by Cathy Porter; and from those of Lev Tolstoy in the original and the translation made by R.F. Christian.

The fictional works of Tolstoy were also consulted in both the original and in various translated versions.

The quotations in the text of my novel are my own except in a very few cases when the original was unavailable.

One *verst* is roughly equivalent to one kilometre.